The Package

Ref. MIX PARCELS

5-8
EC1R 4RG

"EC1R"

SEBASTIAN FITZEK

The Package

Ref: MIX PARCELS

5-8
EC1R 4RG   *EC1R*

Contact ID 372...

translated from the German by

Jamie Bulloch

HEAD
of ZEUS

First published in German as *Das Paket* in 2016 by Droemer Knaur
First published in the UK in 2020 by Head of Zeus Ltd
This paperback edition first published in 2021 by Head of Zeus Ltd

Das Paket Copyright © 2016 Verlagsgruppe Droemer Knaur GmbH &
Co. KG, Munich, Germany
Translation © 2020 Jamie Bulloch

9 7 5 3 1 2 4 6 8

A catalogue record for this book is available from
the British Library.

ISBN (PB): 9781838934491
ISBN (E): 9781838934507

Typeset by Siliconchips Services Ltd UK

Printed and bound in Great Britain by
CPI Group (UK) Ltd, Croydon CR0 4YY

Head of Zeus Ltd
5–8 Hardwick Street
London EC1R 4RG

WWW.HEADOFZEUS.COM

*For my dream team: Manu, Roman, Sabrina,
Christian, Karl, Barbara and Petra*

For the indispensable Carolin and Regine

*And of course for those who I miss even when
I'm hugging them: Sandra, Charlotte, David and Felix*

... all stories, if continued far enough, end in death,
and he is no true-story teller
who would keep that from you.

—*Ernest Hemingway*

It's impossible to observe something
without changing it.

—*Heisenberg's uncertainty principle*

Prologue

When Emma opened her parents' bedroom door she didn't know that it would be for the last time. Never again would she clamber into their bed, toy elephant in hand, to snuggle up to her mother at half past midnight, trying her best to avoid waking her father who'd be kicking about, mumbling random words or grinding his teeth in his dreams.

Tonight he wasn't kicking, mumbling or grinding his teeth. Tonight he was just whimpering.

'Papa?'

Emma toddled into the bedroom from the darkness of the corridor. The light of the full moon, which towered over Berlin like a midnight sun on this spring night, shimmered into the room like mercury through the drawn curtains.

Screwing up her eyes, over which her fringe hung like a chestnut-brown curtain, Emma could make out her surroundings: the rattan chest at the foot of the bed, the glass tables that flanked the wide bed, the wardrobe with sliding doors where she used to hide.

Until Arthur entered her life and spoiled the game of hide and seek.

'Papa?' Emma whispered, feeling for her father's bare foot that was sticking out from under the duvet.

Emma herself was only wearing one sock, and even that was barely attached to her foot. She'd lost the other while asleep, somewhere along the way from the sparkling unicorn palace to the valley of the silver-grey flying spider, who sometimes frightened Emma in her dreams.

But not as much as Arthur frightens me.

Even though he kept assuring her he wasn't wicked. Could she trust him?

Emma pressed the elephant more tightly to her chest. Her tongue felt like a dry lump of chewing gum stuck to the roof of her mouth. She'd barely heard her thin voice, so she tried again:

'Papa, wake up.' Emma tugged at his toe.

As her father retracted his foot he turned to the side with a whine, briefly lifting the duvet and filling Emma's nostrils with his sleepy odour. She was certain that if she were blindfolded she could pick her father out of a dozen men by his smell alone. The earthy mixture of tobacco and eau de cologne, which was so familiar. A smell she loved.

Emma briefly wondered whether she'd be better off trying her mother. Mama was always there for her. Papa often grumbled. Mostly Emma had no idea what she'd done when doors were slammed with such force that the entire house shook. Later Mama would say that her father didn't really know himself. She explained that he was 'earasable', or something like that, and that he felt sorry afterwards. Just sometimes, albeit rarely, he even apologised. He'd come to her room, caress her tear-stained cheek, stroke her hair and say that being a grown-up wasn't so easy, because of the responsibility, because of the problems you had to deal with, and so on. For Emma these select moments were the happiest of her life, and just what she was in need of right now.

Today, especially, it would mean so much to her.

Seeing as how frightened I am.

'Papa, please, I...'

She was moving to the other end of the bed to touch his head when she tripped over a glass bottle.

Oh no...

In her excitement she'd forgotten that Mama and Papa always had a bottle of water by the bed in case one of them got thirsty in the night. When it toppled over and rolled across the parquet floor, to Emma's ears it sounded as if a freight train were ploughing through the bedroom. The noise was deafening, as if the darkness amplified sound.

The light went on.

On her mother's side.

Emma let out a high-pitched cry when she suddenly found herself in brightness.

'Sweetheart?' said her mother, who looked like a saint in the beam of her reading light. Like a saint with dishevelled hair and pillow creases on her face.

Startled, now Emma's father opened his eyes too.

'What the hell…?' His voice was loud, his eyes were scanning the room, trying to get their bearings. He'd obviously woken from a bad dream, maybe it was still in his head. He sat up.

'What's wrong, sweetie?' her mother said. Before Emma could reply, her father shouted again, this time even louder.

'Fucking hell!'

'Thomas,' her mother chided him.

Maintaining his strident tone, he waved his hand towards Emma.

'For Christ's sake, how often have I told you…'

'Thomas!'

'… to leave us alone at night!'

'But my… my… my… cupboard…' Emma stuttered, her eyes welling with tears.

'Not again,' her father scowled. Her mother's attempts to calm him only seemed to make him angrier.

'Arthur,' Emma said nonetheless. 'The ghost. He's back. In the cupboard. You've got to come, please! He might hurt me otherwise.'

Her father was breathing heavily, his face darkened, his lips quivered and for a split second he looked how she imagined Arthur to be: a small, sweating devil with a big tummy and bald head.

'Like hell we have to. Get out, Emma, right now, or *I* might hurt you. No, I *will* hurt you!'

'Thomas!' she heard her mother cry again as she staggered backwards.

Those words had struck Emma hard. Harder than the table-tennis bat she accidentally got in the face last month in games. Tears flooded her face. It was as if her father had slapped her. Emma's cheeks were burning even though he hadn't even raised a finger.

'You can't talk to your daughter like that,' she heard her mother say. Anxiously, with a soft voice. Almost imploring him.

'I'll talk to her as I like. She's finally got to learn that she can't come bursting in here every night...'

'She's a six-year-old girl.'

'And I'm a forty-four-year-old man, but it seems as if my needs count for nothing in this house.'

Emma dropped her elephant without realising it. She turned to the door and left the room as if she were being pulled along like a puppet on a string.

'Thomas...'

'Will you shut up with your *Thomas*,' her father said, imitating his wife. 'I've only been asleep for half an hour. If I'm not on form in court tomorrow and lose this case then that's my practice up the spout and you can wave goodbye to all this: the house, your car, the baby.'

'I know...'

'You know *fuck all*. Emma's already eating us out of

house and home, but you were adamant about having a second kid, who'll stop me from sleeping altogether. For Christ's sake. It might not have escaped you that I'm the only one earning money in this family. And I NEED MY SLEEP!'

Although Emma was already halfway down the corridor, her father's voice wasn't any quieter. Only her mother's. 'Shhh, Thomas. Darling. Relax.'

'HOW THE FUCK CAN I RELAX HERE?'

'Come on, let me, please. I'll look after you now, okay?'

'LOOK AFTER? Ever since you got pregnant again, you've only looked after...'

'I know, I know. That's my fault. Come on, let me...'

Emma closed her bedroom door, shutting out her parents' voices.

Or at least those from the bedroom. Not those in her head.

Get out, Emma, right now, or...

She wiped the tears from her eyes and waited for the roaring in her ears to disappear, but it wouldn't. Just as the moonlight, which shone more brightly here than in her parents' room, wouldn't vanish back out the windows. Her blinds were made of thin linen, while the luminous stars stuck to the ceiling also glowed above her bed.

My bed.

Emma wanted to crawl into it and cry beneath the duvet, but she couldn't do that until she was certain that the ghost wasn't in his hiding place. Certain that he wouldn't pounce on her while she was asleep, certain that he had gone, like he had every time when Mama went to take a look with her.

The old farmer's cupboard was a monstrosity with crude carvings in the oak doors, which mimicked the cackle of an old witch when they were opened.

Like now.

Please let him not be there.

'Hello?' Emma said into the black hole before her eyes. The cupboard was so big that her things only took up the left-hand side. On the other side there was space for her mother's towels and tablecloths.

And for Arthur.

'Hello,' the ghost with the deep voice answered. As always it sounded as if he were putting a hand in front of his mouth. Or a cloth.

Emma let out a short scream. Oddly, however, she didn't feel that profound, all-embracing fear she'd experienced earlier, when she'd heard a clattering inside the cupboard and she'd gone to take a look.

Maybe fear is like a bag of gummy bears, she thought. *I've finished it all in my parents' bedroom.*

'Are you still there?'

'Of course. Did you think I'd leave you alone?'

I hoped you would.

'What if my papa had come to look?'

Arthur laughed softly. 'I knew he wouldn't come.'

'How?'

'Has he ever looked after you?'

Emma hesitated. 'Yes.'

No. I don't know.

'But Mama...'

'Your mother is weak. That's why I'm here.'

'You?' Emma sniffled.

'Tell me...' Arthur paused briefly and his voice went deeper. 'Have you been crying?'

Emma nodded. She didn't know if the ghost could see her, but his eyes probably didn't need any light. Maybe he didn't have any eyes at all. She couldn't be sure as she'd never seen Arthur.

'What happened?' he asked.

'Papa got angry.'

'What did he say?'

'He said...' Emma swallowed. Hearing the words in her head was one thing. Saying them out loud was a different thing altogether. It was painful. But Arthur insisted and, worried that he might become just as irate as her father, she repeated them.

'Get out or I'll hurt you.'

'He said *that*?'

Emma nodded again. And Arthur did seem to be able to see her in the dark, because he reacted to her nodding. He grunted his disapproval and then something quite extraordinary happened. Arthur left his hiding place. For the first time ever.

The ghost, who was much bigger than she'd imagined, pushed a number of hangers aside and as he climbed out he stroked her hair with his gloved fingers.

'Come on, Emma, go to bed now and settle down.'

She looked up at him and froze. Instead of a face she saw a distorted image of herself. As if she were in a chamber of horrors, gazing at a mirror mounted on a long black column.

It took a while before she realised that Arthur was wearing a motorbike helmet and she was staring at her grotesque likeness in his visor.

'I'll be right back,' he promised, making for the door.

There was something about the way he moved that Emma found familiar, but she was far too distracted by the sharp object in Arthur's right hand.

It would be years before she realised that this was a syringe.

With a long needle that glinted silver in the moonlight.

A liar will not be believed
even when he speaks the truth

—*Proverb*

1

Twenty-eight years later

'Don't do it. I was lying. Please don't...'

The audience, consisting almost entirely of men, tried not to show any emotion as they watched the half-naked, black-haired woman being tortured.

'For God's sake, it's a mistake. I just made it all up. A terrible mistake... Help!'

Her cries echoed around the whitewashed, sterile room; her words were clearly intelligible. Nobody present would be able to claim later that they'd misunderstood her.

The woman didn't want this.

Despite her protests, the slightly overweight, bearded man with wonky teeth stuck the syringe into the crook of her strapped arm.

Despite her protests, they didn't remove the electrodes attached to her forehead and temples, nor even the ring around her head, which reminded her of those unfortunate tortured monkeys in animal testing laboratories, their skulls opened and probes inserted into their brains.

Which basically wasn't so different from what was about to be done to her now.

When the sedative and muscle relaxant began to take effect, they began manual ventilation. Then the men started administering the electrical impulses: 475 volts, 17 times in succession, until they triggered an epileptic fit.

From the angle of the closed-circuit camera it was impossible to tell whether the black-haired woman was offering resistance or whether her limbs were twitching spastically. The backs of the figures sporting aprons and face masks blocked the audience's view. But the screaming had stopped. Eventually the film stopped too and it became a little brighter in the hall.

'What you have just witnessed is a horrific case...' Dr Emma Stein began her observations, breaking off briefly to pull the microphone a bit closer so the conference guests could hear her more clearly. Now she was annoyed she'd spurned the footstool the technician had offered her during the soundcheck. Usually she would have asked for one herself, but the guy in overalls had given her such a condescending grin that she'd rejected the sensible option of making herself taller. As a result she was having to stand on tiptoe behind the lectern.

'... a horrific case of coercive psychiatry which had long been thought consigned to history.'

Like Emma, most of those present were psychiatrists. Which meant she didn't have to explain to her colleagues that her criticism wasn't levelled at electroconvulsive therapy. Conducting electricity through a human brain might sound terribly mediaeval, but it produced promising results in combating psychoses and depression. Performed under general anaesthetic, the treatment had virtually no side effects.

'We managed to smuggle this footage captured by a surgery-monitoring camera from the Orphelio Clinic in Hamburg. The patient whose fate you've just witnessed was committed on 3 May last year, diagnosed with schizoid psychosis, based solely on what the forty-three-year-old herself said upon admission. But there was nothing wrong with her at all. The supposed patient faked her symptoms.'

'Why?' a faceless individual from somewhere in the left middle of the hall asked. The man practically had to shout for her to understand him in the theatre-like space. The German Association of Psychiatry had hired for its annual conference the main hall of the International Congress Centre in Berlin. From the outside, the ICC resembled a silver space station, which from the infinite expanses of the universe had spun to a halt directly beneath the television tower. And yet when you entered this seventies building – which was possibly contaminated with asbestos (experts disagreed about this) – you were reminded less of science fiction and

15

more of a retro film. Chrome, glass and black leather dominated the interior.

Emma allowed her gaze to roam across the packed rows of chairs but, unable to locate the questioner, talked in the vague direction she imagined him to be.

'Here's a question of my own: What does the Rosenhan Experiment mean to you?'

An older colleague, sitting in a wheelchair at the edge of the front row, nodded knowingly.

'It was first performed at the end of the sixties, with the aim of testing the reliability of psychiatric prognoses.' As ever when she was nervous, Emma twisted a strand of her thick, teak-brown hair around her left index finger. She hadn't eaten anything before her lecture, for fear of feeling tired or needing to burp. Now her stomach was rumbling so loudly that she was worried the microphone might pick up the noise, lending further succour to the jokes she was convinced were going around about her fat bum. In her eyes, the fact that she was otherwise quite slim only highlighted this bodily imperfection.

Broom up top, wrecking ball below, she'd thought again only this morning when examining herself in the bathroom mirror.

A second later Philipp had hugged her from behind and insisted she had the most beautiful body he'd ever laid his hands on. And when they kissed goodbye at the front door he'd pulled her towards him and whispered into her ear that as soon as she was back he urgently needed relationship therapy with the sexiest psychiatrist in Charlottenburg. She sensed he was being serious, but she also knew that her husband was well versed in dishing out compliments. Quite simply, flirting was hardwired into Philipp's DNA – something Emma had been forced to get used to – and he seldom wasted an opportunity to practise it.

'For the Rosenhan Experiment, named after the American psychologist David Rosenhan, eight subjects had themselves admitted to psychiatric clinics on false pretences. Students, housewives, artists, psychologists and doctors. All of them told the same story on admission: they'd been hearing voices, weird, uncanny voices saying words like "empty", "hollow" or "thud".

'It will not surprise you to hear that all of the fake patients were admitted, most of them diagnosed with schizophrenia or manic-depressive psychosis.

'Although the subjects were demonstrably healthy and behaved perfectly normally after admission, they were treated in the institutions for weeks on end, supposedly taking a total of more than two thousand pills.'

Emma moistened her lips with a sip of water from the glass provided. She'd put on some lipstick, even though Philipp preferred the 'natural look'. She did in fact have unusually smooth skin, although she thought it far too pale, especially given the intense colour of her hair. She couldn't see the 'adorable contrast' that Philipp kept going on about.

'If you think the 1970s were a long time ago, that this took place in a different century, i.e. in the Middle Ages of psychiatric science, then let this video shatter your illusions. It was filmed last year. This young woman was a test subject too; we repeated the Rosenhan Experiment.'

A murmur rippled through the hall. Those present were less worried about the scandalous findings than they were about perhaps having been subjects of an experiment themselves.

'We sent fake patients to psychiatric institutions and once again investigated what happens when totally sane people are admitted into a closed establishment. With shocking results.'

Emma took another sip of water, then continued. 'The woman in the video was diagnosed with schizoid paranoia on the basis of a single sentence when she arrived at the clinic. After that she was treated for more than a month. Not just with medicine and conversational therapy, but with brute force too. As you've seen and heard for yourselves, she was unequivocal about not wanting electroconvulsive therapy. And no wonder, because she is perfectly sound of mind. But she was forcibly treated nonetheless.

'Even though she manifestly rejected it. Even though after admission no one noticed anything else unusual about her and she assured the doctors several times that her condition had returned to normal. But they refused to listen to her, the nurses or fellow patients. For unlike the doctors who passed by only sporadically, the people she spent all her time with at the clinic were convinced that this locked-up woman had no business being there.'

Emma noticed someone in the front third of the hall stand up. She gave the technician the agreed sign to turn up the lights slightly. Her eyes made out a tall, slim man with thinning hair, and she waited until a long-legged conference assistant had battled his way through the rows to the man and passed him a microphone.

The man blew into the microphone before saying, 'Stauder-Mertens, University Hospital, Cologne. With all due respect, Dr Stein, you show us a blurry horror video, the origin and supplier of which we'd rather not know, and then make wild assertions that, were they ever to become public knowledge, would cause great damage to our profession.'

'Do you have a question as well?' Emma said.

The doctor with the double-barrelled name nodded. 'Do you have more evidence than this fake patient's statement?'

'I selected her personally for the experiment.'

'That's all well and good, but can you vouch for her unquestioningly? I mean, how do you know that this person really is sound of mind?'

Even from a distance Emma could see the same haughty smile that had annoyed her on the technician's face.

'What are you getting at, Herr Stauder-Martens?'

'That somebody who volunteers to be admitted to a secure unit for several weeks on false pretences – now, how can I put it carefully? – must be equipped with an extraordinary psychological make-up. Who can tell you that this remarkable lady didn't actually suffer from the symptoms for which she was ultimately treated, and which perhaps she didn't exhibit until her stay at the institution?'

'Me,' Emma said.

'Oh, so you were with her the whole time, were you?' the man asked rather smugly.

'I was.'

His self-assured grin vanished. 'You?'

When Emma nodded, the mood in the hall became palpably tenser.

'Correct,' Emma said. Her voice was quivering with excitement, but also with fury at the outrage that had greeted her revelations. 'Dear colleagues, on the video you only saw the test subject from behind and with dyed hair, but the woman who first was sedated and then forcibly treated with electric shocks against her expressed will, that woman was... me.'

2

Two hours later

Taking hold of her wheelie case, Emma hesitated before entering room 1904, for the simple reason that she could barely see a thing. The little illumination that did penetrate the darkness came from the countless lights of the city, nineteen floors beneath her. The Le Zen on Tauentzienstrasse was Berlin's newest five-star chrome-and-glass palace, with over three hundred rooms. Taller and more luxurious than any other hotel in the capital. And – in Emma's eyes, at least – decorated with relatively little taste.

That, at any rate, was her first impression once she'd found the main switch by the door and the overhead light clicked on.

The interior design looked as if a trainee had been instructed to exploit every possible Far Eastern cliché when selecting the furnishings.

In the hallway, which was separated from the neighbouring bedroom by a thin, sliding door covered in tissue paper, stood a Chinese wedding chest. A bamboo rug extended from the door to a low futon bed. The lamps beside the floor sofa looked like the colourful lanterns that the toddlers carried on St Martin's Day in the parade organised by the Heerstrasse Estate kindergarten. Surprisingly stylish, on the other hand, was a huge black-and-white photograph of Ai Weiwei that stretched from floor to ceiling between the sofa and fitted wardrobe. Emma had recently visited an exhibition by this exceptional Chinese artist.

She looked away from the man with the tousled beard, hung her coat in the wardrobe and took her phone from her handbag.

Voicemail.

She'd already tried calling him once, but Philipp hadn't answered. He never did when on duty.

With a sigh she moved over to the floor-to-ceiling windows, slipped off her peep toes, without which she shrunk to the average height of a fourteen-year-old, and gazed down at the Kurfürstendamm. She stroked her belly, which still showed nothing, although it was a bit too early for that yet. But she was comforted by the idea that something was growing inside her, which was far more important than any seminar or professional recognition.

It had taken a while before the second line on the pregnancy test finally showed up, five weeks ago.

And this was also the reason why Emma wasn't sleeping in her own bed tonight, but for the first time in her life staying the night at a hotel in her home city. Her little house in Teufelssee-Allee was currently like a building site because they'd started extending the loft to make a children's room. Even though Philipp thought it might be a little overzealous to begin nest-building before the end of the first trimester of her pregnancy.

As he was working in another town again, Emma had accepted the overnight package that the German Association of Psychiatry offered all the guest speakers at the two-day conference – even those who lived in Berlin – as it allowed them to have a few drinks at the evening function in the hotel's ballroom (which Emma was bunking off).

'The lecture ended just as you predicted,' she said in the message she left for Philipp. 'They didn't stone me, but that was only because they didn't have any stones to hand.'

She smiled.

'They didn't take my hotel room away, though. The key card I got with my conference documents still worked.'

Emma concluded her message with a kiss, then hung up. She missed him terribly.

Better to be alone here in the hotel than alone at home amongst paint pots and torn-down walls, she thought, trying to put the best possible gloss on the situation.

Emma went into the bathroom and, as she took off her suit, looked for the volume control for the speaker in the false ceiling, which transmitted the TV sound.

Without success.

Which meant she had to go back into the living room and switch off the television. Here too it took a while for her to find the remote control in a bedside table drawer, which was why she was now fully up to speed about a plane crash in Ghana and a volcano explosion in Chile.

Emma heard the nasal voice of the newsreader begin a new item – '... *the police have issued a warning about a serial killer, who...*' – and cut him off at the press of a button.

Back in the bathroom it was some time before she found the temperature setting.

As someone who felt the cold Emma loved hot water, even now in high summer, and it had been an unusually fresh and particularly windy June day at below twenty degrees. So she set the water to forty degrees – her pain threshold – and waited for the tingling sensation she always felt when the hot jet hit her skin.

Emma normally felt alive the moment she was enveloped by steam and the hot water massaged her body. Today the effect was weaker, partly because the dirt that had been hurled at her after the lecture couldn't be washed away with water and hotel soap.

There had been furious reactions to her revelation that,

even in the twenty-first century, people risked becoming the playthings of demigods in white abusing their power just because of sloppy misdiagnoses. The validity of her research findings had been questioned more than once. The publisher of the renowned specialist journal had even announced he would undertake meticulous review before he 'might consider' publishing an article about her work.

Sure, some colleagues had ventured their support after the event, but in the eyes of these few she'd still been able to read the unspoken reproach: *'Why on earth did you put yourself in danger with this stupid experiment? And why are you risking your career and picking a fight with the bigwigs who run the clinics?'*

Something Philipp would never ask. He understood why Emma had for years been fighting to improve the legal status of patients undergoing psychiatric treatment. Because of their mental illness they were usually viewed with more suspicion than patients who, for example, complained of faulty dental care.

And Philipp understood why she also took unusual, sometimes dangerous routes to get there. No doubt because they were so similar in this respect.

In his work, too, Philipp overstepped boundaries that no normal person would cross freely. In truth, the psychopaths and serial killers he hunted as chief investigator in the offender profiling department often left him with no other choice.

Some couples share a sense of humour, others have

similar hobbies or the same political outlook. Emma and Philipp, on the other hand, laughed at completely different jokes, she couldn't stand football and he didn't share her love of musicals, and whereas in her youth she had demonstrated against nuclear power and the fur industry, he had been a member of the conservative youth association. What formed the bedrock of their relationship was empathy.

Intuition and experience allowed them to put themselves in other people's souls and bring the secrets of their psyches to the light of day. While Emma did this to liberate the patients who visited her private practice on Savignyplatz from their psychological problems, Philipp used his extraordinary abilities to draw up behaviour and personality profiles. Thanks to his analyses, some of the most dangerous criminals Germany had ever known had been put behind bars.

Recently, however, Emma had been wishing that both of them would take a step backwards. She was continually nagged by the feeling that in their time off, which was fairly meagre anyway, Philipp was also finding it increasingly difficult to achieve the necessary distance from his work. And she was worried that they were well on the way to proving Nietzsche's dictum about the abyss: if you gazed into it deeply and for long enough, it would start gazing into you.

Some time out, or a holiday at least. That would be enough.

The last trip they'd taken together was so long ago that the memories of it had already faded.

Emma lathered her hair with the hotel's shampoo and could only hope that she wouldn't look like a poodle the following morning. Her brown hair might be strong, but it reacted sensitively to the wrong products. It had taken numerous experiments and tears till she found out what made her hair shine and what turned her head into a ripped sofa cushion.

Emma rinsed her hair, pushed the shower curtain aside and was just wondering why such an expensive hotel hadn't installed glass sliding doors when she was suddenly incapable of another lucid thought.

What she felt was *fear*.

The first thing that came into her mind when she saw the letters was *run!*

The letters on the bathroom mirror.

In neatly written letters, across the steam-covered glass, it read:

GET OUT.

BEFORE IT'S TOO LATE!

3

'Yes?'

'Sorry for disturb. Everything okay?'

The tall, slim Russian woman in the doorway appeared genuinely concerned. And yet the woman who spoke broken German didn't look to Emma like the sort of person who worried unnecessarily about her fellow human beings. More like a model aware of how beautiful she was and who regarded herself as the centre of the universe. Dressed in a close-fitting designer suit, drenched in Chanel and perched on sinfully expensive-looking high heels that would have allowed even Emma to gaze down at others.

'Who are you?' Emma said, annoyed that she'd opened the door. Now she was standing face to face with a Slav beauty, bare-footed, with soaking wet hair and dressed only in a hastily thrown-on hotel kimono. The material was so fine that every curve of her naked body, which was far less perfect than the Russian woman's, must be showing beneath it.

'Sorry. Very thin walls.'

The woman swept one of her blonde extensions from her forehead. 'Hear scream. Come to look.'

'You heard a scream?' Emma said impassively.

In truth, all that she could recall was having felt faint, partly a result of the eerie message on the mirror, but doubtlessly also because the shower had been too hot.

Both these things had well and truly pulled the rug from under her feet.

To begin with, Emma had managed to hold onto the edge of the basin, but then she'd collapsed onto the tiled floor, from where she'd stared at the writing:

GET OUT.

BEFORE IT'S TOO LATE!

'Hear crying too,' the Russian woman said.

'You must have been mistaken,' Emma replied, even though it was perfectly possible that her fall had been accompanied by tears. Her eyes were still burning. The message on the mirror had awoken the darkest memories from her childhood.

The cupboard.

The creaking doors, behind which a man lurked in a motorbike helmet.

Arthur.

The ghost who had spent countless nights with her. Again and again. As a monster at first, then as a friend. Until at the age of ten she was finally 'cured', even though this concept didn't actually exist in psychotherapy. After many sessions the child psychiatrist that Emma visited had succeeded in banishing the demon. From both her cupboard and her head. And he'd made her aware who was really responsible for this phantasm.

Papa!

Ever since that course of therapy, which had first stimulated an interest in her current profession, Emma had known that no ghost had ever existed. And no Arthur. Only her father, who she'd spurned and feared throughout her life, but who she'd have dearly loved as a close ally. For her alone. Always there. To call on at any time, even at night in the cupboard.

But Emma's father had never been a friend. Not in her childhood, not during her studies and certainly not now that she was a married psychiatrist. His work had always been more important. His files, witnesses and cases. Leaving the house too early in the morning, and back too late for supper in the evening. Or not at all.

Although he'd retired a while ago, he only just about managed to send her a card for her birthday. And even that – she would bet – had been dictated by Mama, with whom he now lived in Mallorca. Phrases such as 'I'm missing you' or 'I hope we'll get to spend more time together this year' were simply absent from the lexicon of someone as irascible as him. He'd be more likely to write:

'*Get out, right now, or I'll hurt you.*'

And now a similar threat was scrawled across the mirror in her hotel bathroom.

Could this be a coincidence?

Of course!

Before the knock at her door Emma had already found a logical explanation for the incident.

A trick!

The guest who'd occupied the room before her must have scribbled with their greasy fingers on the dry mirror to give the next person a fright. And they'd succeeded.

So well that she'd practically screamed the hotel down. The joker would no doubt have been shocked by the violence of Emma's reaction, but they couldn't have imagined that the words on the mirror would have awakened an old trauma.

Back then it wasn't what her father said that had unnerved her most, but the fact that Arthur had come out of the cupboard for the first time that night. The motorcycle helmet, the needle, his voice... everything had seemed so real.

And sometimes it still did in her memory.

'You okay?' the woman asked her, continuing to stare at Emma with a mixture of concern and patience. Then she said something that sounded as kind as it did ghastly, and Emma didn't know whether to laugh or cry.

'Client make trouble?'

Oh God.

Of course.

She's a prostitute.

Which explained why she was dressed up to the nines. Half of the conference were staying at Le Zen; the hotel was full of men on their own in single rooms. How many of them had booked an escort for tonight? Scumbags like Stauder-Mertens, for sure, who would definitely use every opportunity they got when away from their wives and families.

'Need help? I can…'

'No, no. It's very kind of you, but…'

Emma shook her head.

… but I'm not a prostitute. Just a jumpy psychiatrist.

How sweet that the woman wanted to help her. How awful that she seemed to have experience of violent punters. *And of beaten-up whores who howl on the floor of hotel bathrooms.*

Emma smiled, but she didn't think it looked sincere. In the woman's dark eyes she could see that her doubts had not been dispelled, which is why Emma decided to tell her the truth.

'Don't worry. I'm alone in my room. But I thought somebody had crept in here and secretly watched me take a shower.'

'Peeper?'

'Yes, but it was just a stupid joke by the previous guest.'

'Okay.'

Although the escort girl still didn't look convinced, she shrugged and glanced at the Rolex on her wrist. Then she left with her first grammatically correct sentence: 'Take care nothing happens to you.' She must have heard this often from colleagues.

Emma thanked her and closed the door. Through the spyhole she saw the woman make her way down the corridor to the right.

The lifts were in the opposite direction, which meant her 'appointment' must be almost at hand.

Her heart pounding, Emma secured the door with all the available locks and levers. Only then did she realise how exhausted she was. First the lecture, then the mirror and now the conversation with the Russian prostitute. She longed to relax. To be able to sleep.

Especially in Philipp's arms.

Why couldn't he be here with her now, so they could joke together about this absurd situation?

Emma briefly toyed with the idea of calling her best friends – Sylvie or Konrad – as a bit of distraction, but she knew that both of them were on a date. Not with each other, of course, as Konrad was gay.

And even if she could get through to either of them,

what would she say? *'Sorry, but I'm slightly anxious because my mirror's steamed up'*?

Was steamed up, she discovered when she went back into the bathroom to clean her teeth.

The steam had vanished, likewise the joke message.

As if it had never existed.

4

Emma froze.

Streaks were all that remained of the condensation that had dissipated, leaving ugly edges on the silvered glass. Without thinking she wiped the patches away with a cloth, but immediately felt annoyed for not having breathed against the mirror to bring the message to life again.

Then she felt annoyed that she wasn't sure of herself any longer.

'What on earth is wrong with you, Emma?' she whispered, her head pressed into a towel.

She hadn't imagined the message. It was just a silly prank. No reason to feel so nervous.

Emma switched off the light in the bathroom without another glance at the mirror. She hung the kimono in the wardrobe and swapped it for some pyjamas. But she couldn't resist the paranoid impulse to check the wardrobe for secret hiding places (there weren't any). And as she was up, she could also take a peek behind the bed, inspect the curtains and try the locks again. All the while watched by Ai Weiwei, whose eyes had been photographed in such a way that they held Emma in his gaze wherever she moved to in the room.

She knew that all of this was displacement activity, but she felt better for having given in to her irrational stress symptoms.

When she finally crawled under the freshly starched bedclothes after her 'patrol', Emma felt tired and heavy. She tried one last time to contact Philipp and left a message on his voicemail that said, 'Dream of me when you've listened to this.' Emma set the alarm and closed her eyes.

As so often when she was overtired yet completely overwrought, flittering lights and shadows filled the darkness she wanted to sink into.

As she drifted off to sleep Emma asked herself, *Why did you say that?* in a woolly memory of her lecture. *Why did you say that you were the patient being tortured in the video?* That had never been her intention, she just acted out of impulse because Stauder-Martens, the narcissistic old goat from Cologne, had pestered her.

Do you have more evidence than this fake patient's statement?

Yes she did. Now it was out. Unnecessary shock tactics.

Emma rolled onto her side and tried to banish the images of the horde of men listening in the conference centre. She felt a pricking in her ear because she'd forgotten to remove her pearl studs.

Why do you always do things like that? she asked herself and, as so often in the transition between being awake and dreaming, she wondered why she was asking this question and what she actually meant by 'always', and while she was stuck in this analytical loop it suddenly happened.

She fell asleep.

Briefly.

Not even for two minutes.

Until the noise woke her up.

The buzzing.

In the darkness.

Very close, right beside her bed.

Emma turned over to the other side, opened her eyes and saw the light on her mobile. She'd placed it on the floor because the charging lead didn't reach from the plug up to the bedside table. Grabbing the phone from the carpet was quite tricky.

Caller unknown.

'Darling?' she said, in the hope that Philipp was calling back from some office phone.

'Frau Dr Stein?'

She'd never heard this man's voice before. Irritation mingled with the disappointment at the fact she wasn't speaking to Philipp. Who the hell was calling her this late at night?

'I hope it's important,' she yawned.

'I'm very sorry to disturb you. This is Herr Eigenhardt from reception at Le Zen hotel.'

On my mobile?

'Yes?'

'We just wanted to see if you'd still be checking in this evening.'

'What?'

Emma groped in vain for the switch to turn on the bedside light.

'What do you mean check in? I'm already asleep.'

Or at least trying to.

'So it's fine if we give the room away?'

Can't he hear me properly?

'No, listen. I already checked in. Room 1904.'

'Oh, please accept my sincere apologies, but...'

The receptionist sounded bemused.

'But what?' Emma asked.

'But we don't have a room with that number.'

What?

Emma sat up in bed and stared at the tiny blinking light on the smoke alarm attached to the ceiling.

'Are you having me on?'

'We don't have a single *four* in the hotel. It's an unlucky number in the Far East and so...'

Emma didn't hear the rest of the sentence as her mobile was no longer in her hand.

Instead she heard something that wasn't possible. Right by her ear.

A man clearing his throat.

And while her own throat constricted with fear, she felt the pressure on her mouth.

She tasted fabric.

Emma was stabbed by something, then she felt a cooling liquid flow into the crook of her arm through the puncture.

The man cleared his throat again and when she was certain she was freezing internally she sensed the blades.

Invisible in the darkness, but unmistakeably close to her face because they were vibrating.

Bzzzzzz.

An electric carving knife, a saw or an electric corkscrew.

Ready to stab, slash or puncture her.

She heard the sound of a zip being unfastened.

'I'm pregnant!' she wanted to cry, but Emma's tongue and lips failed her.

Immobilised, she was unable to scream, kick or thrash about.

Only wait and find out where she'd first feel pain.

And pray that this horror would soon be over.

Which it wasn't.

5

Six months later

Emma opened her eyes and wondered how long the person opposite had been watching her sleep.

Professor Konrad Luft sat in his usual chair, his hands folded in front of his stomach, and his thoughtful gaze lay on her face with a melancholic heaviness.

'Are you okay?' he asked. To begin with she didn't know what her best friend was getting at, but then she noticed the side table by her bed. On it were the pills she'd been given in the psychiatric clinic, where the judge had committed her to the secure unit.

Just in case.

In case she felt pain as soon as she woke up.

She stretched her limbs beneath the covers and with her elbows tried to shift herself up in the hospital bed. Too weak, she sank back down onto the pillow and rubbed her eyes.

She'd slept throughout the journey there, which was no surprise considering all the pills she'd been given. The side effects alone would knock out the strongest elephant, and on top of that she'd been administered a sedative.

After waking up it took her a while to recognise her surroundings. The room where she'd spent so many hours in the past felt unfamiliar, albeit not as unfamiliar as the secure unit she hadn't left over the past few weeks.

Maybe the strange feeling was down to the fact that Konrad had recently renovated his office, but Emma doubted it.

It wasn't the room that had changed so fundamentally, but her.

The smell of paint and freshly oiled walnut parquet still hung in the air, some pieces of furniture had been moved around during the redecoration, but basically everything was as it had been on her first visit almost ten years ago. Then she'd slouched on the sofa in trainers and jeans. Today she was in a nightie on a height-adjustable hospital bed, almost in the middle of the room. At a slight angle, with a view of Konrad's desk and the window behind.

'I bet I'm the first client of yours to have been wheeled in here on a hospital bed,' she said.

Konrad smiled softly. 'I've had some who couldn't be moved so I went to see them. But in the clinic you refused all contact, Emma. You wouldn't even speak to the doctors. So I obtained exceptional judicial authorisation.'

'Thank you,' she said, although there was no longer anything she could be grateful for in life. Not even the fact that she'd been allowed to leave her cell.

She'd refused to receive Konrad in the institution. Nobody was going to see her like that. So ill and broken. Locked up like an animal. The humiliation would have been too much to bear.

'You've lost nothing of your pride, my dear Emma.' Konrad shook his head, but there was no disapproval in his eyes. 'You'd rather go freely to prison than allow me to pay you a visit. And yet now you need my help more than ever.'

Emma nodded.

'Everything depends on how the conversation with your lawyer goes,' they'd told her. The psychiatrists and the police officers, who would surely be waiting outside to take her back.

Did Konrad really have the power to alter her fate? Her old confidant, although 'old' had to be the wrong description for a sporty, almost athletic man of fifty-eight. Emma had met him in the first semester of her medical studies; his name had sounded strangely familiar. Only later did she recall why. Her father and Konrad Luft were colleagues and had joined forces to work together on cases that Emma had read about in the newspaper.

The case that brought her and Konrad together didn't make it into the papers, however.

Emma's ex-boyfriend, Benedict Tannhaus, had drunk one too many and harassed her in a bar near the university. Konrad, who regularly took his evening meal there, saw the guy groping her and actively intervened. Afterwards he'd given Emma his card in case she needed legal assistance, which was indeed the case as her ex turned out to be a persistent stalker.

Emma could have asked her father for help too, of course, but that would have meant swapping one abusive man for another. Although Emma's father had never got physical with her like Benedict, his temper and uncontrolled fits of rage had become worse over the years and she was glad to have avoided contact with him since having moved into her student house. It was a complete mystery to her how her mother managed to stick it out living with her father.

They became friends during the lengthy process by which Konrad obtained a court order against Benedict. To begin with Emma thought that Konrad's interest in her was motivated by other things, and in truth she felt considerably attracted by his paternal charm, despite the big difference in age. As he had in the past, Konrad still kept his prominent chin hidden beneath a meticulously trimmed beard and wore a dark-blue, bespoke double-breasted suit with hand-stitched Budapest shoes. His curly hair was a little shorter now, but still hung over his high forehead, and Emma understood perfectly well why this defence lawyer was contacted so often by well-to-do elderly ladies. They could not suspect that although he loved women, they had no place in his erotic fantasies. Konrad's homosexuality was a secret he'd shared with Emma ever since they became friends.

She hadn't even told Philipp about Konrad's sexual preferences, albeit for selfish reasons, as she had to secretly admit. Because of his appearance and his charms Philipp was frequently the subject of female advances that he wasn't even aware of any more, such as when a sweet waitress would offer him the best table in a restaurant or when he got the friendliest smile in the queue at the supermarket.

This is why it was sometimes good for Emma have her husband react jealously, when Konrad rang yet again to invite her out for brunch. Let Philipp believe that she had admirers too.

Konrad kept his secret to avoid damaging his reputation as a hardcore macho lawyer. He would regularly appear at official functions with pretty law students. *'Better the eternal bachelor unable to commit than the faggot in the courtroom,'* he'd said to Emma as an explanation for his secrecy.

And thus the adventurous, well-coiffed widows showed their disappointment when Konrad told them that he only took on criminal cases rather than divorces, and within his area of expertise only selected the most spectacular, often hopeless-looking cases.

Like hers.

'Thanks for helping me out,' Emma said. A cliché, but she was doing her duty and breaking the silence.

'Again.'

She was now his client for a second time, following the stalking case. Ever since that night in the hotel, when she became the victim of a madman. A serial killer, who'd lain in wait for three women in hotel rooms, then shaven their heads with an electric razor.

... after having brutally raped them...

The hours Emma spent afterwards in hospital were scarcely better than the rape itself. Barely had she regained full consciousness than her orifices were again being manipulated by a stranger. Once again she felt latex fingers in her vagina and objects for taking swabs as evidence. Worst of all, however, were the questions put to her by a grey-haired policewoman with a poker face.

'Where were you raped?'

'In Le Zen. Room 1904.'

'There is no room with that number at the hotel, Frau Stein.'

'They told me that there, too, but it's impossible.'

'Who checked you in?'

'Nobody. I was given the key card along with my conference documents.'

'Did anybody see you in the hotel? Any witnesses?'

'No, I mean yes. A Russian woman.'

'Do you know her name?'

'No.'

'What's her room number?'

'No, she's a...'

'What?'

'Forget it.'

'Okay. Could you describe your attacker?'

'No, it was dark.'

'We couldn't find any defensive wounds.'

'I was drugged. I expect the blood test will reveal what with. I felt a pricking.'

'Did the attacker shave your head before or after penetration?'

'Do you mean before he rammed his dick into my cunt?'

'Look, I understand how upset you must feel.'

'No, you don't.'

'Okay, but I'm afraid I have to ask you these questions all the same. Did the attacker use a condom?'

'Probably, if you say you didn't find any sperm.'

'Nor any major vaginal injuries. Do you frequently change sexual partners?'

'I'm pregnant! Can we please change the subject?'

'Fine. How did you get to the bus stop?'

'I'm sorry?'

'The bus stop at Wittenbergplatz. Where you were found.'

'No idea. I must have lost consciousness at some point.'

'So you don't know for sure that you were raped?'

'*The madman shaved off my hair. My vagina's burning as if it had been poked with a cattle prod. WHAT DO YOU THINK HAPPENED TO ME?*'

The question of all questions.

Emma recalled how Philipp had brought her home by taxi and laid her on the sofa.

'Everything's going to be okay,' he'd said.

She'd nodded and asked him to fetch a tampon. A large one for heavy flow, right at the back of the bathroom cabinet. Emma had started bleeding in the taxi.

It was the first time they'd cried together.

And the last time they'd spoken about children.

The following day Emma lit a candle for the unborn child. It had long burned out.

Emma coughed into her cupped hand and tried to distract herself from these gloomy memories by letting her gaze wander across Konrad's office.

The floor-to-ceiling shelves, which housed not only the leather-bound rulings of the Federal Supreme Court, but also Konrad's favourite works of Schopenhauer, looked slightly lower, probably due to the new coats of paint which made the room appear smaller. And of course the massive desk was in the same place, in front of the almost square windows through which on a clear day you had a view across the Wannsee all the way to Spandau. Today she could see only as far as the promenade on the shore of the lake, along which a handful of pedestrians were struggling through the ankle-deep December snow.

All of a sudden Konrad was beside her bed and Emma felt him gently caress her arm.

'Let me make you a little more comfortable,' he said, stroking her head.

She smelled his spicy aftershave and closed her eyes. Even the idea of being touched by a man had triggered a feeling of revulsion in these last few months. But she allowed Konrad to put his arms around her body and carry her from the bed to the sofa by the fireplace.

'That's better,' he said, as she sank into the soft cushions, half sitting, half lying, and he covered her carefully with a cream cashmere blanket.

And he was right. It *was* better. She felt secure; everything here was familiar. The seating area opposite with the wingback chair to which Konrad returned. The glass coffee table between them. And of course the circular rug at her feet. Fluffy white threads in a black border that looked like a brushstroke thinning out in a clockwise direction. Seen from above the rug appeared to be a hurriedly drawn 'O'. How Emma had loved lying on top of this 'O' in the past and staring into the gas fire as she daydreamed. How happy she'd felt when they ate sushi together. How safe and secure when they discussed relationship troubles, failures and self-doubt and he gave her the advice she wished all her life she'd had from her father.

Over the years the black threads of the rug had faded slightly and assumed a brownish hue.

Time destroys everything, Emma thought, feeling the warmth of the fire on her face, although the cosy feeling she'd always got when visiting Konrad remained absent.

No wonder – this wasn't a visit, after all.

More of a meeting essential to her survival.

'How's Samson?'

'Very well,' Konrad said, and Emma believed him. He'd always had a way with animals. The dog was in the very best hands with him – while she was locked up.

Philipp had given her the snow-white husky with its black-grey mop of frizzy hair soon after that night in the hotel.

'A sledge dog?' she'd said in astonishment when he handed her the lead for the first time.

'He'll get you out of there,' Philipp insisted, by which he meant the *'miserable place'* she was stuck in.

Well, he'd been wrong, and as things looked Samson would have to do without his mistress for quite a while longer.

Maybe for ever.

'Shall we begin?' Emma asked, hoping that Konrad would say no, stand up and leave her alone.

Which of course he didn't.

'Yes, let's,' said the best listener in the world, as a reporter had once described the star lawyer in a newspaper portrait. It was, perhaps, his greatest strength.

There were people who could read between the lines. Konrad could hear between the sentences.

This ability had made him one of the few people Emma could open up to. He knew her past, her secrets and all about her exuberant imagination. She'd told him about Arthur and her psychotherapy, which she believed had liberated her from imaginary friends and other visions. Now she was anything but sure of this.

'I don't think I can, Konrad.'

'You have to.'

Out of a decades-old habit, Emma felt for a strand of hair to twist around her fingers – but her hair was far too short for that.

It had been almost six months ago, but she still couldn't get used to the idea that her long hair, once so splendid, had disappeared. Even though it had already grown back six centimetres.

Konrad gave her such a penetrating look that she had to avert her eyes.

'I can't help you otherwise, Emma. Not after everything that's happened.'

Not after all the deaths. I know.

Emma sighed and closed her eyes. 'Where should I begin?'

'With the worst!' she heard him say. 'Take your mind back to where the memories cause the greatest pain.'

A tear fell from her eyes and she opened them again.

She stared out of the window and watched a man taking a mastiff for a walk along the promenade. From a distance it looked as if the large dog was opening its mouth to catch snowflakes on its tongue, but Emma couldn't be sure. All she knew was that she'd rather be out there, with the man holding the mastiff and the snow at their feet, which couldn't be as cold as the core of her soul.

'Okay,' she said, even though there was nothing about what was to follow that would be okay. Nor would it probably ever be, even if she survived the day, which right now she was not counting on.

'I just don't know what good it will do. I mean you were there during the interrogation.'

At least during the second session. She'd made her first statement alone, but as the officer's questions became more sceptical and Emma started to feel more like a suspect than a witness, she'd demanded her lawyer. Unlike Philipp, who'd had to drive through the night to get to her from where he was working in Bavaria, her best friend had been with her at the hospital at half past one.

'You took me through my statement and you were there when I signed the policewoman's protocol. You know what the Hairdresser did to me that night.'

The Hairdresser.

How the press had made him sound so harmless. Like calling a man who flayed women a scoundrel.

Konrad shook his head. 'I'm not talking about the night in the hotel, Emma.'

She blinked nervously. She knew what he would say next and she prayed she was mistaken.

'You know exactly why you're here.'

'No,' Emma lied.

He wanted to talk about the package, obviously. What else?

'No,' she repeated, less vigorously than before.

'Emma, please. If I'm going to defend you, you have to tell me everything that happened on that day three weeks ago. At your house. Don't leave anything out.'

Emma closed her eyes, hoping that the sofa cushions would swallow her up forever, as the leaves of a carnivorous plant devour a fly, but unfortunately it didn't happen.

And because she probably had no other choice, she started to recount her story in a brittle voice.

The story of the package.

And how, with this package, the horror which had begun that night in the hotel knocked at the door of the little house with its wooden fence at the end of the cul-de-sac and found its way inside.

6

Three weeks earlier

The screw pierced Emma's eardrum and threaded straight into her brain. She didn't know who had switched on the acoustic drill that was puncturing her fear centre. Who it was ringing at her door so early in the morning and throwing her into a panic.

Emma had never regarded her house in Teufelssee-Allee as anything special, even if it was the only detached house in the neighbourhood, the rest of the Heerstrasse Estate consisting of charming 1920s semi-detached properties. And until Philipp turned it into a fortress over the past few weeks, for almost an entire century their small house had been unremarkable, save the fact that you could walk around it without setting a foot on somebody else's land. Very much to the delight of the local children, who on warm summer days used to hold races across their garden. Through the open wooden gate, anticlockwise along the narrow gravel path past the vegetable patch, a sharp left around the veranda, left again beneath the study window and through the overgrown front garden back into the street, where the winner had to tap the old gas lantern and shout, 'First'.

Used to.

In the time before.

Before the Hairdresser.

Now the wooden fence had been replaced by massive grey-green metal struts anchored into the ground and supposedly secure against wild boar, although wild boar were the last things Emma was afraid of.

Her good friend Sylvia thought she was utterly terrified of the man who'd done those dreadful things to her that night in the hotel. But she was wrong. Sure, Emma was afraid that the guy might come back and pick up where he'd left off.

But she was even more afraid of herself than of him.

As a psychiatrist Emma was well aware of the symptoms of severe paranoia. Ironically she'd done her PhD on this subject and it was one of her specialist areas, besides pseudology: pathological lying. She'd treated many patients who got lost in their delusions. She knew how their story ended.

And even worse: she knew how their story began.

Like mine.

The shrill ringing still in her ears, Emma crept to the front door together with Samson, who'd been wrenched from his sleep by the doorbell. It felt as if she'd never get there.

Emma's heart was running a marathon. Her legs were virtually marking time.

A visitor? At this hour? Right now, when Philipp has left?

Samson pushed his nose into the back of her knees, as if encouraging her to go on and saying, *'Come on, it's not that hard.'*

He wasn't growling or baring his teeth, as he usually did when a stranger was at the door.

Which meant she probably wasn't in danger.

Or was she?

Emma just wanted to burst into tears right here in the hallway. Crying – her favourite pastime at the moment. For the last 158 days, 12 hours and 14 minutes.

Since my new haircut.

She felt the hair above her forehead. Felt how much the strands had grown back. She'd already done that twenty times today. In the past hour.

Emma stepped up to the heavy oak door and opened the tiny curtain across the palm-sized pane of glass set into the wood at head height.

According to the land registry, Teufelssee-Allee was in the Westend district, but compared to the villas this posh areas was famous for, her little house looked more like a dog kennel with steps.

It was at the apex of the turning circle of a cobbled

cul-de-sac, which was difficult for large cars to navigate and practically impossible for small lorries. From a distance the house blended in well with the neighbourhood, with its light, coarse render, the old-fashioned wooden windows, a clay-coloured tiled roof and the obligatory reddish-brown clinker steps leading up to the front door, through which she was spying.

Apart from the fence, the most recent modifications were not visible from outside: the glass-break sensors, the radio-controlled locking system, the motion detectors in the ceilings or the panic button in the wall connected to the emergency services, which Emma had her hand on right now.

Better safe than sorry.

It was eleven o'clock in the morning, and a miserable day – the grey, impenetrable cloud seemed almost close enough to touch – but it wasn't raining (it was probably too cold), nor was it snowing as it had done almost uninterruptedly for the past few days, so Emma could clearly make out the man at the gate.

From afar he looked like a Turkish rocker: dark skin, clean-shaven head, ZZ Top beard and silver, coin-sized metal rings that filled the earlobes of his 120-kilo hulk like alloy wheels would a tyre. The man wore blue-and-yellow gloves, but Emma knew that each finger inside them was tattooed with a different letter.

It's not him! Thank God! she thought, a massive weight falling from her soul. Samson stood beside her, his ears pricked in anticipation. She gave him the sign to make room.

Emma pressed the button to open the gate and waited.

Sandwiched between Teufelsberg in the north, several sports grounds and schools in the west, the AVUS Circuit in the south and the S-Bahn and federal railway tracks in the east, the Heerstrasse Estate was home to around 150 mainly middle-class families. A rural community in the middle of the metropolis, with all the advantages and disadvantages of living in a village, such as the fact that everybody knew everybody else by name and what they were up to.

Even the delivery man.

7

'Hello, Salim.'

'Good morning, Frau Doktor.'

Emma had waited for the delivery man to climb the few steps before opening the door a crack, as far as the metal bolt inside would allow.

Sitting beside her, Samson started wagging his tail, as he always did when he heard the delivery man's voice.

'Sorry to keep you waiting so long, I was upstairs,' Emma apologised with a frog in her throat.

She wasn't used to speaking any more.

'No problem, no problem.'

Salim Yüzgec put the delivery on the top step under the porch, kicked some snow from his heels and smiled as he fished the obligatory treat from his trouser pocket. As he did every time, he checked that Emma didn't mind and, as every time, she gave Samson the sign to grab the dog biscuit.

'How are you today, Frau Doktor?' he asked.

Fine. I've just swallowed ten milligrams of Cipralex

and spent from nine o'clock till half past ten breathing into a bag. Thanks for asking.

'Getting a little better by the day,' she lied and felt that her attempt to return his smile was a desperate strain.

Salim was a sympathetic chap, who occasionally brought over a pot of vegetable soup his wife had made. *'So you don't lose any more weight.'* But his concern for the psychiatrist was based on false assumptions.

To stop the neighbourhood from gossiping wildly about why the Frau Doktor no longer stepped outside the house, spent the whole day in her dressing gown and was neglecting her practice, Philipp had told the woman who owned the kiosk that Emma had suffered severe food poisoning, which had attacked her vital organs and almost killed her.

Frau Kolowski was the biggest gossip on the estate and by the time the message had reached Salim's ears, the poisoning had escalated into cancer. But it was better for people to think that Emma had lost her hair through chemotherapy than for them to chinwag about the truth. About her and the Hairdresser.

Why should strangers believe her if her husband didn't? Of course, Philipp tried as hard as he could to hide his doubts. But he'd done his own investigation and found practically nothing that supported her version of the events.

In everyday Chinese, Japanese and Korean the number four has a similarity to the word 'death', which is why it's considered unlucky in some circles. In the areas where Cantonese is spoken, the number fourteen even means 'certain death', which is why the Le Zen owners, who were from Guangdong, not only did away with the corresponding room numbers, but the fourth and fourteenth floors too.

Not even the suspicion that Emma had mistaken her room number was of much help. From her description of the view the only possibilities were rooms 1903 and 1905. Both had been booked for the entire week by a single mother from Australia with three children, who were having a holiday in Berlin. In neither room was there any sign of forceful entry or a physical assault. And neither room had a portrait of Ai Weiwei, which wasn't a surprise as there wasn't a picture of the Chinese artist anywhere in the hotel. This was another reason why the investigating team didn't accord Emma's 'case' a particularly high priority.

And why she increasingly doubted her sanity.

How could she blame Philipp for being sceptical, given such an unbelievable story? A rape in a hotel room that didn't officially exist and which she'd searched thoroughly just before the alleged attack had taken place?

Emma also claimed she'd been abused by a serial killer notorious for shaving the heads of his victims. But all of these so far had been prostitutes and none had lived to tell the tale. For that was another of the Hairdresser's trademarks: he killed female escorts who he'd ambushed in their rooms.

I'm the only one he let live. Why?

It was no surprise that the police were reluctant to attribute her case to the Hairdresser. Amongst Philipp's colleagues she was seen as a self-mutilating madwoman who invented horror stories. But at least she wasn't being hassled by the press.

Only by the delivery man.

'I didn't expect you so early,' Emma said, opening the door to Salim.

'I just fell out of bed this morning,' the delivery man laughed.

Since she'd stopped leaving the house (even walking the dog was Philipp's job), she had many things she needed delivered to her door. Today Salim stood there with relatively few packages. She signed for the receipt of her contact lenses; the online pharmacy had finally sent the painkillers; and the larger, lighter box probably contained the warm slippers you could put in the microwave. Finally there was her daily crate of food for which she'd set up a standing order with the online supermarket.

Philipp was responsible for drinks and all non-perishable items such as preserves, detergents or loo paper. But it was better that vegetables, milk, fish, butter and bread didn't hang around in his car when, as so often, he was suddenly called away and came home hours later than expected.

Recently he hadn't spent several days away at a time, as he did that fateful weekend. Not since the madman had rendered Emma immobile with an injection, stripped off her pyjamas and lain on top of her with all his weight.

In the last few months Philipp had insisted on spending the nights with her. He was even prepared to cancel the Europa Meeting this weekend, even though it was the most important workshop of the year. The leading profilers throughout Europe met only once every twelve months to pool their knowledge. Two days, and a different city every year. This time it was in Germany, in a hotel in Bad Saarow beside the Scharmützelsee. A must-attend event for this sworn band of extraordinary personalities who had to spend every day engaging with the worst things that mankind was capable of – and on this occasion Philipp even had the honour of giving a lecture about his work.

'I insist! If anything happens I'll call you right away. I mean you're practically round the corner, only an hour away,' Emma had said this morning as she gave him a goodbye kiss, while actually wanting to scream, *'An hour? It didn't take that madman much longer to turn me into a psychological wreck.'*

'Step by step I've got to drag myself out of this hole,' she'd said, hoping he'd realise that she was merely parroting hollow phrases from the psychiatry manual that she no longer believed in. Nor did she believe the final lie she sent Philipp off with: 'I'll cope on my own.'

Yes, for five whole seconds as she waved to him from the kitchen window. Then she'd lost her composure and started headbutting the wall until Samson jumped up at her and stopped her from doing herself further injury.

'Thanks very much,' Emma said once she'd taken everything off the delivery man and trudged back into the hallway.

Salim offered to carry the boxes into the kitchen (*I'm not that bad yet*) then slapped his forehead.

'I almost forgot. Could you take this for your neighbour?'

Salim picked up a shoebox-sized package from the floor. Emma had thought it couldn't be for her, and she'd been right.

'For my neighbour?' Her knees began trembling as she evaluated the potential consequences of this dreadful request if she were to be so crazy as to agree to it.

Just like the last time, when she'd kindly accepted the book delivery for the dentist, she'd sit for hours in the darkness, unable to do anything but think constantly about *when* it would happen. *When* the bell would shred the silence and announce the unwanted visitor.

As her hands became clammier and her mouth drier, she would keep counting the minutes and later the seconds until the strange object had vanished from her house.

But that was not the worst thought running amok in

her mind when she read the name of the addressee on the sticker.

Herr A. Palandt
Teufelssee-Allee 16a
14055 Berlin

Having the strange object in her house was one thing – she might be able to cope with that. It would change her routine and throw her emotional balance into disarray, but in itself the package wasn't a problem.

It was the name.

Her pulse racing and hands getting wetter by the second, she stared at the address printed on the package and just wanted to weep.

8

Palandt?

Who... *the hell*... is Herr A. Palandt?

In the past she wouldn't have given the matter a thought, but now her ignorance gave free rein to her darkest fantasies, which frightened her so much that Emma was on the verge of tears.

Teufelssee-Allee 16a?

Wasn't that the left-hand side of the street, three or four houses along, just around the corner? Hadn't old Frau Tornow lived there alone for years? Not...

A. Palandt...?

She knew everybody in the area, but she'd never heard *his* name before, and this unleashed a general feeling of helplessness inside her.

She'd been living in this small cul-de-sac for four years now. Four years since they'd bought the far-too-expensive property, which they'd only been able to afford because Philipp had inherited some money.

'You want me to take it?' Emma asked, without touching the package.

It was wrapped in normal brown paper and the edges reinforced with sticky tape. Two lengths of fibrous string were tied around the package, forming a cross on the front. Nothing unusual.

Apart from the name…

Herr A. Palandt?

'Please,' Salim said, inching his hand with the package closer to her. 'I'll pop a note through his door to say he can pick it up from you.'

No, please don't!

'Why not?' Salim asked in astonishment. She must have spoken her thoughts out loud.

'Those are the regulations, you see. I have to do it. Otherwise the package isn't insured.'

'I understand, but today I'm afraid I can't…'

'Please, Frau Stein. You'd be doing me a huge favour. My shift is almost over. For a very long time, I fear.'

For a very long time.

'What do you mean?'

Emma unconsciously took a step backwards. Sensing her anxiety, Samson sat up beside her and pricked up his ears.

'Don't worry, I'm not getting the sack or anything like that. It's good news for me Naya and Engin.'

'Naya's your wife, isn't she?' Emma said, confused.

'That's right, I showed you a picture of her once. For

the moment there's only an ultrasound thing of Engin.'

A cold draught blew through the door, fluttering Emma's dressing gown. She froze internally.

'Your wife's… *pregnant?*'

The word weighed so heavily inside her that she could barely get it out of her mouth.

Pregnant.

A combination of eight letters that had a completely different meaning today from half a year ago.

Back then, in the time before, the word represented a dream, the future, it was a symbol of joy and the very meaning of life. Today it merely described an open wound, lost happiness, and spoken softly sounded similar to 'never' or 'dead'.

Salim, who'd clearly interpreted her visible bewilderment as stunned delight, was grinning from ear to ear.

'Yes, she's in her sixth month,' Salim laughed. 'She's already got a belly like this,' he added, making the corresponding gesture with his hand. 'It works brilliantly with the admin job. You know, office work? The pay's better, but I'll be sorry not to see you any more, Frau Stein. You've always been really nice to me.'

All Emma could say was, 'What wonderful news' in a rather monotone voice, which made her feel ashamed. In the past she'd responded with enthusiasm to every baby announcement amongst her acquaintances. Even when some of her friends started asking why it was taking her so long, and whether there was a problem. She hadn't once felt envious, let alone bitter, just because it hadn't worked immediately for her and Philipp.

Unlike her mother, who became really irate when others revelled in their delight at being pregnant. The unexpected miscarriage when Emma was six had changed her. And her mother never fell pregnant again.

What about now?

Now was the time afterwards; now she could understand her mother's bitterness.

Fecund? Feck off!

Emma had turned into a different person. A woman with a sore vagina who knew the taste of latex as well as the feeling of vibrating steel on her shaven head. A woman well aware that a single, fateful event could change or even kill off all emotions.

Nice.

She thought of the last thing Salim had said and something occurred to her.

'Just wait a sec, please.'

'No, please don't. It's not necessary, really,' Salim called out after her. He knew what she had in mind when she instructed Samson to sit by the door.

To guard the delivery man too.

In the living room she noticed she was carrying the small package by her chest; she must have taken it from Salim after all – *Christ!*

Now it's in the house.

Emma placed it next to her laptop on the desk, which stood in front of the window that looked onto the garden, and opened the top drawer. She rummaged around for her purse that hopefully had enough for a tip she could give Salim as a parting gift.

The purse had slid into the corner at the very back of the drawer, which meant she had to take out some papers obstinately stuck in front of it.

A letter from the insurance company, bills, unread get-well-soon cards, brochures for washing machines and…

Emma froze as she saw the flyer in her hand.

She was desperate to turn her gaze from the glossy photo.

Bzzzzzz.

A buzzing started up in her head. A loud buzzing. She felt the vibrations on her scalp. It immediately started itching. She wanted to scratch herself but there was as little chance of doing that as there was of freeing herself from the vice that was keeping her head in position and forcing her to stare at the flyer.

Philipp had taken down all the mirrors in the house so that Emma didn't have to be continually reminded of that night by looking at her 'haircut'. All scissors and razors had been banned from the bathroom.

But he hadn't thought about a simple flyer that came with the paper.

Hand-held appliance with stainless-steel blades.

Only €49.90. With hair-cutting function! Save on your hairdressing bills!

Emma heard a soft click, which always preceded the avalanche of her nightmares, right before they fell from the precipice of her soul.

She closed her eyes. And as Emma collapsed to the floor she fell into the rats' nest of her memories.

9

Most people think that sleep is death's little brother, whereas in fact it is his arch enemy. Not *sleep*, but *tiredness,* is the vanguard of eternal darkness. It is the arrow the man in the black hood shoots unerringly at us every evening, and which sleep endeavours with all its might to pull out of us every night. Unfortunately, however, it is poisoned, and however much the flow of our dreams tries to wash the poison away, a residue always remains. The older we get, the more difficult it becomes to climb out of bed feeling recovered and rested. Like a once-clean sponge, the capillaries of our existence soak up a black ink, and the sponge becomes ever more saturated. The dream images that were once happy and colourful turn into nightmarish distortions until sleep finally loses its battle against tiredness and one day, exhausted, we pass over into a dreamless oblivion.

Emma loved sleep.

Only she didn't like the dreams that the poison of exhaustion had transformed into horrific visions.

Horrific because they were so real, and this reflected what had actually happened to her.

As every time when she was unconscious, it began with a sound.

Bzzzzzz.

Not with the violent penetration, the heavy breathing in her ear or the fitful coughing that thrust waves of peppermint-smelling breath into her face while the Hairdresser pinched her nipples as he came inside his condom. She couldn't be certain if these visions were real memories or the excruciating attempt by her brain to fill with nightmares the lost hours between the attack in the hotel and waking up at the bus stop.

It always began with the buzzing of the razor, which grew shriller and sharper when the vibrating blades touched hair.

Hair.

Symbol of sexuality and fertility since the dawn of time. The reason why women in many cultures cover their heads to avoid arousing the devil inside men. The devil, who otherwise...

... would overwhelm, rape and then scalp me...

The Scalper, an awkward but far more accurate term for the attacker than *the Hairdresser*, because he didn't style his victims' hair, he tore their lives from their heads.

As ever, Emma was unable to distinguish between dream and reality when she felt the cool blade on her head, paralysed as she was either by exhaustion or an anaesthetic in her bloodstream. She felt the electric blade vibrating on her forehead, and it didn't hurt when it moved upwards and to the back of her head. It didn't hurt and yet it felt like dying.

Why does he do it?

A question to which Emma thought she'd found the answer.

The attacker had raped her and he felt ashamed. An intelligent man, well aware of what he'd done, he wasn't trying to undo the crime, but to shift the responsibility to the victim.

Emma hadn't covered herself; her plainly visible, abundant locks of hair had enticed the male animal from his lair. For this she didn't have to be punished, but made to look respectable so that no man gazing at her could possibly get wrong idea.

That's why he shaved my head.

Not to humiliate me.

But to drive out the devil that led him into temptation.

Emma heard a crackling whenever the blades hit a crown, felt her head being turned to the side so he could get at her temples, felt a burning when the foil went in too deep and caught a bit of skin, felt a latex glove on her mouth, smelled the rubber covering her lips which would have probably opened to scream, and it dawned on her...

... that he waited for me...

He'd sought her out. He knew her!

He'd been watching her beforehand. Her hair when she twisted a strand around her finger. Her locks that danced on her shoulder blade when she turned around.

He knows me. Do I know him too?

At the very moment she asked herself this question, Emma felt the tongue. Long, rough, full of spittle. It was licking her face. Slobbering over her nose, closed eyes and forehead. This was new.

This had never happened before.

Emma felt a damp pressure on her cheek, opened her eyes and saw Samson above her head.

It took a while for her to realise that she was lying on the living-room floor beside her desk.

She was awake. But the arrow of tiredness had buried itself deeper than before. Her body felt as if it were full of lead, and she wouldn't have been surprised if her own weight had dragged her down into the basement, if she'd crashed straight through the parquet floor into the laundry room or into the study that Philipp had set up down there so he didn't have to keep on going to the office at weekends.

But of course she didn't crash through the robust parquet; she stayed where she was, lying on the ground floor, a couple of metres away from the sizzling fireplace, its flames flickering with unusual vigour.

They were being stirred, as if by the wind. Immediately Emma felt a breath of cold on her face, then on the whole of her body.

A draught.

The fire dancing in the cold draught could only mean one thing.

The front door!

It was open.

10

sorry, had to go.

take care!

A tiny Post-it note with little space, which was why
Salim had written his farewell note in small letters.

With clammy fingers Emma removed the yellow
sticker from the wooden frame of her front door and
screwed up her eyes. It had started snowing again. At
the other end of the street, just before the junction,
children were playing 'It' between the parked cars, but
there was no sign of the delivery man or his yellow van.

How long was I out of it?

Emma checked her watch: 11.13.

So she'd been unconscious for almost a quarter of
an hour.

During which the front door had been open.

Not wide open, just a few centimetres, but still.

She shuddered.

What now? What should I do?

Samson was rubbing up against her legs like a cat. It was probably his way of saying it was bloody cold, so she finally went to shut the door.

Emma had to brace herself against it, for all of a sudden a violent gust of wind blew straight at the house, howling and hurling a few snowflakes into the hallway before the lock clicked and the room fell silent.

She looked to her left, where the mirror that had been left in the wall unit would have shown her red cheeks had it not been covered in packing paper.

It would have probably been fogged up by her breath too.

With writing on it?

Emma was briefly tempted to rip the paper from the mirror to check for hidden messages. But she'd done this so often and never found any writing on the glass. No *'I'm back'* or *'Your end is nigh'*. And Philipp had never complained about having to repaper the mirror.

'I'm sorry,' Emma told herself, unsure what she was referring to. The conversations she had with herself, which ran into the dozens per day, were making less and less sense.

Was she sorry that she'd abandoned Salim without giving him a tip? That she was causing Philipp all this trouble? Ignoring his suggestions, avoiding being intimate with him and having refused him her body for months now? Or was she sorry that she was letting herself go? As a psychiatrist she knew, of course, that paranoia wasn't an illness but a weakness, for which you needed therapy. *If you've got the strength for it.* And that the overreactions were a symptom of this suffering, which wouldn't go away of its own accord, just because she 'got a grip on herself'. Those who weren't afflicted were often suspicious of the mentally ill. They would wonder, for example, how a world-famous actor or artist who 'had it all' could possibly commit suicide, in spite of their fame, wealth and endless 'friends'. But these people knew nothing of the demons that would embed themselves, particularly into sensitive souls, then at the moment of that person's greatest happiness whisper into their ear and reel off their shortcomings. Psychologically healthy people would tell depressives to stop being so miserable all the time, and urge paranoid individuals like her to stop making such a fuss and checking the front door every time the beams creaked. But that was a bit like asking a man with a broken shin bone to run the marathon.

What now?

Unsure, she looked at the post by her feet, which Salim had delivered. The narrow, white packet of contact lenses could stay in the hallway for the time being, as could her medicines and the slightly larger box with the gloves. The food had to be put into the fridge, but at the moment Emma felt too weak to drag the crate into the kitchen.

I can't be afraid and carry stuff at the same time.

At her ankles, Samson shook himself and Emma wished she could do the same, simply shake her entire body and cast off everything that was currently bearing down on her.

'You would have barked, wouldn't you?' she asked him. Samson pricked up his ears and put his head to one side.

Of course he would have.

Samson was so attached to his mistress that he growled whenever a stranger approached the house. Never in his life would he allow an intruder to enter.

Or would he?

Although she was paralysed by the thought that she couldn't be one hundred per cent sure she was alone in the house, she could hardly call Philipp and ask him to come back for no reason at all.

Or was there a reason?

She had an idea.

'Don't move!' she ordered Samson, and opened the fitted cupboard by the front door, which housed the small white box that controlled the alarm system. The digits on the control panel lit up as soon as her hand moved close.

1 – 3 – 0 – 1

The date they met. At Sylvia's birthday party.

The alarm was programmed to call Emma's mobile at the sign of a break-in. If she wasn't available or didn't give the correct code word (*Rosenhan*), a police patrol would be dispatched immediately.

Emma pressed a pictogram showing an empty house, thereby activating all motion detectors. With a second button (G) she switched the ground-floor sensors back off.

'Now we can move around,' she said. 'But we're staying downstairs, do you hear me?' If anyone entered unauthorised, she'd hear as soon as they moved upstairs or in the basement.

It was highly unlikely that anyone was hiding on the ground floor. There were no curtains in the living room, no large cupboards, chests or other hiding places. The sofa was right up against the wall, which itself had no nooks and crannies.

But better to be safe than sorry.

Emma took her mobile from the pocket of her dressing gown, opened her list of favourites and pressed her thumb on Philipp's name, so she could contact him in an emergency. She was about to go back into the living room with Samson, but had to turn around again because she was no longer certain if she'd turned the key twice.

Once she'd had another check and again resisted the impulse to look in the mirror, she followed Samson who'd already pattered noisily back to his sleeping blanket beside the fire.

I really ought to get his claws cut, she thought, but

not out of concern for the parquet, which was tatty anyway and urgently needed a good polish as soon as she could cope with people in the house again.

In another life, perhaps.

She was ashamed that he got so little exercise. This morning a mere quarter of an hour, when Philipp had taken him once around the block before leaving for the conference. Emma herself always let him out on his own in the garden, where he did his business like a good dog at the rhododendron beside the tool shed, while she waited behind the locked door for him to come back.

The fact that the dog was behaving so peacefully was a sure sign that they were alone, at least here downstairs. A mere fly would get Samson worked up and he'd start wagging his tail excitedly. He was so fixated on Emma that even in Philipp's presence he never relaxed completely. She was never far from Samson, which meant that her husband automatically assumed the role of a guest who was watched affectionately, but without a break.

Emma sat at the desk, its drawer still open. She managed to stuff back in the flyer that had triggered her memory, without looking at the razor advertisement again. Then she decided to break from her usual routine and take a closer look at the package before embarking on her 'work'.

Taking it in both hands she turned it around. It couldn't weigh more than three bars of chocolate, perhaps less, which probably made it a parcel, although

Emma wasn't an expert in these matters. As far as she was concerned, anything in a solid container and larger than a shoebox was a package.

She shook it beside her head as a barman might a cocktail mixer, but she couldn't hear anything. No ticking, no humming, nothing that suggested an electrical item or (God forbid) a creature. All she could feel was that something light was moving inside. Sliding back and forth. It didn't seem particularly fragile, although she couldn't say this with any certainty.

Emma even gave the package a sniff, but couldn't detect anything out of the ordinary. No pungent, acrid smell of some caustic chemical or maybe a poison. Nothing that pointed to anything dangerous inside.

Apart from the fact that Emma found its mere existence threatening, it appeared to be a perfectly normal package, of the sort that is delivered in Germany every day by the tens of thousands.

You could get that packing paper in any stationer's or at the post office, if you could still find one open. In *the time before*, Emma remembered, they were closing at an alarming rate.

The string tied around the package looked exactly like the stuff she used to make things out of as a child: grey, coarse strands.

Emma studied the sticker on the front, which gave A. Palandt as the addressee, but oddly the box for the sender's details was empty. No company or private address.

It must have been dispatched via an automated Packstation, the only way of sending packages anonymously, something Emma had discovered this last Christmas when wanting to send her mother a package without her immediately realising who it was from. All the same Emma had entered an invented name *(Father Christmas, 24 Santa Street, North Pole)*. On this package, however, the address box was completely empty, which nearly unnerved her more than the fact that she didn't know of a neighbour by the name of Palandt.

She put the package aside again, almost in disgust, pushing it well away from her to the far end of the desk.

'Do you really not want to keep me company?' Emma said, turning back to Samson. In all her hours of loneliness she'd become used to talking to him as if he were a small child carefully watching whatever she did during the day. Today, however, he seemed peculiarly sleepy, having snuggled up so peacefully next to the fire rather than at her feet beneath the desk.

'Oh well,' Emma sighed when he continued to make no reaction. 'The main thing is you don't snitch on me. You know I promised Philipp I wouldn't.'

But today of all days she couldn't help herself. No matter how angry he'd get if he found out.

She simply had to do it.

Feeling as if she were betraying her husband, she flipped open her laptop and began her 'work'.

11

There was only one photo of her with Philipp that Emma didn't hate, and that had been taken by a two-year-old thief.

Around five years ago, on the way to an exhibition of a photographer friend of theirs, they'd taken refuge from a downpour in a tourist trap on Hackescher Markt – a 'potato restaurant' with long benches lined up along a sort of trestle table, which they had to share with a good dozen other fugitives from the weather.

Obliged by the waiting staff to order more than just drinks, they opted for potato cakes with apple sauce. It is unlikely that this unspectacular late-April afternoon would have branded itself on her memory if Emma hadn't found these strange photos on her mobile the next day.

The first four were completely dark. The fifth showed the edge of a table, as did the six that followed, plus the individual responsible for these blurred pictures, starting with just the thumb and ending with the entire person:

a blonde girl with sticking-up hair, a semolina-smeared mouth and the sort of diabolic smile that only small children are capable of. She must have stolen the phone without them noticing.

Seven photographs taken without a flash showed bits of Philipp and Emma. On one of them they were even smiling, but the nicest picture was the one in which time seemed to have fled into another room: Emma and Philipp standing side by side, gazing into each other's eyes while both their forks had spiked the same piece of potato cake. It was as if the image were from a film in which the sound – restaurant guests yelling over one another, children bawling and the noisy clatter of cutlery – breaks off abruptly and the freeze frame is accompanied by a romantic piano melody.

Emma had no idea that she and her husband still exchanged such loving glances, and the fact that this photo had been taken unawares, free from any suspicion that it might have been staged, made it all the more prized in her eyes. For Philipp too, who loved the picture, he thought there was something 'James Dean' about his gangly poise, whatever he meant by that.

Earlier, in the time before, Emma looked at the photograph every day at five o'clock, when Philipp called her to say if he'd be back for dinner or not, because she'd selected the image as the contact photo for his number. She kept a copy of the picture in the inner pocket of her favourite handbag, and for a while it had even been the screensaver on her notebook, until a system update inexplicably wiped it from the computer.

Just like my self-confidence, my zest for life. My life.

Sometimes Emma wondered whether the Hairdresser had also given her a system reboot that night in the hotel and restored her emotional hard drive to its factory settings. And clearly she was a dud: defective goods that unfortunately couldn't be exchanged.

Emma clicked the Outlook icon on the taskbar, the standard screensaver vanished and now she could focus on her unpleasant, but necessary daily task.

Her daily 'work' consisted of trawling the internet for the latest reports about the Hairdresser. Philipp had expressly forbidden her to do this after the papers had got hold of the criminal profile he'd drawn up thanks to an indiscretion by the public prosecution department. They'd slugged it out for days. Philipp was worried that the sensational tabloid reports would unsettle Emma even more, and so she had to proceed with caution.

Secretly, like an adulteress.

She surfed in private mode via a search engine that didn't save browser history. And the folder where she chronologically stored all the reports and information about the case was labelled 'Diet' and password protected.

Currently the internet was awash with another flood of speculation because the Hairdresser had struck again the previous week. Again in a five-star Berlin hotel, this time on Potsdamer Platz, and once more a prostitute had been poisoned with an overdose of gamma-hydroxybutyric acid. Residues of it had been identified in Emma's blood test too, but the investigating officers didn't see this as conclusive proof. She was a psychiatrist, which meant that it was easy for her to get hold of this product, which in small doses was a stimulant and often used as a party drug. Even easier than shaving her hair off.

The tabloid articles gave more details about the sexual preferences of Natascha W. (22) than the person who'd lost her life in agonising pain. A study of readers' comments in internet forums gave the impression that the majority pinned at least some of the blame on the women, for who offered themselves to total strangers for money?

It didn't occur to most of the commentators that the victims were sentient beings. The Russian woman who'd knocked at Emma's hotel door that night had more empathy than all of them put together.

It was just bad luck that the investigation team hadn't been able to find her. But hardly a surprise. What female escort would give their real name to reception or say which room they were booked in? In luxury hotels such 'girls' were unavoidable but invisible guests.

Crack.

A log fell from its burning pile in the fireplace, and whereas Samson's nose didn't even twitch, Emma jumped in fright.

She glanced out of the window, staring at the fir she decorated as a Christmas tree every year. Its branches were weighed down by the snow.

The sight of nature was one of the few things that calmed her. Emma loved her garden. To be able to get back outside and tend to it was a major impetus to ridding herself of this ridiculous nuisance in her head. At some point she was certain she'd find the strength to go into therapy and let an expert check her self-medication.

At some point, just not today.

In her inbox Emma found what was obviously a spam email threatening to block her bank cards, as well as several news alerts for the keyword 'hairdresser', including an article in *Bild* and one in the *Berliner Zeitung*, which she opened first. When she established that it didn't say anything new, she copied it as a PDF in the 'Hairdresser_THREE_Investigations_ NATASCHA' folder.

In truth she'd taken the place the Hairdresser had earmarked for Emma. Natascha was already number four.

I'm just the woman who doesn't count.

For each victim Emma had subfolders for 'Private life', 'Professional life' and 'Own theories', but those dedicated to the official investigations were obviously the most important.

Here there was also the *Spiegel* article about Philipp's initial profile, which characterised the killer as a psychopathic narcissist. Affluent, cultured and with a high level of education. So in love with himself that he was incapable of forming a firm relationship. Because he believed himself to be perfect, he blamed women for his loneliness. Women who gave men the come-on, but who only wanted one thing from them: money. It was their fault that such a handsome chap like himself couldn't control his urges. He regarded the act of shaving as a service he was performing for the world of men by making the women ugly.

It was possible that there were other victims, like Emma, who'd 'only' had their hair shorn off after the rape. Maybe he didn't necessarily want to kill his victims, only if he still found them attractive when they were bald.

This idea had led Philipp to the suggestion that the Hairdresser might have worn a night-vision device during his attacks to assess the end results. A supposition that Emma had put in the 'Theories' folder, along with the one that the attacker could be repulsed by the sight of blood. But he'd cut Emma while shaving her head. In hospital they'd treated the wound on her forehead and washed away the encrusted blood. This had possibly been the reason for her survival, for the wound and the blood might have disfigured her in such a way that the Hairdresser considered his deed complete.

Philipp was not officially on the case because of his personal involvement, although 'involvement' was a polite euphemism for 'crazed wife with madcap violent fantasies'.

Unofficially, of course, Philipp was tapping all his sources to keep abreast of the investigations. Emma was convinced he wasn't telling her everything he knew, otherwise she wouldn't have gasped when she opened the *Bild* home page.

Jesus Christ!

Emma slapped a hand over her mouth and blinked.

The headline above the photograph consisted of only three words, but these filled two thirds of her monitor:

IS THIS HIM?

The green-tinged colour photo had been taken by a camera in the ceiling of a lift.

From the back right-hand corner a man in a grey hoodie was visible. His face was three quarters covered and the rest could have belonged to pretty much any white adult male wearing jeans and sneakers.

What unnerved Emma wasn't the sight of the slim, average-height man about to step into the lobby of the hotel where victim number two had lost her life.

But what the man was holding as he left the lift.

'Here you can see a man who wasn't registered as a guest leaving the hotel on the night that Lariana F. died,' the article said. As it was not certain that this man was the killer, they had refrained earlier from publishing the photograph for reasons of data protection. Now, however, they were doing it given the lack of alternatives.

The usual telephone numbers were listed for information relevant to the case, as well as a direct link to the police.

God almighty! Are my eyes playing tricks on me, or is that…?

Emma looked on the desk for a paper bag she could breathe into. When she couldn't find a bag she considered going into the kitchen to fetch one, but then decided to enlarge the photo first.

Zoom into the hands that were still wearing latex gloves.

Into the fingers.

Into the object they were gripping.

'*The authorities are working on the assumption that this is the Hairdresser making off with his trophies,*' the lurid text continued.

Her hair? In a package.

Emma looked up. Her eyes wandered across the desk, then back to the picture.

A small package wrapped in plain brown paper.

Roughly like the one in front of her. The anonymous package that Salim had given Emma for her neighbour.

A. Palandt.

Whose name she'd never heard before.

Emma felt a small bead of sweat drip from the back of her neck and trickle down her spine, then she heard Samson growl before the alarm sounded in the attic.

12

What was that?

Once the fear had coursed into her limbs, Emma forced herself not to panic but to find out what was going on.

The noise was too quiet and too distant for the shrill din that the motion detector would have set off. Captured by the infra-red sensors, a single movement would trigger a deafening interval alarm throughout the entire house. Not just on one of the upper floors.

Besides, the sound was too rich, almost melodic.

Like a...

Emma had an inkling, but couldn't put a finger on it. Her thoughts dissipated almost simultaneously with the beeping that stopped as abruptly as it had started.

'What was that?' she asked out loud, but Samson remained horizontal, not even raising his head from his fat paws, which was very unlike him and caused Emma to worry that she might have imagined the sound.

Am I suffering from aural hallucinations now too?

Emma shut her laptop, pushed her chair from the desk and stood up.

The parquet creaked beneath her feet, which is why she tiptoed her way to the stairs in her ballerina slippers. Leaning against the wooden banisters in the hallway she listened, but could hear nothing save for a soft whooshing in her ear, the tinnitus that everyone experiences when they focus too hard on their own hearing.

Emma switched off the motion detectors using the control panel by the front door.

Then she crept upstairs to the first floor, where there was the bedroom, a dressing room and a large bathroom.

She'd forgotten to turn on the light by the stairs, and up here (she was just two steps from the first-floor landing) the roller blinds were still down (sometimes when the migraine side effects of her psychotropic drugs set in she blocked out the light all day long), so it felt as if Emma were climbing into the darkness.

Bugger this, she'd go into the basement. At least there she could defend herself with the fire extinguisher that was hanging on the wall by the stairs.

'Samson, come here, boy!' she called out without turning around because she was suddenly afraid that someone might slip out of the black hole and come at her on the stairs. And then, as if Philipp had also installed a voice detector for her security, these words set the alarm off again.

Oh God!

Emma bit her bottom lip to stop herself from screaming.

It could, of course, be pure coincidence that she was hearing it again now. But there it was: the mysterious sound. And she wasn't imagining it.

A high-pitched beeping, somewhat louder now because she had moved towards the source, which evidently wasn't on the first floor, but higher up, below the roof. And the alarm reminded Emma of her incomplete thought from a few minutes ago, with a number of associations.

An alarm clock was the most harmless, but also the most unlikely, explanation, because up in the attic there was nothing but paint pots, pulled-up floorboards, a torn-down drywall and all manner of tools dotted about the place. But no clock! And even if there had been, why should it start ringing today, half a year after they'd abandoned their renovation?

No, there wasn't an alarm clock in the nursery building site, which Emma secretly called BER after the capital's airport which probably would never be finished either. That night her desire for children had been shorn along with her hair.

'*For the time being,*' Philipp had told her. '*For good,*' her soul said.

But if it wasn't an alarm clock, then it could only be a...

... *mobile phone.*

'Samson, come on!' Emma called out again, louder and more energetically. She was unsettled by the thought of a mobile ringing in the attic above her head. The inevitable conclusion that it must belong to somebody pushed Emma to the edge of panic.

Which she toppled over when the bathroom door slammed shut only a few metres ahead of her.

13

She ran. Without thinking, without making any rational decisions or even weighing up her options, because then she would have certainly hurried downstairs, back to Samson. To the exit.

Instead she leaped up the last couple of steps, crossed the narrow landing virtually blind, losing a slipper, yanked open her bedroom door and shut it again behind her. Emma locked the door with the simple key which – thank God – was on the inside. She grabbed a chair and wedged the backrest under the handle, as she'd seen in films…

… *but does that make any sense?*

No, nothing made sense here, it hadn't for a long while. Ever since she'd been picked up off the ground by the bus stop outside Le Zen.

Without hair.

Without dignity.

Without reason.

Emma's eyes slowly became accustomed to the darkness.

In the scant daylight that seeped through the slats of the roller blind she could only make out shapes. Shadows. Vague surfaces. The bed, the wardrobe, the heavy door.

Squatting down beside a chest of drawers, an heirloom from her grandmother where she kept her underwear, Emma fixed her gaze on the door handle, the only reflective object in the room.

What her eyes had forfeited in vision, her ears had evidently made up in hearing. Besides the fitful noises of her own breathing, which was going far too fast, and the rustling of her dressing gown rising and falling over her pumping torso, dull thuds were sounding in the background.

Footsteps.

Heavy footsteps.

Coming up the stairs.

Emma did the worst thing she possibly could.

She screamed.

A high-pitched, piercing scream. She heard her own mortal fear wresting from her throat. Despite the fact that she was only drawing attention to herself, she couldn't stop.

Sinking to her knees, Emma pressed her hand to her mouth, bit her knuckles, whimpered and despised herself for such weakness.

How proud she used to be of her ability to keep

her feelings under control, even in the most emotional situations. For example when the jealous borderliner who she was referring to a colleague punched her goodbye in the face. Or when an eleven-year-old patient died of a brain tumour and she'd held her mother's hand in the clinic until it was over. She'd always managed to put off her collapse till she was home alone, where, at a time and manner of her own choosing, she could bawl her anger or grief into a pillow pressed onto her face. But this form of self-control was history now and she hated herself for it.

I'm a wreck.

A screaming, howling misery guts who starts crying every time she sees an advertisement with a baby in it. Who thinks of the Hairdresser every time she meets a man.

And who anticipates certain death when the handle is being shaken on the other side of the door.

The last thing she saw was the door trembling from the hammering it was getting. Then Emma closed her eyes, tried pulling herself up on the chest of drawers, but slipped feebly like a drunkard unable to keep her balance.

Howling, she sank to the floorboards again, tasted her tears, smelled the sweat dripping from her eyebrows *(why didn't he shave those off too?)* and couldn't help thinking of the roller blind, *which I didn't open this morning, stupid cow.* Now there wasn't enough time to pull the heavy thing up. And jump.

SEBASTIAN FITZEK

It wasn't so far from the first floor, especially with all that snow on the ground in the garden.

Maybe I could have done it…

Her screams and thoughts broke off when the door splintered and at once a cold draught cooled her tear-stained face.

Emma could hear panting. Footsteps. Shouting. Not coming from herself. But from the intruder.

Male shouting.

Two hands yanked away her arms which she'd wrapped over her head in protection, crouched like a little child waiting to be punished.

No, more like a woman waiting for death.

Finally she heard her name.

Emma.

Being yelled again and again by a voice, the last voice she'd been expecting in what were likely to be her last few seconds without pain.

Then the blow came. Straight to the face.

Her cheek burned as if it had been stung by a jellyfish and her tears bit open her eyelids from the inside. Through the blur she could see that she had two intruders to deal with.

The two men were standing close beside one another. Despite the meagre light and veil before her eyes she recognised both faces.

Which was hardly surprising.

She was married to one of them.

14

Philipp was no dream husband, or at least not by the apparent standard of the average woman's dreams. He wasn't a shining prince who called three times a day just to say 'I love you' before stopping on the way home at a florist's, jeweller's or lingerie boutique to pick up a small token to surprise his beloved, every day till their golden wedding anniversary and beyond. He wasn't a husband who never argued, never glanced at other women, was always kind to his mother and loved nothing better than to cook for her friends.

He was, however, a reliable partner by her side.

Someone who voiced his opinions, a man with a mind of his own, which she found more important than being helped into her coat.

He gave her security and trust. In spite of all the difficulties that had marked the start of their relationship.

It had taken him months to disentangle himself from his ex, and he ended up two-timing Emma with 'Kilian' for weeks.

SEBASTIAN FITZEK

That wasn't his ex-girlfriend's real name, of course, but at the time Philipp had stored Franziska's number on his mobile under the name of a football chum, so that Emma wouldn't get suspicious if there was another call or text message. When she by chance discovered the truth, they had their first major row, which almost brought an end to their relationship. Finally, however, she believed Philipp that the ploy hadn't been an attempt to keep something going with his ex. Because it wasn't possible just to change his work number, Philipp couldn't prevent Franziska's wine-fuelled, sometimes hysterical calls. What he'd been trying to do was at least to protect Emma from unnecessary hurt, and himself from unnecessary arguments. In vain.

In the end the problem solved itself: Franziska found a new boyfriend and moved with him to Leipzig. There were no more calls from 'Kilian'.

Otherwise he possessed the usual male quirks. Philipp enjoyed staying out late with friends without sending her a text to tell her they were moving on to yet another pub. He snored, flooded the bathroom and put his elbows on the table when they were eating. Once he forgot their wedding anniversary and, in a fit of rage, hurled a full cup of coffee at the wall (the stain was still visible), but he'd never, ever hit her.

But Emma had never given him such a compelling reason to do so before.

'I'm sorry,' he said, a few minutes later. He'd helped

108

her downstairs into the kitchen, where she'd sat at their square wooden table. In the past they loved having breakfast there at the weekends because it offered such a pretty view of the garden. The neighbouring one was totally overgrown, giving the impression that you were gazing into a forest.

Emma nodded and tried to say, 'It's okay,' but her voice sank back down into her throat. She was clutching a bulbous cup of coffee, but wouldn't take a sip. Philipp was leaning against the work surface by the sink. Keeping his distance.

Not because he wanted to, but because he knew this was what she needed right at the moment. For a few minutes at least, until the voice of terror in her head was screaming not quite so loudly.

'Jesus, I'm really sorry,' Philipp said, grinding his teeth and staring at his hands as if unable to comprehend what he'd done.

'No.' Emma shook her head, pleased to have found her voice again, even if it emerged from her mouth as little more than a croak. 'What you did was absolutely right.' The slap that was still burning her cheek had smothered the flames of panic. It was only afterwards that she'd stopped screaming and calmed down again.

'I was completely off my rocker,' she admitted, while thinking: *So that's how my patients feel when they confide in me.*

Do they also realise how absurd their behaviour is in hindsight?

Emma had thought a stranger had slammed the bathroom door, but Philipp's sudden return explained everything.

Having forgotten the papers for his lecture in the study, he'd turned off the motorway and headed back immediately. He'd even called Emma to let her know, but the call had gone straight to voicemail when she was lying unconscious in the living room.

'I came straight upstairs when I heard you screaming.'

Her husband looked as if he'd aged several years, and Emma was worried that this wasn't just an effect of the pendant light. His temples appeared grey, his hair slightly thinner and his brow furrowed. All this, she suspected, was less a result of his forty years than what had completely changed half a year ago: their life.

Emma wanted to stand up, put her hand out to Philipp, stroke his chin – hastily shaven early this morning – and say, *'Don't worry, everything's fine now. Let's go to Tegel and take the first plane to somewhere we've never been before. It's just got to be far away. Let's leave fate behind us.'*

But she couldn't. Emma wouldn't make it to the front door. Christ, she couldn't even move the kitchen stool. So all she said was, 'I thought somebody had broken in.'

'Who?'

'No idea. Somebody.'

Philipp gave a sad sigh, like a young boy who's been hoping that the toy he's carefully mended will finally work again, only to discover when he tries it out that it's still broken.

'There's nobody here, Emma. The bathroom door slammed when I opened up downstairs. You know how draughty it gets here.'

She nodded, but with a grimace. 'That doesn't explain the ringing.'

'What sort of ringing?'

Emma turned to the voice behind her. Jorgo Kapsalos, Philipp's best friend and partner at the Federal Criminal Police Office, was standing in the kitchen doorway. He was the second man she'd seen in the bedroom.

This morning when he'd come to pick Philipp up, Jorgo had stayed in the car. Now he'd come in and was gazing at her as he always did when they met: wistfully and with subliminal hope.

Philipp overlooked his partner's secret looks, or misinterpreted them, but Emma guessed what was going on in Jorgo's mind when he eyed her so melancholically. If Emma sometimes used Konrad to stir Philipp's jealousy, she'd never abuse Jorgo's feelings for such a purpose. For unlike the defence lawyer, her husband's partner was anything but gay. The poor guy was hopelessly in love with her, something Emma had known even before her wedding day when a totally drunk Jorgo slurred into her ear as they danced that she'd married the wrong man, *for heaven's sake!*

'What sort of a ringing?' he repeated.

'No idea. An alarm clock or a mobile phone. I think it was coming from the attic.'

She hadn't heard anything since the two men had broken down the bedroom door and rushed in to her.

'Would you mind checking the rooms?' Philipp asked his partner.

'No, please don't!' In vain Emma racked her brain for words to explain that she'd been through all this once before.

Once before she'd searched a room and convinced herself that she was alone, only to be raped afterwards. Of course it was totally irrational and illogical, but Emma was worried that another search would summon the evil back and the horror would repeat itself. As if there were a times table of evil. An equation with an unknown by the name of 'danger' and a foregone conclusion: 'pain'.

Emma knew better than anyone else that this reasoning was pathological. Which is also why she didn't verbalise it to the two psychologically stable men, but just said, 'You've got to go. I've detained you long enough.'

'Don't be silly,' Jorgo said with a dismissive wave of the hand. 'It's not a problem.' He was incredibly well built, a compact, muscular man you'd be very glad to have at your side on a dark underground platform when a horde of drunks were coming your way. 'We can miss the first seminar. It's not that important anyway.'

Philipp nodded. 'My lecture's not indispensable either. Maybe it would be best if you went without me, Jorgo.'

'If you say so.' Jorgo shrugged, looking not particularly pleased. Emma guessed why. *He* would rather stay alone with her. Her husband's best friend had sent her several emails offering her his help in the wake of her great misfortune. She'd deleted them all, the last few without even reading them.

'Yes, I think it's better if I stay here.' Philipp nodded once more. 'You can see how distraught she is.'

He pointed to Emma and spoke as if she weren't in the room. Another of his non-dream-husband habits. 'I can't leave her here alone.'

'Of course you can. It's not a problem,' Emma protested, even though *'It's not a problem'* expressed roughly the opposite of what she thought.

Philipp went over to her and took her hand. 'Emma, Emma, what was it that upset you so much today?'

Good question.

The advertisement for the electric razor? Her fainting? Salim's farewell? The photo of the Hairdresser in the lift?

Or… wait, no…

'What sort of a package?' she heard Philipp say,

realising that she'd thought out loud for the second time this morning.

'The food crate in the hall?' he asked.

'No, I'm sorry, I haven't unpacked it yet.'

The fact that she'd almost forgotten to tell her husband about the strange package on her desk made her aware of just how all over the place she was. Deep inside she sensed that she was overlooking something different, something crucial, but she couldn't work out what for the moment. And the package was probably far more important.

'Salim asked me to look after something for our neighbour.'

'And?' Jorgo and Philipp chorused in unison.

'But I've never heard the name before,' Emma added.

Bloody hell, what's he called again? In her distress, Emma had actually forgotten, but then recalled the name. 'Do you know an A. Palandt?'

Philipp shook his head.

'There you go. Nor do I.'

'Maybe he's new to the area?' Jorgo suggested.

'We would know,' Emma said, almost truculently.

'And this is what worked you up?' Philipp squeezed her hand more tightly. 'A package for a neighbour?'

'An *unknown* neighbour. Darling, I know I overreact...'

She ignored Philipp's slight sigh.

'... but we really do know everyone here, and—'

'And maybe he's subletting, perhaps he's a son-in-law living with his fiancée's parents for a while and having his post sent here,' Philipp said. 'There are hundreds of potentially innocent explanations.'

'Yes, you're probably right. But still I'd like you to take a look at the package. You must know that photograph from the security camera in the lift at—'

Philipp's face darkened and he let go of her hand. 'Have you been on the internet again?'

As if he'd given the magic word it happened again.

Two floors above them.

There was a beeping.

The sad look with which Jorgo, leaning against the doorframe, had listened to their conversation, vanished and was replaced by expression of hard concentration.

Philipp, too, had put on what Emma called his 'policeman's face': narrowed eyes, knitted brow, head to one side, lips slightly open, tongue pressed against the upper incisors.

After a brief exchange of glances in the interval between two rings, the two men nodded to each other and Jorgo said, 'I'll take a look.'

Before Emma could object, Philipp's partner disappeared into the hallway. He climbed the stairs with confident steps, his hand on the belt holding the holster of his service weapon.

15

'It can't go on like this, Emma,' Philipp whispered, as if he were worried that Jorgo might hear him two floors up. 'You've got to make a decision.'

'What do you mean?'

The distant beeping was gnawing at Emma's nerves and she couldn't concentrate on her husband's voice. Nor could she deal with the horrific images in her head. Images of what might happen to Jorgo up there – a slit throat, for example, opening and closing, and each time the policeman unsuccessfully tried to scream a torrent of blood spurting onto the floor of the children's room that would forever remain unfinished.

'What are you talking about, Philipp?' she asked again.

Her husband came up close and bent down so that his cheek touched her slapped one. 'Therapy, Emma. I know you want to get over this alone, but you've crossed a line.'

Emma shuddered when she felt his breath on her earlobe. For a moment she thought she was remembering the tongue that, in the darkness of the hotel room, had buried itself in her ear, while she, paralysed, had only been capable of muffled cries. But then Philipp said softly, 'You've really got to look for a therapist, Emma. I've spoken to Dr Wielandt about this.'

'The police psychologist?' Emma asked in horror.

'She knows your case, Emma. Lots of people are familiar with it. We have to check the...' He faltered, obviously because he realised he couldn't finish the sentence without hurting his wife.

'... check the facts of my statement. Say no more. So what does Dr Wielandt think? That I'm a pathological liar who invents rape stories for fun?'

Philipp took a deep breath. 'She's concerned that you were deeply traumatised as a child...'

'Oh, shut up!'

'Emma, you have a lively, exuberant imagination. In the past you saw things that weren't there.'

'I was six years old!' she yelled.

'A child neglected by her father, making up an imaginary substitute to compensate for his lack of affection.'

Emma laughed. 'Did Dr Wielandt have to write that out for you or did you learn it by heart first time?'

'Emma, please...'

'You don't believe me then?'

'I didn't say that—'

'So now you also think I suffer from hallucinations,

don't you?' she hissed, interrupting him. 'I imagined the whole thing? The man in my hotel room, the injection, the pain? The blood? Oh, what am I saying, perhaps I wasn't even really pregnant. Maybe I made that up too? And the alarm in the attic, that's just in my head too…'

She fell silent abruptly.

Oh God.

The beeping wasn't even in her head any more.

It had stopped.

Emma held her breath. Looked up at the ceiling that was urgently in need of a coat of paint. 'Please tell me you heard it too,' she said to Philipp and pressed her hand to her mouth. After her outburst the sudden silence felt like a harbinger of dreadful news.

'You heard it, didn't you?'

Philipp didn't answer her, but Emma heard footsteps coming down the stairs. She turned to the door, where Jorgo appeared with a red face.

'Have you got any batteries?' he asked.

'Batteries?' she repeated, confused.

'For the smoke alarm,' Jorgo said, presenting her with a small nine-volt battery in the palm of his hand. 'You need to change these every five years at the latest, otherwise they start to beep like the one in your attic.'

Emma closed her eyes. Happy that there was a harmless explanation for the beeping, but also disappointed in an irrational way. Basically, she'd had a nervous breakdown because of the signal from a smoke alarm, and this overreaction can only have reinforced her husband's doubts about her mental faculties.

'Strange,' Philipp said, scratching the back of his head. 'That can't be right. I only checked the things last week.'

'Not thoroughly enough, so it seems. So, Emma?' she heard Jorgo ask, and for a moment she had no idea what he was getting at.

'Batteries?' he repeated.

'Wait, I'll have a look.' She pushed past Jorgo and Philipp and was on her way into the living room when she suddenly remembered what she'd forgotten earlier.

Samson!

In all the kerfuffle she'd completely forgotten about him, and only now that she was looking at his sleeping blanket by the fireplace did she realise what her subconscious had been nagging her for.

Why didn't he come when I called him?

Samson just raised his head wearily and seemed to smile when he saw his mistress. Emma was horrified by his sad expression. His breathing was shallow and his nose dry.

'Are you in pain, little one?' she asked, wandering over to the shelves where the electric thermometer was in the bottom drawer. She glanced at the desk and all of a sudden was unable to think about Samson's condition any more.

Not when she saw the desk.

Where the package was that Salim had given her earlier.

Wrong.

Where it ought to have been.

Because in the place where she'd put it before opening up her notebook, to take yet another look at the lift photo of the Hairdresser, there was nothing to be seen now.

The package for A. Palandt had vanished.

16

Three weeks later

'And then they left you alone?'

Konrad had barely moved while listening; he hadn't even uncrossed his legs or unclasped his hands in his lap. Emma knew why: he'd told her when she'd once remarked on his bodily control.

With difficult clients – those who had something to hide – the merest distraction would disturb their flow.

I'm one of those for him now.

Emma was no longer a daughter-like friend, she was a difficult client whose statements had to be meticulously scrutinised.

'So in spite of the fact that the package had disappeared without trace Philipp and his colleague left?' Konrad clicked his fingers. 'Just like that?'

'No, of course not just like that.'

Emma turned to look at the window. The lake was

buried beneath a thin layer of snow. From this distance
it looked inviting for ice-skating, but Emma knew how
deceptive the appearance could be. Every year people fell
through the ice on the Wannsee, having overestimated
its strength. Luckily she didn't see anyone bold or
reckless enough to tempt fate today, the miserable
weather playing a part. There wasn't a soul to be seen
on or around the lake. Only a few ducks and swans had
flocked by the shore, defying the prevailing sleet that
bathed the entire scene in a sad grey.

'I lied to Philipp,' Emma said by way of explanation.
'I told him that my nerves must have been playing a
trick on me and probably I hadn't drunk enough. Hence
I blacked out and hallucinated about a package that
never existed.'

'And he believed *that*?' Konrad asked doubtfully.

'No, but when I took a diazepam in front of him he
knew I'd sleep half the day.'

'You take that for anxiety disorder?' Konrad asked.
Emma remembered he was a lawyer rather than a
doctor. In her head she could already see him working
on a theory of diminished responsibility due to excessive
tablet consumption. And yet he had far more in his hand
than paltry substance abuse to plead mental incapacity
on her behalf. But they'd come to that in good time.

'Yes. Lorazepam would have actually been my drug
of choice. It's newer, takes effect more rapidly and
doesn't sedate you as much as diazepam, which makes

you incredibly tired. But unfortunately it was all I had in the house.'

'So you took your pill and then the two of them went to the conference in Bad Saarow?'

'After they'd checked the smoke alarms in every room and thus done a search of the entire house including the basement, yes.'

Emma couldn't say whether it was his tightly pressed lips or the growl in his voice, but she clearly sensed that Konrad seriously frowned on her husband's behaviour. The two men had never got on, which wasn't helped, of course, by the fact that Emma had ignored Philipp's 'sugar daddy' comments and had even cultivated his jealousy. For his part, Konrad had often raised an eyebrow about the vulgar 'peasant' who would pass over the phone without saying hello or barely shake his hand on the rare occasions they met.

In this specific instance, however, Konrad's criticism of Philipp as an oaf was unjustified. If he'd been in Philipp's shoes and she'd implored him in the same way, he'd have found it difficult to refuse her request too.

'I need my peace and quiet, Philipp. I'd be even more stressed if I knew you were missing your lecture just because of me. I've taken my medicine now. You've searched the entire house and, anyway, Sylvia's popping by this afternoon to check on me, so please do me and yourselves a favour and leave me alone. Okay?'

None of that was a lie, and yet none of it was honest.

'Did the medicine work?'

Konrad poured her some tea. He'd soon have to replace the tealight in the warmer as the wick was virtually swimming in wax.

'Oh boy, did it work.'

'You felt tired.'

Emma took the cup offered to her and sipped some tea. The Assam blend tasted bittersweet and furry, as if it had been left to brew for too long.

'The diazepam almost floored me. I felt sleepy like before an operation.'

'And free of anxiety?'

'Not to begin with. But that was also because...'

'What?'

'Something... something happened. As they were leaving.'

Konrad raised his eyebrows and waited for her to continue talking.

'Jorgo. He gave me his hand...'

'And?'

'And he put something in mine.'

'What?'

'A note.'

'What did it say?'

'The nicest thing that any man had said to me in ages.'

'I love you?' Konrad asked.

Emma shook her head.

'I *believe* you,' she said, pausing to allow the words to take effect.

Konrad didn't appear surprised, but with his well-trained poker face that didn't mean much.

'I believe you,' he repeated softly.

'Jorgo had scribbled that on a tiny piece of paper. And that I should ring him. I was speechless when I read the message as soon as they were out of the door.'

'What happened then?'

Emma winced before answering Konrad. 'You know what happened.'

'I want to hear it from your mouth.'

'I, I...'

She closed her eyes. Pictured her front door. From the inside. Saw her hand stretching out for the handle, turning the key twice.

'I did the unthinkable,' she said, completing her sentence.

Konrad nodded slowly. 'For the first time in six months?'

'Yes.'

Konrad bent forwards. 'Why?'

She raised her head and looked him straight in the eye. She could see herself as a tiny reflection in his pupils.

'Because of the blood,' she whispered. 'All of a sudden there was blood everywhere.'

17

Three weeks earlier

Emma was kneeling in a pool of red in the middle of the living room, halfway between the fireplace and her desk. She felt strangely calm. The blood had gushed out, completely unexpectedly in spite of the wheezing and panting that had preceded it.

A deep breath, a spastic convulsion of the upper chest muscles. A sound as if a living creature were being breathed out of the body, then Samson vomited at her feet.

'My poor darling, what's wrong?'

As she stroked his head she could feel him shivering, as if he were just as cold as her. Philipp and Jorgo had been gone barely half an hour, in which time she'd turned the house upside down again looking for the package that had actually disappeared.

But that's impossible!

Unbelievably tired, her back soaked with sweat, Emma had returned to the living room from the hallway, having searched it yet again. In a moment of desperation, she was going to check beneath Samson's blanket to see whether the dog might have thought to take the package to his sleeping place. Instead she'd found him in this pitiful state.

'Hey, Samson. Can you hear me?'

The husky started retching again.

In normal circumstances Emma would have been scared witless and slapped her hands over her mouth, terrified that this desperate situation was too much for her. But now the first diazepam tablet was smoothing the largest waves of anxiety without eliminating them altogether. It was like being anaesthetised at the dentist's. You no longer felt the shooting pain, but there was a general, dull ache just waiting to flare up again the moment the injection wore off.

What now?

She looked outside. A jackdaw came to rest on a bare magnolia and seemed to wave at her, but of course Emma was imagining it. Heavy snow was still falling and Emma couldn't make out the bird's eyes.

It was more her subconscious telling her what she had to do.

'You've got to leave the house!'

'No!' she said, but she could barely hear herself because Samson was being sick again. This time it was accompanied by less blood, but that didn't make it any better.

'*Yes, and you know it. You've got to get out, Samson needs help!*'

'No way.' Emma shook her head and went over to the desk where her mobile was.

'*Who are you going to call then?*'

'Who do you think? The emergency vet.'

'*Are you sure?*'

'Of course, just look at him.'

She looked at Samson.

'*I hear what you're saying,*' said the voice in her head, which sounded like a precocious version of her own. '*He probably doesn't have much time left. But is that what you really want to do?*'

'Save him?'

'*Put yourself in danger,*' the voice said.

As if thunderstruck, it took Emma a while to digest these words. Then she put her mobile back on the desk.

'You're right.'

I can't call anyone.

Because it wouldn't just be that one call. At some point there would be a stranger at her front door. A vet she didn't know, but who she'd have to let in, because she could hardly send Samson out into the cold to be examined. And in the end she'd have to go with him to the veterinary clinic after all when it turned out that they wouldn't be able to treat him at home.

'Fuck,' she cursed.

Samson was now lying on his side, almost in a foetal position, and panting. His tongue was hanging wanly out of his mouth and his nose was completely dry. A string of blood ran from his black muzzle to the parquet floor.

'What on earth is wrong with you?'

And what should I do?

She couldn't let a stranger into the house, not in her condition. But the only logical alternative – to leave the house – was at least as terrifying.

For a moment Emma wondered whether she ought to ring Philipp, but that would put paid to his conference for good, and Emma didn't want that.

Maybe it's just a virus?

As Emma stroked Samson's white coat she was hardly able to feel his ribs when he breathed. It could be a lung inflammation, but the symptoms were too drastic and had come on too suddenly.

At least she now knew why Samson had been so limp the whole time.

My poor bear, it looks more likely that someone…

She jumped to her feet, flabbergasted by this shocking thought.

… that someone poisoned you!

Emma couldn't get out of her head the image of Salim asking her if it was okay and giving Samson a treat.

No, no, no. That's nonsense.

Emma's thoughts were flowing into her consciousness at half speed, a typical effect of the sedative. She was still capable of reasoning, but everything took twice as long.

But not Salim. He gives Samson something every time, and nothing ever happened before.

Outside, the jackdaw had left its perch. Emma could see just its tail feathers as it flew exactly in the direction she had to move in now too.

Dr Plank's veterinary practice was just one block towards Heerstrasse.

But she'd have to wear something warm, put Samson on a lead, even carry him perhaps, although this was not what made her so worried.

The biggest problem was that she'd have to open the front door and leave the protection of her own four walls for the first time in almost six months.

'No, I can't. It's inconceivable,' she said, which of course was a paradox because she'd just been mulling it over in her mind. She was also thinking that she'd never manage to tear down the wall that had built up between her and life outside, and take not just one but several steps into a world she wanted nothing more to do with.

No, I won't manage it.

Even though Dr Plank was the closest vet, only five minutes' walk away, and his practice stayed open till six o'clock, whereas most others in Berlin were closed on Saturdays.

I still can't.

It's inconceivable.

Emma stood motionless for a quarter of an hour beside the suffering animal at her feet, until she made the decision to try and cope without outside help for the time being.

Then Samson had his first respiratory arrest.

18

Anxiety eats into the soul and hollows people out from the inside. It also feeds on human time: it took Emma half an hour to put on something warm, and she needed several attempts just to lace up her boots before her clammy fingers pulled up the zip of her puffer jacket and, dripping with sweat, she opened the door, which required another eternity, or so it seemed to her.

At the moment the diazepam that she'd washed down with a gulp of tap water was having more side effects than direct ones. Emma was incredibly tired, but the iron ring around her chest would not loosen its grip.

Luckily Samson had started breathing again, although he couldn't stay on his feet for long. So to make matters worse Emma had to make a detour to the shed, a small, grey, metal shack that stood at the back of the garden. If she wasn't mistaken, the sledge was still hanging on the wall in there. Philipp had bought it when they moved, on the erroneous assumption that they'd use it regularly, given that they were now living so close to the Teufelsberg.

Well, maybe it was paying for itself today as transport for Samson.

Emma was breathing heavily and focusing on her path across the snowy lawn. Shuffling tentatively, like a patient attempting her first step after a major operation, she teetered forwards.

Each step was a test of courage.

The walk was so arduous, as if she were having to make it with diving cylinders on her back and wearing flippers. Her feet sank to her ankles and more than once she had to stop to regain her breath.

At least she wasn't shivering, which may have been because her soul was already so frozen that there was no room left to feel the cold physically.

Or I'm already suffering from 'hypothermic madness', the name given to a psychological phenomenon whereby some people on the point of freezing to death believe they're terribly hot. Which was why sometimes you found frozen corpses naked outside. As they died, the poor souls ripped the clothes from their bodies.

Well, if fear were a shirt, I'd be happy to take it off, Emma thought, surprised that she couldn't smell anything out here in the garden. No snow, no earth, not even her own sweat. The wind was blowing in the wrong direction, bringing the rattling of the S-Bahn from nearby Heerstrasse station into the gardens. Although her hearing was a little better than usual, her sight was worse.

The garden seemed to get narrower with every step. It took her a while to realise that the panic was constricting her field of vision.

First of all the bushes disappeared, then the cherry and rhododendron, and in the end there was just a long, black tunnel leading straight to the shed.

Visual disorders.

Emma knew the symptoms of an oncoming panic attack: dry mouth, racing heart and a change in the perception of colour and form.

Worried that she'd never get any further if she stopped again now, Emma staggered onwards until she finally reached the shed.

She jerked open the door and grabbed blindly for the sledge which Philipp had hung neatly on the wall beside the door.

A bright-red plastic object that was light, wide and shaped like a shovel. Thank goodness it wasn't one of those old-fashioned, heavy wooden things with runners, which Samson could very easily have fallen off.

On the way back Emma felt a little better. Her success in having found the sledge immediately imbued her with some confidence.

Her field of vision had widened again too. The bushes were in their place, although they were moving about in a most unnatural fashion. Not sideways, as if being blown by the wind, but up and down like an accordion.

Disconcerting, but nowhere near as terrifying as the footprints that Emma hadn't noticed on the way there.

She looked at the heavy boot prints in the snow in front of her. They couldn't be her own as they were at least three sizes too big. They were only going in one direction.

To the shed.

Emma turned back to the grey shack. She'd left its door open.

Was it moving?

Was anyone in there?

Had she maybe grabbed the sledge in the darkness and just missed a man crouching behind the lawnmower?

Emma couldn't see anything or anyone, but the feeling lingered that she was being watched.

GET OUT!

'Samson,' she called, speeding up. 'Samson, come here! My poor thing, please come!'

The suffering creature did her bidding, struggling up from the doormat where he'd been waiting for her. It sounded as if he had whooping cough.

'Thank you, my darling. Good dog.'

She tapped on the seat of the plastic sledge and he dragged himself onto it, then slumped, sniffling.

'Don't worry,' Emma said comfortingly to the dog and herself. 'I'll help you.'

She patted his head, gritted her teeth and pulled Samson with a rope towards the road. Unwisely, she turned back and thought she saw a shadow behind the small window in the door.

Did the curtain just move?

No, it was hanging serenely and there was no light behind it that could have cast a shadow.

And yet. Emma felt as if she were being followed by invisible eyes.

GET OUT

BEFORE IT'S TOO LATE.

And these eyes opened wounds, out of which all her courage seeped.

If my will to live were fluid, I'd leave a red trail behind me, she thought. *Which would be practical; I'd only need to follow it to find my way back.*

She took hold of the sledge rope, which had briefly slipped from her hand, and forced herself onwards again. To the vet.

Away from the dark house behind her, from which she believed she was being watched by dead eyes at the window. Waiting for her to come back.

Assuming she ever did.

19

'How long has he been in this condition?' Dr Plank asked as he listened to Samson's chest.

The poor creature was on a drip providing him with electrolytes and a substance that should induce him to vomit in a few minutes' time. Ever since the vet had heaved the husky onto the treatment table with Emma's help, Samson had barely been conscious. Now and again he shuddered as he exhaled, but that was the only sign of life.

'How long? Well, I, I think...' Emma's voice was trembling as badly as her knees.

She felt as if she'd run for her life, rather than merely having gone three hundred metres around the corner. In her mind, three hundred metres equated to a marathon.

My first time outside alone, and with a dog as close to death as I am to insanity.

Contemplating her feat in the harsh light of the halogen lamp that hovered above Samson, she could scarcely believe that she'd made it. Made it here, to the broad, end-of-terrace house with its cream façade and green shutters. The garage had been converted into a waiting room years ago. Fortunately Emma didn't have to spend too much time there. With the exception of a small girl, who'd sat crying with a cat basket on her lap, she was the only patient. And because of the severity of Samson's symptoms she'd been shown in immediately.

'I'm not sure. He's been droopy since this morning,' Emma finally managed to complete her sentence. 'I think it started around eleven.'

The vet grunted and Emma couldn't tell if it was a grunt of satisfaction or concern.

He'd put on a bit of weight since she'd last seen him, but that was a while ago now, in the time before, at the neighbourhood party organised every year by the residents' association. The freshly starched apron was a little tight around the tummy of the 1.90-metre man. He'd developed a slight double chin and fuller cheeks, which made him appear more affable than before. Now Plank resembled a large teddy bear with light-brown, unkempt hair, a broad nose and melancholic button eyes.

'Did he eat anything unusual?'

Emma felt nervously for the headscarf covering her short hair. If Plank was wondering why she hadn't taken it off he wasn't letting it show.

'Yes, I mean, no. You know Salim, don't you?'

'Our delivery man?'

'He gave Samson a dog biscuit, he always gives him one.'

'Hmm.'

Plank was wearing latex medical gloves, similar to those that had stroked her head. Back in the darkness of the hotel room.

'What's going to happen now?' she asked the vet, one hand on Samson's chest, gazing at a white, glass-front cabinet, her eyes fixed on packets of gauze bandages and surgical collars as if they were as captivating as a work of art.

'We're going to have to wait to begin with,' Plank replied, checking the drip with a critical eye. He pointed to the drain of the table. 'We're treating him on spec; there are lots of signs that he's been poisoned. As soon as he's been sick we'll give him some charcoal to bind any toxins. My assistant is just calling the laboratory courier. Once that's done we'll hook Samson up to a urinary catheter to prevent the toxin from being reabsorbed by the bladder wall. Then, of course, there's the usual cocktail of medicines.'

Emma nodded. The same procedure as for humans.

'Everything on spec until we have the haemogram.'

'Could it be anything else apart from poisoning?'

Plank managed to nod and shrug at the same time. 'Unlikely. We'll know in more detail when the lab results are back.'

He patted the plaster covering the injection site on Samson's hind leg, from where he'd taken the blood.

'I've got good contacts at the veterinary clinic in Düppel, I'll have the results tomorrow morning at the latest.'

Emma noticed that her eyes were filling with tears. She couldn't say whether this was due to exhaustion or fear that it might be too late and the poison had already worked its way irreparably through Samson's body.

'The best would be if you left him here under observation for the next twenty-four hours, Frau Stein.'

Plank paused and accidentally brushed her hand briefly as the two of them stroked Samson's head together. 'He's better off here than at home.' He followed this up with a baffling question.

'Talking of home. Is your basement dry again?'

'I'm sorry?'

'The water that got in last month. The same thing happened here once. It was ages before we could get rid of the fan heaters. *Dearie, dearie me,* I thought, *poor old Frau Stein.* I mean, first your illness and then something like that. Nobody needs that. Your husband told me all about the palaver with the burst pipes.'

'Philipp?'

The door to the treatment room opened and a plump elderly woman in a nurse's coat entered. She gave Emma a cheery smile as she walked over to the medicine cabinet in her squeaky Birkenstock sandals, presumably to get everything ready for Samson's treatment.

Plank kept talking regardless.

'I met him in town by chance. It must have been four weeks ago pretty much to the day. A freaky coincidence. I was on call and that evening I had to go to a hotel, the chihuahua, do you remember?' he said to the nurse, who nodded wearily.

Plank grinned, shaking his head. 'An American woman's plaything had stepped on a piece of glass. As I left I saw your husband sitting in the lobby.' As Emma listened to the vet's words a wave of heat surged against her ribcage from the inside.

'My husband? In the lobby?' she repeated as if in a trance.

'Yes. *Well, well,* I thought, *I wonder what Herr Stein's doing here.* Then I saw the two drinks on the table and when I said hello he told me that the two of you were having to spend the night here until the worst was over.'

There was a ring at the door and Plank's assistant returned to the reception.

'Not that I was being nosy, mind, or thinking he was up to something, but afterwards I thought one could easily have drawn the wrong conclusions. I mean, who sleeps in a hotel in their own town, if...'

'... they haven't got the builders in?' Emma completed his sentence flatly.

Converting the nursery.

Which will never be used.

Or repairing water damage.

Which never happened.

'Well, I hope the pumps are out and your floor is dry again. Frau Stein?'

Emma removed her clenched fist from Samson's coat, realising that she must have been gaping at Plank for quite a while with an expressionless face. Without the sedative she would have probably screamed the place down, but the diazepam had deadened her emotions.

'Is everything okay with you?'

She forced a smile. 'Yes, everything's fine. I'm just a bit out of sorts because of Samson.'

'I understand,' Plank said, softly stroking her hand. 'Don't worry about him. He's in the best hands. And take a card with my mobile number from reception. If you have any questions you can call me at any time.'

Emma nodded. 'I've got one question already,' she said, on her way out.

'Go ahead.'

'The hotel.'

'Yes?'

'Where you bumped into my husband. Do you remember the name?'

20

Emma opened her mouth and waited to taste her child-hood as soon as the snowflakes landed on her tongue.

But this sensuous experience failed to occur.

The fragrance of winter, the smell of the wind, the taste of the snow and all other sensations that could only be experienced rather than described, and which would bring back memories of her first sledge ride, difficult walks with wet socks and falling off her bike, but also a comforting hot bath in the evening, dunking lebkuchen into warm milk on the bench by the window while watching the tits pecking at the feed scattered from the birdhouse – Emma couldn't recall any of this.

She just felt cold. The way back was long and arduous, even without the sledge that she'd left behind at the practice. She felt her way forwards circumspectly, step by step on the pavement, which was icy in parts, listening to the crunching of her boots.

In her first December here in Teufelssee-Allee, Emma thought the estate could have been made for Christmas.

Small, cosy houses with fat candles in the windows, evergreen firs in the front gardens that needed merely a chain of lights to look Christmassy. Hardly any cars to spoil the atmosphere with their noise and which the foxes would have to watch out for as they scurried into the road from the Grunewald early in the afternoon.

Even the local residents, most of them slightly older, fitted the picture perfectly. Old Mother Frost type women in their pinafores returning with their shopping trolleys from the weekly market in Preussenallee, white-haired men in billowy cords, puffing on pipes as they cleared the snow from the pavement, and who you wouldn't be surprised to hear say 'Ho, ho, ho' as a greeting.

At the moment, however, there wasn't a soul about, except for a teenage boy who'd obviously been forced by his parents to grit the driveway.

This is something at least.

Emma couldn't have coped with being stopped by a neighbour for some small talk.

'Well, Frau Stein, what a nice surprise this is. We haven't seen you in ages! You must have missed at least four community breakfasts.'

'Yes, I'm sorry. A rapist stuck his penis in my far too dry vagina and then cut my hair off afterwards. I've been a bit all over the place since then, but if you don't mind me suddenly getting up and screaming during the meal, smashing my head against the edge of the table or pulling out clumps of hair, just because for a

second it occurs to me that the man opposite could be the instigator of my paranoid panic attacks, then I'll happily turn up to the next breakfast and I'll bring some croissants with me. How does that sound?'

Emma smiled briefly at this absurd inner dialogue, before starting to cry. Tears ran down her face, already damp from the snow. She went around the corner, turned into her street, then, after a few short steps, had to cling onto a fence and regain her breath.

She couldn't, no, she didn't *want* to comprehend just how far she'd fallen. Only a few months ago she'd been running an excellent practice. Today she couldn't complete even the most basic of everyday tasks and was being defeated by a pavement of no more than a few hundred pathetic metres.

And all because I didn't go back home that night.

Pitying oneself. Reproaching oneself. Killing oneself.

Emma knew the tragic trinity, and she'd be lying if she claimed never to have considered the last option.

'*How absurd,*' said her reason.

'*How inevitable,*' said that part of the human system that essentially makes all the decisions and which cannot be monitored nor cured, but only ever damaged: the soul.

The problem with psychological illnesses was that self-diagnosis was impossible. Trying to understand your brain using your brain held out about as much hope as a one-armed surgeon trying to sew back their own hand. It didn't work.

Emma knew that she was overreacting. That there must be a harmless explanation for why the vet had met Philipp in the hotel.

'*Le Zen. A palace of Oriental kitsch, don't you think?*'

And in all likelihood the mystery of the package would have a ridiculously simple explanation too.

It was pointless to spend hours poring over whether Salim really had given her a delivery for the neighbour, because her brain would never accept the alternative conclusion – that she'd lost her mind. Perhaps she hadn't seen Salim at all today; perhaps it wasn't the delivery man who rang at her door, but a stranger who'd given Samson poison rather than a biscuit?

Maybe she hadn't been to the vet either today, and instead she was strapped to a bed in the secure unit of the Bonhoeffer psychiatric hospital?

Emma didn't think this very likely. Such serious, audiovisual schizophrenic episodes were extremely rare and weren't triggered by a single traumatic incident. They were preceded by years and years of the most horrific damage. But maybe she *couldn't help* thinking this and it was a lie to protect herself.

Deep down she was convinced that although her self-control and communication skills had gone, she hadn't lost all relation to reality. But there was never a one hundred per cent certainty, especially when one's soul had suffered as severe damage as hers.

'The package was there!' she exclaimed, to tear

herself from the vicious circle of her thoughts. She repeated the words, as if to give herself courage. 'The package was there. I had it in my hand.'

Emma said it three more times and with each repetition she felt a little better. With rediscovered determination she took her mobile from her pocket and called her husband's number.

It beeped and went to his voicemail.

There was poor reception on sections of the A10 motorway; maybe they were going through a tunnel. At any rate Emma was grateful that she could deliver her message without being interrupted by critical questions.

'Darling, I know this is going to sound strange, but do you think it's possible that our delivery man isn't completely kosher? Salim Yüzgec. Is there any way you could run a background check on him?'

She explained the reason for her suspicion and finished with the words, 'There was one more thing. The vet says he saw you in Le Zen. You mentioned something to him about water damage. Could you tell me what that's all about?'

She put the phone back into her trouser pocket and wiped the snow from her eyes.

It was only when she took a step backwards that she realised which fence she'd been gripping onto all this time.

The garden gate, which had seen better days, was hanging crookedly from a rusty post. It was lined with chicken wire, the holes far larger than normal. For a name plate someone had simply stuck some tape to the edge of the door and written on it in permanent marker.

The letters were somewhat faded and, just to make sure, Emma looked up again at the ancient enamel sign which, as was customary in this area, was affixed between the kitchen window and the guest lavatory: Teufelssee-Allee 16a.

No doubt about it.

Her gaze returned to the fence. For a split second she was afraid that the letters on the sticky tape might have vanished into thin air just like the package on her desk, but they were still there, unchanged:

A. P.

Like 'A. Palandt'.

In the twinkling of an eye Emma made a momentous decision.

21

The logic was straightforward: *if the card exists, so does the package*.

Simple proof.

If, as he claimed, Salim had posted a delivery note through A. Palandt's door, then he must have given Emma the package beforehand.

So simple. So logical.

To be certain, the most obvious thing Emma could do was ring the doorbell and ask for Palandt, assuming he was back home now. But after everything Emma had seen on the internet this morning, that was out of the question. She felt sick with fear at the idea that the door might open to reveal a man only vaguely resembling the guy in the lift.

No, the only possible option was to take a quick glance in the post box which – and here Emma was confronted with another problem – appeared to be non-existent. Like much about this house, it seemed to have gone missing.

Emma recalled that the delicate widow who lived here alone had always kept the house in good nick. Now there were bulbs missing from the outside lights and the small, clay garden ornaments had disappeared. As far as Emma could see, there were no longer curtains inside the windows either, which was why the plain, grey house with its coarse, pockmarked render didn't just look uninviting, but abandoned.

I don't think there's anyone here.

The garden gate she'd been leaning against was stuck, but the entrance to the carport was wide open. She should abort her plan and go back home. But Emma felt magically drawn to the open gates. And if she were being honest with herself she'd know the reason why. It wasn't just about proving the existence of the package; she was being driven by the paranoid compulsion to gain some certainty about the identity of A. Palandt.

As improbable as it was that this individual had anything to do with the Hairdresser and what Emma had suffered, she was sure that she'd be driven mad by the thought of the stranger and the contents of that package if she didn't investigate further.

And so Emma sank into the ankle-deep snow on the way up to the house. She didn't mind the wet that crept into her boots through the eyelets, nor the fact that the snow was making her headscarf damp, flattening her hair beneath.

More uncomfortable were the penetrating looks she

thought she could feel in her back. Neighbours standing at the window, watching Emma make her way to the entrance, which unusually was at the side of the house, rather than the front. It was covered with corrugated iron and stood in the shade of a fir tree whose branches drooped like a curtain over the steps leading up to the house.

Emma climbed the four stairs and looked back at the street, but couldn't see anyone. Nobody watching her from a car or a neighbouring garden, not even any passers-by wondering why the woman who hadn't shown her face in public for half a year was suddenly crouching beside a stranger's front door.

As she'd feared, the post was delivered directly through an aperture in the door at A. P.'s house.

Shit.

If he'd had an external post box, she might have been able to feel the card with her slim fingers, *but like this?*

Emma lifted the metal flap, peered through the hole and of course she saw nothing. Inside the house it was darker than outside.

She took out her mobile and with her clammy fingers switched on the torch function.

In the distance a dog barked, and the sound mingled with the ever-present drone of Heerstrasse, which she only ever noticed when friends visiting for the first time brought the subject up while they were sitting in the garden.

Or when fear sharpened her senses.

Not just the fear of being discovered (for what was she supposed to say if the door suddenly opened?), but also the fear of being totally overwhelmed psychologically. Until this morning the world outside her front door had seemed like a raging ocean, with her as a non-swimmer on the beach, and now she was about to venture way too far out into the wide-open sea.

But I don't have a choice.

The light from her smartphone torch didn't get her any further. Given the narrow aperture and the oblique angle available to her, all she could make out were some floorboards and something that did actually look like paper or letters scattered on the floor. But was the card for the missed delivery amongst them? It was impossible to tell.

Okay, that's that then.

Emma felt relieved when she stood back up. Her brain had identified an acceptable reason for her not being able to conclude her plan. It was a good sign, a healthy sign that she wasn't so driven by impulse as to look for spare keys hidden beneath the mat, shake the side window of the guest room, or simply try the doorknob, which...

... turned without any resistance!

Emma withdrew her hand. There was a loud creaking as the door ground across the dark floorboards, pushing the post inwards.

She glanced over her shoulder, but nobody was

behind her, or at least nobody she could see. When she turned back she realised that it wasn't as dark inside the house as she'd first thought. A wan, yellowish light fell into the hallway from one of the rooms, and in the glow Emma could see that the front door was wedged by a pile of bulk mail.

There was something else too.

Something that made her take two steps into the unfamiliar house, even though she found the slim, metre-tall object she was heading towards more repellent than attractive.

But Emma couldn't believe what she was staring at here in the hallway, right beside the coat stand. And as she was worried that it might be her imagination, a vision dreamed up by her deranged brain as further fuel for her paranoia, she *had* to inspect it close up to be sure.

Emma stretched out her hand.

Noticed her own breath, as here inside it was barely warmer than outside.

Touched the cold polystyrene.

And felt a strip of adhesive tape on the replica of the human head, to which a few hairs were stuck.

No doubt about it.

That's a wig stand.

As she came to this realisation, which induced a numbness in Emma's hands, her mobile phone started to buzz.

Luckily she'd switched it to vibrate, otherwise

the sound would have echoed through the hallway like church bells.

'Hello,' she said, when she saw it was the veterinary practice on the line. Besides the wig stand, her concern for Samson was another reason to leave this house as quickly as possible.

'Frau Stein? It's Dr Plank's practice here. I'm very sorry to disturb you, but we've got a problem with the payment for the laboratory analysis. The animal clinic at Düppel says your credit card has been blocked.'

'That must be a mistake,' Emma whispered on the way back out, which was now obstructed. Not by a person, nor an object, but by light.

Bright, white xenon light, flooding the driveway and pouring into the house she had just entered illegally.

Broad headlight beams swept across the hedge as the vehicle, its engine gurgling, slowly turned into the entrance to the carport.

22

Back entrance.

This was the only thing she could think of as soon as she'd cut off the call.

Emma's body had switched into flight mode, and now her head felt clear. The fear of being discovered tore through the fog she'd been drifting in thanks to the diazepam.

For the time being at least.

There must be a back entrance here somewhere, she thought.

No way was she going to leave via the front door. Back past the mail, down the steps and straight into the arms of the owner of the wig stand as he was getting out of his car.

Out the back then.

And fast.

If, like most of the houses on the estate, this one was from the 1920s, it would have a similar floor plan with a living room that led onto a terrace.

Emma hurried down the hallway and opened the first door on the right into a large room that was even darker.

Initially she was worried that the external blinds might be down, but she only had to yank the heavy curtains stinking of dust and cold smoke to the side of the French doors.

These did indeed lead into the garden, which stretched out before her like a long, narrow towel.

The doors were old and their wavy glass panes made it seem as if you were looking at the world through a fisheye lens. But Emma wasn't in the slightest bit interested in the distorted view of a massive weeping willow, several gnarled fruit trees and a scattering of snow-covered boulders.

Hearing footsteps in the doorway, she breathed in the particle-heavy air, suppressed a cough and tried to make as little noise as possible as she slowly turned the handle of the French doors anticlockwise. The piercing sound when she pulled the jammed door tore painfully at her eardrums. Louder than a school bell signalling break time, the noise resonated throughout the entire house.

An alarm system?

Surely Palandt hadn't left the front door open, but secured the exit to the garden electronically?

It didn't make any sense, particularly as there was nothing to protect here, going by the squalor of the living room.

The sofa to Emma's left was half covered in old

newspapers. On the other side a spring had worn through the fabric cover. An upturned beer crate served as a coffee table. Unsophisticated drawings of horses' heads gaped from the walls, there was no dining table, no bookshelves, no rugs or chairs. An ugly statue of a dog stood on a mat right beside the door, a porcelain Labrador that could be used as an umbrella stand. She was reminded of Samson.

What I'd do to have him beside me now!

Otherwise there was just an empty chipboard display case, sitting diagonally in the room, as if it had been hurriedly dumped there by packers.

Certainly nothing that might interest a burglar, and yet an ear-splitting ringing had just shredded the silence.

Emma was sweating and her mouth felt parched, but the diazepam and adrenaline were performing great teamwork. Fear was spurring her on, her tiredness taking a break. It now dawned on her that it had only rung once, which was also unusual for a burglar alarm.

Emma let go of the handle and was just about to shove the door, clearly stuck, with her shoulder when she heard voices.

Foreign voices.

Albanians, Slovenes, Croats?

She couldn't tell; all she could say was than none of them could be A. Palandt because the two men who must have first rung at the front door and were now coming down the hall, were shouting the house owner's surname loudly and aggressively over and over again. 'PAAALANDT? PAAAAALANDT!'

One of them had a hoarse rattle, as if he'd just had surgery on his larynx. The other man's barking could have been coming straight from the stomach of a bull terrier.

Between the shouting, the two men hissed at each other in their native language, which sounded anything but friendly.

'AAANTON?'

So now she knew his first name, but not the way out of here.

In vain Emma pushed and pulled at the door to the terrace. It was stuck fast, as if it had been glued or nailed to the floor, unlike the living-room door through which she'd just entered. This was kicked open with a fury that almost threw it off its hinges.

If the first of the two men hadn't turned back to his accomplice because he couldn't understand what he was saying, Emma would have been discovered immediately. But now she had a second or two to dart past the empty cabinet, where she'd intended to hide until she suddenly realised that it had been blocking her view of something which was, temporarily at least, her salvation: a connecting door.

It was open and Emma slunk through it while behind her the men seemed to be cursing in their mother tongue.

Did they see me?

She didn't waste time thinking, nor did she look back,

only forwards, where she saw a staircase. It led upstairs along the internal wall of the house.

Up is good…

… Better, at least than down… *into the cellar.* People in danger only went into the cellar in horror films. *But not in a strange house, escaping from strange men looking for a strange neighbour, to do something to him they'd probably rather have no secret witnesses to.*

So Emma held onto a narrow banister and tried to climb the old, well-worn wooden stairs as quietly as possible.

Behind her came a crash – had the men pushed over the cabinet? Glass shattered but the loudest sound was her breathing.

On the first floor, equally sombre, Emma felt her way along the ingrain wallpaper on the landing to a door.

Locked. Just like the second one, directly opposite.

That's not possible.

She kept walking, towards a bright slit at the end of the landing. Another door, from beneath which the light slanted into the otherwise dark corridor that seemed like a tunnel to Emma. But this one wouldn't open either.

Emma wanted to scream with fury, fear and despair, but the men downstairs were already doing just that.

'PAAALAAANDT!'

Not just their bellowing, but their footsteps were approaching too. Hard, heavy boots climbing the stairs quicker than she had just done.

She turned to the left, having completely lost her bearings – she didn't know whether she was facing the street or the garden – and shook another door handle.

Nothing.

With the strength of desperation she finally threw herself against it in one last attempt, and almost flew into the room.

Emma tripped, slipped from the handle, her knees crashed on the floor that was covered with a rug, and she used her elbows to prevent her from hitting her head.

Shit.

She immediately got up again and closed the door from the inside.

Did they hear me?

Overcome by faintness, Emma looked for something to hold onto and came across a small chest of drawers. She kneeled beside it, unaware that she'd hidden in exactly the same position only hours ago.

Her back to the wall, her eyes fixed on a large bed.

It was warmer than in the rest of the house; she could smell sweat and another slightly rotten odour.

Either the curtains here weren't as thick as in the living room, or the tension had sharpened her senses. At any rate, Emma could see more than just shadows and shapes now.

She was obviously in Palandt's bedroom, which was dominated by an antique four-poster bed.

It had been freshly made; a patchwork quilt bulged over a thick duvet that peeked out at the foot of the bed.

At the other end, cushions of various sizes were neatly arranged in three rows that took up a third of the bed.

Like in a hotel, Emma thought, detesting the comparison.

'PAAALAAANDT?'

The men, now upstairs, rattled the same door handles she had only moments ago, except less gingerly.

Wood splintered, hinges creaked.

And Emma didn't know where to go.

Under the bed?

No, that would be the first place they'd look.

There weren't any large cupboards, just a clothes rail on wheels, a valet stand and a bedside table, right next to her, holding half a pharmacy's worth of pillboxes, sprays, tablets in foil packaging and other medicines.

All of a sudden she couldn't hear anything apart from the constant humming of fear inside her ears, then the proverbial calm before the storm was past. The bedroom door crashed open, knocking into the side of the chest of drawers she was hiding beside, and Emma was blinded.

Bright, glowing. Light.

From the ceiling it shone far too brightly and mercilessly onto the bed and everything else.

Including me.

Emma closed her eyes, not in that sort of childish reflex hoping nobody could see her just because she couldn't see anything herself, but because she'd been mistaken.

The thing next to the window wasn't a valet stand, but another wig stand. And it wasn't as bare as the one in the hall downstairs; this polystyrene head wore a long, blonde, lustreless woman's wig.

What the hell have I done? What sort of place have I entered?

Caught between two attackers and a pervert?

Hearing a pair of boots enter the room she still didn't dare open her eyes... and then her mobile rang.

Shit.

A loud, piercing ring. Like the alarm.

Shit, shit, shit!

Sweat was oozing from her pores as if the room had been turned up to sauna temperature.

She knew the game was up. That she wouldn't have time to grab the phone from her pocket, take the call and scream for help. She tried anyway.

Too late.

She held the telephone and stared at a dark display, cursing the caller who'd only let it ring twice to give her away. Then she heard the man with the bull terrier bass give a filthy laugh.

She opened her eyes, in the certainty that she'd be staring at her own death, but nobody was there.

The laughing grew quieter, moved away from the bedroom and down the landing, along with the sounds that the second man's boots made on the floorboards.

It was only when the two of them were back downstairs that Emma realised it wasn't her phone that had rung, but the bull terrier's.

It had the same standard ringtone as her own. The man had been called by someone who'd made him laugh and had evidently said something to make them abandon their search.

'Get outta there, we've found Palandt.'

or

'Forget the neighbour, there's something else for you to do.'

or

'Hi, it's me, Anton Palandt. They also call me the Hairdresser. I know we'd arranged for you to come here, but could we meet somewhere else? Right at this moment I've got problems with a dying tart.'

Whatever the message, Emma felt as if the caller had saved her life.

For now.

She got to her feet, gripped onto the chest of drawers, and wondered whether to grab one of the pillboxes that, as she could see now in the harsh light of the overhead lamp, all had Cyrillic writing on them. But there was no time to translate her decision into action.

Right in front of her the cushions jerked.

The quilt arched, bulging in some places like a pregnant woman's belly where the unborn baby kicks.

Then an arm emerged from beneath the exposed duvet and a bald, skinny man sat up.

23

His torso was bare and bony; he looked like a prisoner on the verge of starvation.

His eyes were wide open, swimming in a pool of tears. He didn't blink once.

Not when he turned his head to Emma.

Nor when he fixed his stare on her.

Not even when she let out a high-pitched scream and tore from the room. Along the landing, down the stairs to the front door where initially she thought she'd run slap into the two men. But it was just the wig stand, which she knocked to the ground, falling over herself in the process. She got up again at once and rushed into the street, without a thought for the neighbours or anyone else who might be watching. Emma slipped several times on the icy cobbles, but not so badly as to fall a second time.

Emma ran and ran and ran... Startled by the crunching gravel her feet was spraying up. By the panting of her own lungs.

She pressed her hand to where the stitch hurt most and kept running until she finally came to her house. The only detached building in the area, which Philipp had made as secure as a bank, with electronic locks she needed a transponder to open. This was a round, coin-like chip you had to hold beneath the lock before it beeped twice and now Emma pulled it from her pocket as she went up the steps.

She almost dropped it when she noticed that the LED light on the lock was green. And then Emma saw a dim glow coming through the curtain behind the small pane of glass in the door.

No. That's impossible, Emma screamed silently.

That *has* to be impossible!

Someone had switched off the alarm system, opened the door and turned the light on inside.

And it wasn't Philipp, because his car wasn't there.

24

'Where are you going?'

Emma, who'd made a sharp about-turn and was searching in vain for her mobile to call the police, was infinitely relieved to hear her best friend's voice behind her.

She turned back to the door, which was now open. 'Christ, Sylvia. You gave me a fright.'

Instead of an apology or at least a normal greeting, Sylvia just left her standing on the step and went back into the house without a word.

Emma followed her, now overcome with sheer exhaustion. Samson, stealing into Palandt's house, the intruders, the way back when she'd overexerted herself – all this had taken Emma to her limits. She could happily do without another problem, which her friend's strange behaviour suggested was on the cards.

Emma closed the door.

Her fingers trembling, she hung her coat on the rack, took off her snow-drenched boots and went into the living room. With the sudden change in temperature blood shot to her cheeks.

'Are you alright?'

Sylvia shook her head angrily. Her dark hair, which was usually pinned up, hung limply on her shoulders.

Normally when she came to visit Sylvia would make herself comfortable with her legs up on the sofa. She'd ask Emma for a macchiato before chatting about the most trivial things that had happened over the past week. Today she was wearing a mouse-grey tracksuit instead of the habitual designer clothes, and she sat as stiff as a statue on the edge of the sofa, her gaze fixed on the glowing embers in the fire.

'No, I'm not. Nothing's alright,' Sylvia said, as if to explain her unusual outfit and strange behaviour.

Sylvia Bergmann was not only her best friend, but the tallest too. Even amongst her widest circle of acquaintances, there was no woman on a par with her, and not just metaphorically speaking. The fact that she wore size forty-two shoes said a lot, as did the fact that she might have become a professional basketball player if her conservative parents hadn't insisted on a proper career, although as far as study was concerned they'd been thinking more on the lines of medicine rather than physiotherapy. The patients in Sylvia's practice on the Weinberg loved her because of her huge, magical hands that, as if equipped with a sonar, first felt for tension and blockages, then made them vanish by pressing energy and reflex points known to her alone.

Today, however, Sylvia looked as if she could do with one of her own treatments. Everything about her appeared cramped and tense.

'Sit down,' she demanded gruffly, as if this were her house and Emma a summoned guest.

Emma was fighting a wave of tiredness that was causing her to sway now that she was back within her own four walls. The house didn't feel as safe as it had this morning, partly because Sylvia had opened the door to her.

'Sylvie, I hate to say it, but you know that I gave you the key only for emergencies?'

'Sit down!' Sylvia repeated in a cold voice. 'This *is* an emergency.'

'What's wrong with you?' Emma asked, deciding to stay standing. Despite her wobbly knees she thought it was important to keep her distance. If necessary she could hold onto the mantelpiece above the fire.

'What's wrong, you ask?' Sylvia achieved the impossible and managed to sound even less friendly. 'Why are you doing this to me?' she blurted out.

'What are you talking about?'

'This!'

Her friend took a white pillbox with a red cap from the pocket of her tracksuit top.

'You know what this is?' she asked.

Emma nodded. 'Looks like the progesterone I gave you.'

A drug that increases the chances of pregnancy. The medicine stimulates circulation in the uterus. Women who've been unable to have children are encouraged to take this before conception and also afterwards to prevent them from miscarrying. Emma had it prescribed by her gynaecologist after the first ultrasound scan and gave the opened packet to her friend.

After the bleeding, *after the night in the hotel*, she'd had no further use for it.

'Why are you doing this to me?' Sylvia said again, putting the pillbox onto the coffee table.

'What the hell are you talking about?'

'Do you not want me to have any children?'

'I'm sorry?'

'Do you want me to suffer the same fate as you?'

'What on earth has got into you?' Emma raised both hands, opened and closed her fingers and kneaded the air like invisible dough, feeling helpless, with no idea how to respond to this unbelievably hurtful accusation. 'Why should I think that?' she asked, tears welling in her eyes. 'I love you, Sylvia. I wouldn't wish a night with the Hairdresser on my worst enemy.'

Sylvia looked at her in silence for a while, then nodded scornfully, as if she'd been expecting a lie like that. 'Over the last few weeks I've been suffering permanent sickness, headaches and tiredness,' she said flatly.

Welcome to the club.

'I was delighted to begin with, because I thought it

had finally worked. But the tests remained negative and I got my period. So I went to the doctor and he asked me if I was taking any medicines. Only Utrogestan, I said, which he approved of. *Yes, that can help.*'

As Sylvia's eyes wandered across Emma's face they felt like acupuncture needles. Her best friend opened her mouth and Emma took an involuntary step backwards, as if Sylvia were a growling dog baring its teeth.

'That's assuming that the packet your dear friend gives you *is* progesterone. And not Levenor-something,' Sylvia said in a voice that was too quiet for such an outrageous accusation.

'Levonorgestrel?' Emma became hot. She started sweating for the first time that day. 'That's impossible,' she spluttered. She wobbled over to the mantelpiece and felt even hotter.

'What were you thinking?' Sylvia asked. 'When the bleeding got heavier, Peter took a look at the pills. His ex-wife had taken them too, you see, and he said hers looked very different.'

Peter!

Sylvia's boyfriend with no surname. Or at least Emma didn't know his surname, which might have been because she barely listened to her best friend when she talked about him. Sylvia had only met him in the time afterwards, when Emma didn't mind listening to anything apart from relationship stories. She hadn't even wanted to see a photo of him. All she knew about

Peter was that he was supposedly 'the one', the dream man she wanted to have children with.

'So I took the pills to a pharmacist and he analysed them.'

Her best friend started to weep. In tears, she grabbed the packet from the table and flung it in Emma's direction, missing her head by miles and crashing into shelves behind her. As it hit the ground the box opened and the pills rolled across the parquet floor like tiny marbles. 'You swapped them,' Sylvia screamed. 'You gave me the morning-after pill, you crazed bitch!'

25

From a slight distance Emma stared at the packet that looked exactly like the one she'd given Sylvia a good three months ago.

The morning-after pill?

'There's got to be a logical explanation,' Emma said, without having the slightest clue what it might be.

'Why doesn't it surprise me that you're going to try to come up with one of your stories?'

'Sylvia, you know me.'

'Do I?'

I don't know. I don't even know if I know myself.

Emma scratched her forearm nervously. Suddenly she felt her whole body itching. 'If what you're saying is right, then someone else must have swapped the pills.'

'Oh yes, an ominous somebody. Like the somebody who supposedly raped you.'

Ouch!

Now it was out in the open. *Supposedly.*

A single word. That was all it needed to toss their friendship into the bin and put the lid on.

'I didn't mean it,' Sylvia croaked. She looked as if she'd just awoken from a bad dream. With a different, slightly softer expression, she put her hand to her mouth in regret.

'But you said it,' Emma said impassively.

'I know. But just put yourself in my situation. What am I to think?'

'The truth.'

'But what is the truth, Emma?'

The brief pause for breath was over. Sylvia now talked herself into a rage again, and every word brought her closer to the fury of a few moments before.

'A hotel room that doesn't exist? A witness who can't be found? For Christ's sake, Emma, you don't even fit the profile. The Hairdresser kills whores. You're the most faithful wife I know. And you're alive.'

'I was shaved and raped. There was a man in my room…'

'Yeah, like Arthur in your cupboard…'

Ouch again!

The dustbin where their friendship was festering was ready to go to the tip.

'What are… you… you…?' Emma felt so hurt she couldn't speak. She closed her eyes and was in danger of getting lost in a maelstrom of memories.

Letters on a mirror flashed in her mind.

GET OUT.

She heard her father's voice.

GET OUT RIGHT NOW. OR I'LL HURT YOU.

Heard the vibrating blades.

BZZZZ.

Heard a door slamming. So hard that the whole living room shook.

'That night I didn't just lose consciousness and my hair, but my baby too,' Emma screamed with her eyes closed, striking her stomach in anger. Once, twice. Until the pain was so intense that she sank to her knees.

She retched, gasped and was on the verge of throwing up.

'Help me,' she said, the words coming from her lips as if spontaneously. 'Help me. I don't know what's happening to me.'

She opened her eyes, put her arms out and groped for her friend.

But there was nobody there to help her any more.

Sylvia had already gone.

26

Emma dragged herself coughing to the sofa.

Her throat burned from the retching and her stomach felt inflamed as a result of the blows. She thought of Samson, who was in a far worse state, but who was hopefully in good hands and being treated.

With pills.

You swapped them! You crazed bitch...

Sylvia had gone, but her voice lingered in Emma's head where it continued to level accusations that Emma couldn't make head nor tail of.

She'd never even taken the morning-after pill, let alone built up a supply she could have passed on. As a doctor she felt she had a duty to life. She'd never intentionally give her best friend the wrong medicine. Not Emma, who'd revived the Rosenhan Experiment as a protest against the abuse of patients.

And yet, although Sylvia's accusations were terrible and her suspicion had hurt Emma deeply, their argument was nothing compared to what she'd experienced in Palandt's house.

Emma hauled herself to her feet again.

She had to call Philipp.

He would of course take her to task as soon as he heard about her solo effort. But in the end he'd have to admit she was right: Anton Palandt was a very strange neighbour, who they ought to keep an eye on.

She shuffled to the coat rack.

'Hello, Philipp? Can you please tell the investigators they should check out the resident of Teufelssee-Allee 16a? A bald man who swallows mountains of pills, lives in a gloomy house, is obviously being threatened by someone and – just listen to this – stuffs his house with wig stands. There's even a woman's hair in the bedroom – don't ask how I discovered that.'

This, or something along those lines, was what she wanted to tell him on the phone, but she couldn't, as she realised to her horror when she felt her coat pocket. Because her mobile had disappeared.

No! No, no, no…

In distress, Emma let her hands fall to her sides.

'Disappeared' was the wrong word for what had happened to her mobile.

I've lost it, she thought, then cursed out loud when it dawned on her that there was only one likely place where it could have fallen out of her pocket.

At A. Palandt's house.

When I tripped over the wig stand on my way out.

27

Emma felt as if she were being buffeted by a cold draught, a psychosomatic stress reaction. One part of her brain told her she had to go back to fetch her mobile; the other asked if she was seriously so insane as to want to return to the lion's den.

She froze and took her thick, sky-blue towelling dressing gown from the cupboard in the hall. It smelled of the perfume that she'd fished out again only yesterday, in the hope that the scent Philipp had bought her on the first day of their honeymoon in Barcelona would remind her of the happiest days of the time before. At that moment, however, all the mixture of cassis, amber and lotus did was to confirm Emma in her belief that she'd irretrievably lost the happiness of the past.

With sluggish steps she dragged herself to the kitchen, where she took the cordless house telephone from its charging station beside the coffee machine.

Her back leaning against the vibrating fridge, she looked out into the garden and keyed in Philipp's number.

SEBASTIAN FITZEK

Please pick up. Please pick up…

A crow landed in the middle of the garden on the splintered trunk of a headless birch tree, which had been hit by lightning years before, and which they ought to have removed ages ago. Outside it was already getting dark and the lights of the neighbouring houses were shimmering cosily between the trees like small sulphur lamps.

In the time before, she would have poured herself a cup of tea at this hour, lit a candle and put on some classical music, but now the only soundtrack accompanying her depressive mood was the endlessly ringing telephone.

She was expecting to hear it go to voicemail when there was a click on the line and she heard a cough.

'Yes? Hello?'

Emma moved away from the fridge, but the vibrations in her back remained. They got stronger when she realised who had answered her husband's mobile.

'Jorgo?'

'Everything alright?' the policeman whispered.

'Yes. Where's Philipp?'

'He's… hold on a sec.' She heard a rustling, then footsteps and finally something like a door closing. Jorgo spoke louder now; his voice sounded strangely distorted, as if he were standing in an empty room.

'He can't talk right now.'

'I see.'

'He's just giving his lecture. I've had his mobile all this time.'

Was that an excuse?

Emma pressed the receiver closer to her ear, but couldn't detect any background noises that might either confirm or refute Jorgo's claims.

'And you don't want to listen to your best friend talk?'

'I left the room especially because of you. Is there a problem?'

Yes. My life.

'How much longer will it go on?' she asked.

'A while yet. Listen, if it's about his visit to Le Zen again…'

An icebox opened in Emma's stomach.

'How do you know about that?' she gasped.

The explanation was as simple as it was embarrassing. 'Philipp had his phone on speaker in the car when he listened to his messages earlier.'

She blinked nervously.

Shit.

She'd completely forgotten her first call. And Jorgo had heard everything.

'Four weeks ago Philipp was at the hotel in a professional capacity. I know, because I accompanied him. We got them to show us all the rooms on the nineteenth floor again. What else could he have said when he suddenly found himself face to face with that vet? *Hello, I'm waiting for the hotel manager? We want to find the room where my wife was raped.*'

Emma gave an involuntary nod.

The icebox in her stomach closed again.

'Haven't you listened to your voicemail?' Jorgo asked after a slight pause.

'Sorry?'

'Philipp called you back a number of times. But you didn't answer your mobile or landline.'

Because I broke into Palandt's house, where I lost my phone, Emma almost said.

What a fuck-up.

As soon as her neighbour found it in his hallway it was just a matter of time until he discovered who'd made their way into his house.

He also saw me in his bedroom!

Emma froze at the memory of those wide, unblinking eyes.

'Could you please tell Philipp that I'm contactable again. He should call me on the landline. And thanks for your note.'

It grew louder in the background, as if Jorgo had put the phone on speaker.

'Which note?' he asked.

'You know, the one you put in my hand earlier. Thanks for believing me.'

'I'm sorry, but I don't know what you're talking about.'

'What?'

Emma felt woozy, as if she'd been running too quickly. She sat at the desk and stared out into the garden, looking for a fixed point that at least her eyes could latch onto, even if her mind had become derailed.

She saw the splintered birch again.

The crow had gone.

'But you... you gave...'

The note!

Emma hastily felt in her trouser pockets, but couldn't find it. She tried to concentrate, but couldn't remember where she'd put Jorgo's note. Far too much had happened in the meantime; maybe she'd lost it at the vet's, on the way to Palandt's or even in his house with her mobile.

'I didn't give you any note,' she heard Jorgo say, his voice suddenly sounding strangely irritable.

'*YOU'RE LYING!*' she was about to yell, but then noticed an object on the desk, so large that it would have been impossible to miss. Like the proverbial wood you fail to see for the trees. Emma shuddered.

'Is there anything else?' she heard Jorgo ask as if from a great distance.

Emma couldn't prevent her shudder from intensifying into a shake.

'No,' she croaked and hung up, even though what she really wanted to scream was, '*YES. THERE IS SOMETHING ELSE. SOMETHING DREADFUL!*'

She was shaking so badly now that she dropped the cordless phone. This extreme reaction had nothing to do with Palandt's eyes or her escape from his house.

But with the package.

The item that Salim had given her this morning for her mysterious neighbour.

It was there again.

On the desk.

In the very place she'd put it earlier.

As if it had never been anywhere else.

28

Just as an alcoholic knows what they're doing when they lift the glass for their first sip, so Emma knew what she was doing when she untied the string around the package. She was embarking on the most dangerous leg of her self-destructive journey, deep into the slums of her pointless existence.

One of the first things she had learned in her psychiatry lectures was the meaning of the word 'paranoia', which comes from the Greek and is best translated as 'contrary to all reason'. Which was exactly how she was behaving at the moment: contrary to all reason. She was even committing a crime, although violating the law on the privacy of correspondence was the least of her worries. She was far more afraid of herself. What if everyone else was right? The police psychologist who'd claimed Emma had invented the rape to get attention. Jorgo who'd sworn he'd never given her a note.

But the package had turned up again.

Emma was sure that it contained the key to solving all

the puzzling events of the last few hours, if not weeks.

But how many people had she met with a completely distorted sense of reality? How many patients had she treated, lost souls who did nothing all day long apart from mentally twisting their observations and experiences until eventually they could serve as proof for the most malicious conspiracy and persecution theories? Had she changed sides? Was she now doing the same?

Emma knew that you could see things differently. That although she'd discovered a number of 'discrepancies' in the past few hours, she hadn't found an ounce of proof to suggest that this package was connected with what had been done to her. Even so, she cut her thumb on the edge of the paper as she tore it open.

She yanked the flaps apart, virtually breaking the package open, and with her right hand burrowed amongst the polystyrene balls that protected the contents during transit. Emma excavated boxes about the size of tablet packets with foreign writing on the top:

МОРФЕЙ N6o ТАБЛ.

There were at least ten packets, white cardboard with a sky-blue stripe, and Emma opened one of them.

Medicines after all.

Tear-sized, ochre pills in a transparent strip.

But what sort?

Emma had learned English and Latin at school, but no Russian. She picked up the open box again.

МОРФИЙ N6o ТАБЛ.

Some of the writing was a reference to the dosage of the pills, she could work that out, but not the brand name or what it contained.

Emma found an instruction leaflet, squashed rather unprofessionally into the box. She unfolded it and the Cyrillic characters reminded her of the medicines on Palandt's bedside table. She rummaged further in the polystyrene balls and came across something that curiously didn't cause her to scream, even though she found herself holding a deadly weapon.

A plastic-handled scalpel.

Emma only gasped when she undid the already torn cellophane wrapping to expose a coloured blade.

Is that blood?

Struck by the surreal feeling that someone behind Emma was stretching out their hand towards her, she turned around, but nobody was there. Not even Samson, who she wished was here right now.

She pushed the knife aside in disgust and kept searching through the package.

Emma found a brown bottle, its label without a logo or anything printed on it, just some handwriting:

ГАММА-ГИДРОКСИМАСЛАЯНЯ КИСЛОТА

Emma rubbed her eyes and had to force herself not to close them for more than a moment. She felt like a car driver trying to avoid a microsleep.

I ought to pull over and take a break. Good idea.

She longed for her sofa *(oh yes, just a little lie down, wouldn't that be lovely?)*, but that was out of the question. *What if Palandt comes to pick up his package?*

Emma picked up the scalpel with the smeared blade and put it in her dressing gown pocket.

Despite the weapon she felt totally defenceless, for quite apart from the fact that she was hardly in a fit state to handle a blade should it come to that, the scalpel would be useless against the most terrifying of all enemies.

The demons corroding my mind.

What if she had a rest and the package had disappeared again once she'd slept off the diazepam?

Emma toyed with the idea of taking photographic proof of the medicine packets scattered across her table, *but with what?*

Her mobile was at A. Palandt's house, where the brutal foreign visitors sounded as if they'd be able to read these hieroglyphics that Emma couldn't decipher... *Hang on...*

She looked at her laptop.

... the computer can!

She opened her notebook, went to the country settings and put a tick next to 'Russia'.

That was quick.

It took her considerably longer to find the right characters on her keyboard. She could only proceed using trial and error, so it was some time before she'd managed to type МОРФИЙ N60 ТАБЛ and ГАММА-ГИДРОК-СИМАСЛАЯНЯ КИСЛОТА into Google Translate.

When she saw the results in the right-hand box she wished she'd never done it:

Morphine & gamma-hydroxybutyric acid.

Every child knew the first of these, every doctor the second.

GHB. A liquid anaesthetic that in higher doses made patients not only limp and defenceless, but also impaired their memory. Sadly the drug had gained notoriety in the press as the 'date-rape drug' after numerous rapists had secretly mixed it into their victims' drinks.

Emma panted, gasping for air.

The package contained the drug that the Hairdresser had used on all his victims.

There was a shimmer before her eyes, as if she were staring at the hot tarmac of a road in high summer.

She'd reached the point where this solo effort at research had to stop. Strictly speaking, she'd crossed that point some time ago. Terribly lonely, utterly shattered and with an almost painful feebleness, Emma stood up from the desk, dragged herself over to the sofa and sank exhausted into the cushions.

She thought about the package and its contents, which she'd hoped would dispel her morbid suspicions, only to achieve the opposite.

She thought about A. Palandt who, threatened by

thugs, wept silently in the darkness of his bedroom, and about Philipp, who'd left her on her own with her inner emptiness and who she couldn't get in touch with now.

Not because her mobile phone was lying next to Palandt's wig stand in the hallway, because she had her landline. Nor because she was afraid of his anger when he found out that she'd already committed three crimes today: trespass, violation of correspondence privacy and wilful damage to a package.

No, there was a very simple reason why Emma couldn't phone her husband – her eyes were closing.

The last thing she saw of her surroundings was a shadow moving a few metres to her right at the door to the living room. A shadow that seemed to be in the form of a dark, male figure. Although Emma was deeply troubled by the apparition, it couldn't keep her awake. With every step he came closer, Emma slid further from consciousness. Even the shuffling sound of his boots couldn't stop her from drifting into a dreamless sleep.

29

Three weeks later

When Emma opened her eyes she had difficulty getting her bearings. She knew where she was (in Konrad's office), who she was (a paranoid patient in the dock) and why she was here (to make an important statement – much was at stake). But she didn't have a clue where the last few minutes had disappeared. The hand of the clock on the shelf had advanced a quarter of an hour and the Assam tea in her cup, which Konrad had just poured, was no longer steaming in spite of the fact that she'd only blinked.

'What happened?' she asked Konrad with a yawn.

'You fell asleep,' he said. His legs were no longer crossed, but that was the only change in his otherwise flawless poise. He sat as straight as a die in his seat, without looking the least bit tense. Emma knew that he'd been a passionate advocate of autogenic training for years and he'd perfected the mindset for keeping calm.

'I fell asleep? During our conversation?' she asked in disbelief, massaging her tensed neck.

'In the middle of a sentence,' he asserted. 'The medication is making you tired and it's also very hot here. I've turned down the fire.'

What a pity.

Emma looked at the glass panel in the wall, behind which the gas flames were lapping with less vigour, and couldn't help yawning again.

Raising his eyebrows, Konrad asked gently, 'Maybe we should stop there today, Emma.'

'Do I have to go back?'

She swallowed. The very thought of her 'cell' produced a lump in her throat.

'I'm afraid so, but I guarantee that they won't sedate you tonight.'

Wow, what progress!

'I think I'd like to stay for bit longer.'

'Okay, but...'

'No, it's fine. Tiredness isn't an illness, is it? I've still got some strength left, so we should make use of the time. It does me good to tell you everything.'

'Everything?' Konrad pressed her.

'What are you getting at?'

He took a deep breath and paused. 'Well, I note that there are some things you merely touched upon before quickly changing the subject.'

'Like what?'

'The money, for example.'

'What money?'

Konrad gave a mischievous smile, as if this question were the proof of his assertion.

'Didn't you say that the vet was complaining your credit card was blocked?'

'Oh, that.' Emma folded her hands in her lap.

'What was that all about? Was it a bank error?'

'No,' she admitted softly.

'So it really was blocked?'

'Yes,' she said with a nod.

'And the email you casually mentioned before. The one referring to the blocking of your account, which you thought was spam…'

'It was real, yes.'

Konrad narrowed his eyes. 'Did you and Philipp have financial problems?'

'No.'

'What, then?'

Emma cleared her throat in embarrassment, then pulled herself together. 'You asked if *we* had financial problems. I said no, because it was just me in trouble.'

It was barely conceivable that Philipp would ever get into financial difficulties. His parents had left him a fortune they'd accumulated from building motorway service stations, before the two of them were swept away by cancer.

'I'd ordered too much, all manner of rubbish teleshopping and on the internet, from expensive cosmetics to microwavable slippers. Useless stuff I was buying to try and take my mind off things. Meanwhile my practice wasn't earning a cent.'

'But surely Philipp didn't leave you in the lurch?' Konrad asked.

'No, you know how generous he is. We didn't sign a pre-nuptial agreement, even though he brought all the money into our marriage. But he was already paying the loan on my practice. I used my own account for my shopping addiction.'

'And when it was empty you were too ashamed to tell him?'

Emma lowered her gaze. 'Yes.'

'Okay,' Konrad said as if ticking off an item from the list, and indeed he did change the subject.

'Let's discuss what you told me about Sylvia. What got you more worked up? When she alleged you swapped the pills, or when she talked of the "supposed" rape?'

Emma swallowed. 'I don't know. I think they're one and the same. She called me a mad liar who was out to hurt her.'

'Did she?' Konrad put his head to one side. 'Didn't she in fact doubt your sense of perception?'

Emma frowned. 'I don't see the difference.'

'Oh, it's huge. You know very well how three witnesses to a car crash can sometimes come up with four different accounts of the accident. None of them is lying, but in stressful situations the brain often plays tricks.'

'Maybe, but I'd definitely know if I'd deliberately swapped her pills and whether or not I was raped.'

Konrad nodded and something uncanny occurred. He changed, and so rapidly, as if a switch had been pressed. His paternal smile vanished as quickly as the laughter lines around his eyes. His expression became tight, almost rigid, as sharp as the drawing pins on his desk. His jawbones stuck out and his breathing grew very calm.

That's what a fox looks like just before it pounces on the rabbit, Emma thought, and indeed her kind mentor had become the notorious star lawyer whose cross-examinations were feared by witnesses and public prosecutors throughout Germany.

'So you're sure?' he asked.

'Yes.'

Beneath the cashmere blanket Emma clenched her fists.

'As sure as you were that you were forcibly treated during the Rosenhan Experiment?'

'Konrad, I...'

'At least that's what you told the audience at your lecture. You showed them a video. Although the woman had different-coloured hair, you explained that it was you being given electric shocks.'

'Yes, but...'

And with that the cat was out of the bag. The 'but'

that changed everything. Emma rubbed her eyes in the vain attempt to hold back the tears.

'But even I don't know why I fibbed about that,' she said, then corrected herself straight away. 'Well, yes, I do. I wanted to take the wind out of the sails of a colleague by the name of Stauder-Mertens. He's an arrogant arsehole who was trying to make me look ridiculous with his questions. It was really stupid of me, but…'

She left the second 'but' hanging in the air, because there was nothing that could undo her deception.

'Those critical questions from a colleague may have been the trigger for your lie. But not the cause,' Konrad said.

'I know that.'

She turned to the window and gazed at the snow on the lake. Wished she could be out there. Floating lifelessly, beneath the ice.

'Of course you do,' Konrad said, still pressing her. 'Pseudology is your specialist subject. You know the circumstances that can give rise to pathological lying.'

'Konrad, please…'

Emma turned back and looked at him imploringly, but the criminal defence lawyer knew no mercy and enumerated the symptoms: 'Neglect in childhood. Rejection by one's parents, one's father, for example. A highly fertile imagination that allows one to escape into a world of make-believe where one invents a substitute attachment figure, who might be called Arthur.'

'STOP!'

Emma threw the blanket from her knees. 'Why are we bothering to talk if you don't believe a word I say?' she cried and was about to leap up from the sofa. But, overestimating her strength, she teetered back, knocking over her teacup.

Fat drops fell from the coffee table onto the white part of the rug. A stain wouldn't have been so obvious on the once-dark black threads that had faded to brown over the years.

'I'm really sorry, Konrad. Christ, I didn't mean it.' More tears filled her eyes, and this time she didn't bother fighting against them.

'It's not a problem,' she heard Konrad say, who'd jumped up instinctively, and basically he was right. It was a minor stain, which would easily come out in cleaning, yet she felt as if she'd defiled the thing most sacred to him.

Why did it have to be the O rug?

She knew what the old, round thing meant to Konrad. He'd brought it back decades ago from a trip to Tibet when he was a student. It had been his first major acquisition, his lucky charm – and she'd soiled it.

'Where are you going?' Konrad asked, when she tried to get up from the sofa again.

She pointed at the door beside the exit that led to Konrad's private loo.

'To get some water and soap.'

He shook his head gently, her old friend and mentor

once more. Again the change had occurred in a split second, and even if he wasn't smiling he sounded as warm and friendly as before: 'The rug isn't important, Emma. What is important is that you tell me the truth.'

'I *am* trying, but you're scaring me.'

Konrad shrugged as if meaning to say, *'I know, but what can I do?'*

'Don't feel intimidated by me,' he said gently and sat down again. 'I'm just playing the *advocatus diaboli* here. During the trial the public prosecutor will try to faze you with quite different tricks.'

Emma swallowed, wishing he'd hug her, or at least hold her hand, but he just watched her sit back down. Only then did he stand up again, take a large handkerchief from his trouser pocket and wipe the glass table. He ignored the dark stain on the floor. 'The prosecutor will reveal all your dark secrets, which is what he must do. After all, he wants to see you locked up in prison for life.'

'I know.'

Emma scratched the top of her forehead, resisting the urge to check the length of her hair. She wiped her nose with a tissue, then said, 'I didn't intend any of it to happen, do you believe me?'

Konrad tapped his lips, then pursed them and replied after a brief deliberation, 'Normally at this point I always say that it's not important. That it doesn't matter to me whether my client's lying or telling the truth. But in this case it's different.'

'Because we're friends?'

'Because I don't yet know the whole story, Emma. Tell it to me! And not just what I already know from the files. You need to go deeper and talk about things that you find painful.'

Emma's eyes glazed over.

Looking right through Konrad, of course she understood what he meant. He wanted to hear about the bodies.

Alright then...

Her eyes focused again, wandered across the fire and the huge desk to the window, beyond which lay a lake she'd probably never walk on again in her life.

On the other hand she had pictures in her head that would accompany her everywhere, no matter how fast she ran away from herself.

For example, the barrel with the severed limbs.

Yes, that's a good idea.

Why don't I tell him about the barrel?

But before that she had to explain how she'd come to be in the shed in the first place and why she'd had to leave the house for a second time, without noticing that she was being watched by the delivery man... Everything in good time.

And so Emma lay back on the sofa and obliged Konrad by going where she found it most painful.

Back to the house in Teufelssee-Allee, where soon she'd lose everything that had once been important to her.

30

Three weeks earlier

She stayed quite calm.

Emma had fallen asleep sitting up, her head had slipped to the side and was now resting on the edge of the sofa cushion, tipping the room about forty-five degrees anticlockwise.

The cup on the coffee table, the photo frame on the mantelpiece, the vase with dried flowers in the window – everything appeared to be defying gravity.

Including the man three paces away from her.

For a moment Emma thought she was trapped in a dream and to begin with she was surprised that she *could* dream with the sleeping pill. Then she was surprised that she was surprised, because normally she tended not to reflect on her state of consciousness while asleep. Eventually she realised that she'd opened her eyes and everything around her was real: the dust on the coffee table, the burned embers in the fire, the dressing gown that she'd soaked through with sweat in her short, but intense sleep. And the man with the chunky winter boots, dripping melting snow onto the floorboards.

The man!

Emma sat up so quickly that she momentarily felt giddy and the world started to spin.

She reached for the switch on the standing lamp and clicked it on. Warm, soft light flooded the living room, which had been in a dusky gloom.

'Hello,' the man said, raising his hand.

'What do you want?' Emma said, feeling for the scalpel in her pocket. Strangely she was far less frightened than she ought to feel looking at a man who'd entered her house while she was sleeping.

She was agitated, nervous, felt as she might before an exam she hadn't revised for, but she was far from becoming paralysed with shock or even screaming. Not because she was resigned to her fate, but because the man looked less scary than the first time she'd seen him.

Not an hour ago.

Weeping in his bedroom.

'Herr Palandt?' she said, and the intruder nodded silently.

He'd been bald before, but now he was wearing a short, dark-brown wig that had turned black in the sleet.

He was tall, almost Sylvia's height, and slim, even

gaunt. His black raincoat hung over his sunken shoulders like a tarpaulin. It had yellow buttons, which looked curiously fashionable for someone who otherwise didn't seem to care about his appearance. His cords, which were also far too thin for this weather, were several sizes too big, as if Palandt was having to wear an elder brother's clothes. Yet he must be at least sixty.

The most striking thing about him were his glasses. Beige, plastic monstrosities with lenses so thick you could hardly make out his eyes behind them. Could he see anything at all without them?

'What do you want?' Emma asked again in the hope that Palandt hadn't recognised her in his bedroom. 'How did you get in here?'

Emma pushed herself up from the sofa cushions and felt as if she had to apologise, even though it was her neighbour who had intruded into *her* house, *and trespass is a more serious offence than criminal damage, isn't it?*

'I'm sorry. I hope I haven't frightened you, but your front door was open.'

The front door?

Emma recalled lying howling on the floor and hearing Sylvia angrily slam the front door. So hard that she'd felt it in the living room.

Maybe it had jumped out of the latch again.

I didn't check – stupid cow!

Palandt turned away from her and looked over at the desk.

At the package!

Ripped open as if by an impatient child at Christmas, its contents lay scattered amongst polystyrene balls on the desk.

'I'm sorry,' she said guiltily, pointing at the package. 'I'm... well... I'm not in a good way. It was a stupid idea to look through the post after taking a sleeping tablet. I thought the package was for me. Sorry.'

'No problem,' Palandt said. His words sounded friendly and warm, but his voice was weak. 'As I said, it's me who should apologise.'

Emma unconsciously shook her head, and so Palandt went on: 'Yes, yes. I should never have just burst in here to pick up my package.' He put his hand in the back pocket of his cords and pulled out Salim's card. 'I knocked, but couldn't find a bell...'

'It's out by the garden gate.'

'Oh, yes, right. I didn't go back to the gate once I'd climbed the steps. I'm a bit unsteady on my legs, you see.' He looked down as if checking that his scrawny legs were still attached to his emaciated body.

'Anyway, when nobody answered I was worried that this house had been burgled too.'

'Too?' Emma asked, and all of a sudden it was there, the fear. Because of course she knew what Palandt was talking about.

'Oh, I've been robbed several times, including today,' her neighbour said, scratching the back of his head.

'Today they even came into my bedroom and watched me.'

Emma turned cold. She opened her mouth, intent on posing the questions that an innocent person would ask immediately: 'Who are you talking about? What did they want from you? Have you called the police?' But no sound would issue from her lips.

Not when she saw the wig moving on Palandt's head while he kept on scratching.

He muttered something that sounded like 'this damned itching…' and at the same time his monstrous glasses turned into an aquarium of tears.

Palandt had started to cry.

31

'Would you mind…?' Palandt sniffled and looked around as if he were searching for something specific in the living room, then he appeared to have found it, for he turned away from Emma and took a step to the right. 'Would you mind if I sat down?'

Without waiting for an answer, he slumped into the armchair that stood at an angle to the sofa and where Philipp liked to read the paper on a Sunday. It was made of dark-green leather with concrete-coloured armrests, an ugly industrial look, Emma thought, that was totally out of place in this otherwise rustically furnished house. But it was an heirloom from Philipp's mother and he was attached to it. Palandt appeared to be comfortable in it too; at any rate he gave a sigh of relief, wiped the tears from his cheeks with the back of his hand and closed his eyes.

Emma, who was standing indecisively beside the coffee table, was worrying that her neighbour would fall asleep when Palandt opened his eyes again. 'I find it very embarrassing, Frau Stein, but I'm not especially well, as you can perhaps see.'

Frau Stein.

Emma wondered momentarily where the neighbour could know her name from, because it wasn't on the door. Then it occurred to her that Salim must have written it on the delivery note.

'What's wrong with you?' she asked, although she was actually seeking other answers. Whether he'd found her mobile phone, for starters. What was wrong with his hair. Whether he was playing a game of cat and mouse with her and they'd just entered a quiet phase in which Emma was supposed to think that the weak, suffering Palandt represented no danger, whereas in truth he was just waiting for the right moment to go for her throat.

'I've got cancer,' he said tersely. 'A tumour in my liver. Metastases in the lungs.'

'That's the reason for the medicines?' They both looked over at the desk.

'Morphine and GHB,' Palandt said outright. 'One takes away the pain, the other either stimulates me or helps me get to sleep depending on the dose. Today I probably took too much and missed the delivery man.' He laughed sadly. 'I'd never have thought I'd become a junkie one day. All my life I've played sport, eaten healthily, never drunk – well, I wasn't allowed to in my profession.'

Palandt spoke quickly with that mixture of excitement and shame so typical of lonely people who after a long time finally find the opportunity to talk to someone, even if it's a total stranger.

'I was in the circus,' he explained. 'Daddy Longlegs they called me. Perhaps you've heard of me. No? Oh well, it was a while ago. Anyway, Daddy Longlegs like the spider, because I've got long legs too, but I can make myself very small. My God, I was really flexible. I used to get the loudest applause for my suitcase routine.'

'Suitcase routine?' Emma asked.

'Yes, I could bend my body to fit into a small suitcase.' Palandt gave a sad smile. 'I had rubber bones back then. These days it hurts when I tie my shoelaces.'

Emma swallowed. She couldn't shake off the thought of a man squashing himself into the farthest corner of a room to avoid being discovered before its occupant went to bed.

But in Le Zen there wasn't a single corner to hide in. Not even for a contortionist.

Emma looked at the window. Snowflakes spun beneath the head of the streetlamp like a swarm of moths around the light in summer. She felt a dull ache pressing against her forehead from the inside. Emma couldn't help thinking that even half of one of those pills on her desk would be enough to kill the pain, however severe the migraine became that was now brewing.

Noticing that Palandt had followed her pensive gaze over to the package, she said, 'It's none of my business, but, well, I'm a doctor.'

Palandt gave a squeaky laugh. 'And you want to know why I order these cheap copycat drugs on the black market?'

Emma nodded.

'It was a stupid idea,' Palandt explained. 'I never had any health insurance, you see. What was the point? All my life I was healthy and if things took a bad turn, I thought, I could live off my savings in my mother's house.'

'Frau Tornow?'

'That was her maiden name. She took it again after the divorce. Did you know her?' Palandt appeared to be delighted and he smiled softly.

'We bumped into each other on the street from time to time,' Emma said. 'I haven't seen her in ages.'

'She's in Thailand,' he said. 'In a nursing home right on the beach.'

Emma nodded. That made sense. More and more German pensioners were spending their retirement years in Asia, where you could get better healthcare for far less money. And where it didn't get as cold in winter as at home. 'I'm supposed to be looking after the house in her absence.' Palandt was about to add something, but put his hands to his mouth abruptly. A sudden coughing fit shook his entire body.

'Sorry...' He tried to say something, but had to keep interrupting himself and didn't seem to be getting enough air.

Emma fetched him a glass of water from the kitchen. When she came back his face was bright red and he was scarcely intelligible as he wheezed, 'Would you mind giving me a pill?'

She handed him the morphine from the desk.

Eagerly he swallowed two pills at once, then coughed for a further thirty seconds until eventually settling down and relaxing.

'Excuse me,' he said with jittery eyelids. He'd briefly removed his glasses to dry his tears with the back of his hands. 'Sometimes I wake up with such bad pain that I can't help crying.'

Palandt put his glasses back on the bridge of his nose and smiled apologetically. 'I know I look like a scarecrow with these on, but if I didn't wear them you could get up and leave the room and I'd continue chatting to the sofa cushions.'

Emma spontaneously wrinkled her nose and sat back down on the sofa.

Is that true?

It was probably the reason why he was behaving so naturally towards her. Particularly as when he woke up earlier he may have been suffering the pain he was talking about. Without his glasses and with tears in his eyes he wouldn't have been able to see her standing beside his bed.

Maybe he hasn't found my mobile yet?

Emma's paranoid self wanted to see things in a

different light, of course, with Anton Palandt as a gifted actor merely feigning his illness to lull her into a false sense of security, *after all, he is wearing a wig!* But she was longing for a harmless, logical explanation for all the mysterious occurrences she'd experienced and witnessed today, and so Emma asked her neighbour bluntly, 'Did you lose your hair because of the chemotherapy?'

Palandt nodded. 'Yes, it looks ghastly, doesn't it?' He lifted the toupee briefly and Emma could see age spots dotted all over his head. 'It's a cheap thing off the internet and itches like hell. But I don't dare go out into the street without it. With a bald head I look like a rapist.'

He gave a throaty laugh and Emma tried to put on a brave face by raising the corners of her mouth too.

A coincidence, her hopeful self said. *'He's playing with you,'* her paranoid identity countered.

Emma bent forwards on the sofa, as she used to do in her therapy sessions when she wanted patients to believe they had her undivided attention. 'You said the foreign medicines were a bad idea? Do they not work?'

Palandt nodded. 'They're cheap copies. I should never have got involved with the people who supply me with them.'

'Russians?'

'No. Albanians. They get them on the black market and send them by post, anonymously of course, because they haven't obtained them strictly legally.'

'So what's the problem?'

'Those bastards are scammers. When you order the medicines, they cost less than a third of the normal products, which is why I opted for them. I can't afford anything else, you see. All my money has gone on alternative therapies. Shamans, gene therapy, miracle healers – I wasted all my savings and hopes on these. But after the first delivery the bastards suddenly demanded more than a thousand euros from me. I don't have that sort of money.'

'And so they burgle your house?'

With this question Emma had flicked a switch. Palandt's good-natured, grandfatherly facial features hardened. His lips turned to lines, then vanished, while his eyes assumed an other-worldly expression. 'Yes, to collect the cash.'

He raised his right hand and pointed in Emma's direction. His fingers were shaking like someone with Parkinson's.

'The threats were more subtle to begin with,' he said, upset. His fury at the people who were blackmailing him made him forget his polite choice of words from earlier. 'Those fucking arseholes continue to send me drugs. The quality keeps on deteriorating. They barely work any more, they just do enough to stop me from kicking the bucket before they get their money.'

Palandt wiped some spittle from his lower lip, then he appeared to notice how tense Emma was. Bewildered and shocked by his sudden mood swing, she was holding her breath.

'I'm sorry, I got carried away,' Palandt said, and the anger in him died down as quickly as it had flared up.

Emma wondered whether his illness might have set off a bipolar manic-depressive disorder. Deciding not to underestimate him, she invited Palandt to continue.

'Well, Frau Stein, what should I say? They are doing all they can to intimidate me. For example they'll put newspaper cuttings about gruesome murders in a package.'

Or a bloody scalpel.

'As a warning that my name might appear in print too, do you see? But they're not sticking to hints any longer. They're rummaging through my house, threatening to beat me up. I can't close my door any more, they broke it last time. And they were back there today.'

'Why don't you go to the police?'

Palandt sighed feebly. 'There wouldn't have been any point up till now. I mean, I don't know who they are or where they live. Don't know any names. What could the police do? Keep a round-the-clock watch on the house of a cancer patient? I fear they've got better things to do.'

'How did they get onto you?'

'I ordered via a Russian website.'

'And what do you mean by *till now*?'

'Pardon?'

'You said you couldn't report them till now. What's changed?'

'Oh, I see. Yes, the blackmailers made a mistake. They lost a mobile phone.'

Palandt gave a smile of triumph, while Emma's body temperature rose by several degrees.

'A mobile phone?' she echoed.

'Yes. I found it in the hall. You can get the owner's number from it, can't you?'

Emma shrugged. Her right eyelid started to twitch.

Yes, you can. Like a good girl I put in my contact number in case it ever got lost.

She felt sick.

'Have you informed anyone about the break-in yet?'

To Emma's relief he shook his head.

'No. When I found the delivery card I decided to come to you first to pick up my medicines. I've got morphine at home, but I'm running out of drops.'

Palandt stood up. 'Thanks so much for listening to me. And, of course, for the water. And please excuse me again if I gave you a fright by just coming in like that. Oh, would you have a bag by any chance?'

'A bag?'

Palandt pointed at the torn package.

'For my medicines. Then I can go back home and examine the phone.'

'Why?' Emma asked uneasily.

'No idea. I'm not really sure yet. In truth I'm not a great fan of the police. But perhaps they can do something if I give them the name of the person whose mobile it is.'

32

Emma had rarely felt so unable to deal with a situation as this one. She wasn't really tired any more, even though the sleep her neighbour had torn her from had been far too short to be at all restorative. But, just as in Palandt's house earlier, the fear of being caught had a revitalising effect.

Emma had to prevent her 'break-in' from becoming public knowledge. Palandt must under no circumstances call the police. What would it look like if it got out that because of a mental aberration on her part she'd intruded into the house of an old, terminally ill man? Most people already doubted her sanity. Even Philipp had suggested quite openly today that she get some therapy, and her best friend was accusing Emma of having poisoned her.

If her intrusion became known, her reputation would be destroyed for good. And everybody would say that the doctors unwittingly involved in the Rosenhan Experiment would have been better off giving her forced therapy after all. Because she really was a basket case.

'Are you alright?' Palandt asked, when she came out of the kitchen with a plastic bag. 'You look so pale.'

'What, oh, yes, no, I'm fine. I was just thinking.'

She handed him the bag and he went to the desk while she stayed by the fire.

'What about?' her neighbour asked, as the bag rustled each time it swallowed a box of pills.

I didn't ask him whether he wanted to take his coat off, Emma thought as she stared at his bony back. Suddenly she had an idea.

'Have you touched it yet?' she asked.

'I'm sorry?'

Palandt turned to her.

'The mobile,' she said. 'Have you already held it?'

'I'll be honest with you, yes. Why?'

'Well, my husband's a policeman.'

He didn't seem fazed by this rather strange answer.

'Oh, really?'

'Yes, Philipp often deals with these sorts of blackmail cases,' she lied. 'Usually they're linked to organised crime.'

Palandt coughed, them said, 'I can imagine. I bet that those brutes persecuting me are part of an organised gang.' He put away the last packet and turned to go.

Emma stood in his way. 'I work as a psychiatrist and sometimes help my husband out when he's compiling reports, so I know a bit about his work. I'm afraid you've just caused a problem for the investigation.'

'Because of my fingerprints?' Palandt took off his glasses and rubbed his tired eyes.

'Yes. They've got top lawyers, these Mafiosi. They were probably wearing gloves, which is why your prints might be the only ones on the phone.'

'But that doesn't matter, because if they trace the number they'll see it's not my phone, won't they?' Palandt said, but he sounded slightly unsure.

'If the burglars were so stupid as to use a mobile with a contract. But I'd lay money on it being a prepaid phone.'

'Oh.'

The floorboards beneath his feet creaked as Palandt put his weight on one leg, then the other. His eyes still looked friendly, but his expression was tense. Standing was clearly uncomfortable for him. 'Oh well, doesn't matter. It's worth a try, isn't it?' he said, putting his glasses back on and making to leave finally, but she made herself touch his arm.

'I'd be careful, if I were you.'

He stopped again. 'Why? What can happen?'

'Okay. You ring the police, they come by, examine the phone, run a check on the numbers dialled, but can't prove anything in the end. But because the officers have checked those numbers, you've flushed out the rats, Herr Palandt, and ultimately you've achieved nothing except for making your medicine dealers even more angry at you.'

'Hmm.'

Her words had hit their target. His head was processing them.

'Maybe you're right. I should let it rest; I don't want any more trouble. Having said that...' He looked Emma uncertainly in the eye. 'Dammit! I want it all to stop. They're bound to come back to fetch the phone, aren't they? I can't just carry on, hoping that everything will work out fine on its own.'

'I understand,' Emma said, without being able to offer Palandt a solution to his quandary that would get her out of trouble too.

'Give it to me,' she suggested, devising a plan even as she was talking.

'You?'

'Thanks to my husband I know a little police trick that can tell you if the phone is registered or not. Every manufacturer has a hidden system function.'

That was of course nonsense, a complete pack of lies, but it had the desired effect.

'You'd do that for me?'

'Sure.'

I'll do a few things before you find out who the mobile really belongs to.

She turned to the window, snowflakes were spattering the glass as if it were the windscreen of a moving car. She briefly wondered whether she could ask Palandt to bring the phone to her. But before he could change his mind it would be better if they lost no time.

'Right then…' Emma picked at her sweaty and now damp dressing gown. 'I've just got to put on something warm before we go.'

33

Arthur once told her about a weather switch her parents had hidden in the cellar. That was some time after Emma had stopped being afraid of her imaginary companion, not least because he hadn't appeared to her again in his terrifying helmet. Emma chatted to the voice in the cupboard, in secret so her parents wouldn't find out.

Ever since that night when she'd seen Arthur for the first time, she'd never entered her parents' bedroom again. Not even during the day.

Nor did Mama come into her room any more to read her a goodnight story. That stopped the day she lost the baby – for a while Emma blamed herself for this, even though she didn't know exactly why. Arthur comforted her and said it wasn't her fault that she wasn't going to have a baby brother. And he took over the job of reading the goodnight stories. Or at least until one night her father noticed that Emma was talking to the cupboard, and the very next morning arranged an appointment with the child psychiatrist.

After more than twenty sessions her father was pleased that his daughter had abandoned her flights of fancy. In truth, however, Emma felt as if she'd lost a friend. She missed the voice that told her all those funny stories, such as the one about the weather switch that allowed you to change seasons, so that fathers who didn't want to go the playground with their daughters could switch from sun to sleet.

And because this theory sounded no less plausible than the story of the man with the white beard who managed to deliver millions of presents to all the children in the world in a single night, one day Emma went down into the cellar to look for the legendary switch.

All she found, sadly, was the isolation valve in the boiler room, which is why it turned much colder in the house for a while once she'd successfully turned off the heating.

The weather switch remained undiscovered. Unfortunately. Because even today Emma would love to have something to turn off the early onset of darkness, the frost and especially the biting wind that sunk its sharp teeth into her face the moment she closed the front door and left the protection of the porch.

'That's what I call weather,' Palandt complained ahead of her. She pulled up the collar of her puffer jacket and had trouble keeping pace. Emma couldn't help feeling respect for her neighbour's straight back and controlled movement. Cancer or no cancer, Palandt's former life as an artiste still seemed to be paying off today. Unlike her, he wasn't shuffling forwards shakily and tentatively, nor did he adopt the cowering posture of a beaten dog against the gusts of snow. He swapped the bag with his medicines from one hand to the other and glanced back over his shoulder. 'It's very kind of you. But you don't have to do this for me.'

Get my mobile back before you identify it? Oh yes, if only you knew just how much I have to do it.

There was no 'wanting' to do it, however. It was bad enough that Emma had already exposed herself to the horror of the outside world once today, and she wasn't thinking of the weather, but the streets, lamps, *strangers!*

The effect of the diazepam continued to wear off, which meant she was no longer yawning every few seconds, but fear was once more perched on her shoulders.

In every parked car a shadow was lurking on the back seat. The light from the streetlamps illuminated the wrong sections of her route, leaving an entire world full of dangers in the dark. And the only reason the wind driving the snow was blowing so loudly was to swallow all those sounds that could warn her of impending disaster. In fact it was blustering so violently about her unprotected ears (in her hurry Emma hadn't put on a headscarf this time) that the wind even drowned out the ever-present drone of traffic on Heerstrasse.

They were passing the open drive of a corner house whose owners had wisely scattered grit, when Palandt gave Emma a shock. He turned to her and shouted, 'Have you been to my place before?'

Emma made the mistake of looking up at him, and so failed to see the snowed-over pothole and tripped. She felt a sharp pain shoot up to her knee, threw her hands up and lost her balance. Then a ring closed around her wrist like a handcuff and brute force pulled her forwards, where she hit something hard that also wrapped itself around her like a collar.

Palandt!

He'd grabbed her arm, yanked her towards him and prevented her from falling.

'Thanks,' Emma said, far too quietly for the wind, and far too uncertain about being in the arms of her bony neighbour, whose strength she must have completely underestimated. She felt for the scalpel in her pocket and groaned when she realised that of course she wouldn't find it in her winter jacket. Now the scalpel was in the washing basket on the steps down to the basement, where she'd thoughtlessly stuffed it in her clammy dressing gown before putting on the puffer jacket.

I'm unarmed, she thought.

And this thought heightened her fear.

'*I think, perhaps, that this wasn't such a good idea. I'd better go home now,*' was what she wanted to say before turning around and running back.

'I think… that was close,' was all she manged to utter.

Emma had tears in her eyes, from pain, fear and of

course the weather. She blinked because she was terrified that the water could freeze on her contact lenses.

'I mean, to my mother's,' Palandt said when she'd regained her balance and he let her go, his hands still stretched out protectively, like a father standing beside his child the first time they ride without stabilisers.

'Did you ever visit my mother when she lived here?'

Emma shook her head.

'That figures,' Palandt said, and if Emma wasn't mistaken he seemed to chuckle quietly, but that too was swallowed by the wind. 'She's always been a bit of a loner.'

They walked the rest of the short way side by side in silence, until Emma was standing outside 16a for the second time that day. She went up the covered steps for the second time, and a few moments later saw the inside of the house for the first time in the light. 'Do excuse me, my place isn't as cosy as yours,' Palandt apologised, making to take Emma's puffer jacket, but she was far too cold.

According to an old mercury thermometer on the wall it was a scant sixteen degrees in the hall. Nor was it better in the other rooms, as Palandt acknowledged.

'I'm afraid my finances don't allow me to heat all the rooms day and night. But how about I make us some tea and we sit by the stove in the living room?'

She declined politely but firmly. 'Have you got the mobile?'

'Yes, of course. Please wait a minute.'

Palandt put his medicines on a chest of drawers and went through a door to the left, leading to what she imagined must be the bathroom.

That's where he's keeping my mobile?

Emma used his temporary absence to have another look around the hallway.

The post was no longer on the floor by the front door and the coat stand was still empty. As was the stand with the mouthless, eyeless polystyrene head that was presumably for Palandt's chemotherapy wig.

In the flickering light of the old incandescent bulb hanging bare from the ceiling, the wig stand cast what looked like a living shadow. Emma stepped closer and saw something flash briefly, a shimmer on the otherwise dull surface.

She put out her hand, stroked the rough polystyrene and then looked at her fingers.

No! she cried silently to herself. She hit her chest, rubbed her hand on her thigh, tried again on her coat, but the hair, *the long, blonde WOMAN'S HAIR* that she'd picked up from the wig stand wouldn't come off her finger.

'Everything okay?' said Palandt behind her, who'd come back out of the bathroom. Emma turned to him, to his bespectacled eyes, his strained smile – and his slim surgeon's fingers in skin-tight latex gloves, holding a freezer bag.

34

'I found them in the cupboard under the sink,' Palandt said, smiling one second, then with watery eyes behind his glasses the next. 'I'm sorry,' he said, sniffling. 'I always get sentimental when I think of my mother. She's so far away now.'

He raised his hands and wiggled his fingers in the surgical gloves. 'Mother always used them to dye her wigs.'

Emma felt like screaming, but fear has its own fingers, which at that moment were slithering around her neck and cutting off her air.

'Unlike me she likes wearing these hairy things.'

Palandt strode down the hallway to the chipboard chest of drawers, on top of which was the bag. His raincoat crumpled with every step.

Emma recoiled, her hands pressed defensively to her chest, beneath which her heart was galloping with wild hoofbeats. As Palandt was now blocking her way out the front door, she scanned her surroundings for other escape possibilities. Or for weapons to defend against the attack she was anticipating. *The coatrack?* Too heavy and anyway it was screwed to the wall. *The polystyrene head?* Useless – too light.

The door ahead on the left? With a bit of luck and legs that weren't so paralysed by fear she might make it to the kitchen, but what guarantee did she have that she'd find a knife block she could reach before Palandt grabbed her by the hair? It was now long enough for a man's fist to grasp hold of it.

'Would you hold this for a sec?'

Emma flinched.

In her hand she felt a piece of flexible plastic, a small bag. Palandt had given her the freezer bag and turned back to the chest of drawers. He opened the top drawer.

A few seconds later he turned around with a smile of satisfaction on his dry lips. And Emma's mobile in his hand.

'Here it is.'

He gave her a nod of encouragement. Clearly he misconstrued Emma's expression, for he said, 'Yes, I know. The gloves are probably unnecessary, but at least there won't be any new fingerprints on it. May I?'

He pointed to her hand.

Emma looked at her fingers that were holding the freezer bag.

Palandt asked her to hold the bag so he could put the phone inside it.

'That's how you handle evidence, isn't it?' he said, then paused. 'When will he be able to examine it?'

Emma blinked nervously and bit her lower lip, which had started to tremble uncontrollably.

Panic was like an invisible night-time monster. Even if you'd checked that it wasn't hiding in the cupboard or under the bed, you would still lie there for a while in the darkness, your heart pounding, unable to trust the tranquillity.

'Examine?' asked Emma, who'd momentarily forgotten the lie she'd served up. Her face was bathed in sweat, but even with his thick glasses Palandt seemed not to notice, or he thought it was the rest of the snow melting on Emma's forehead.

'The special function,' he reminded her. 'That lets you find out who the phone belongs to...'

He fell silent and flinched, as if he'd received an electric shock. This involuntary reaction matched the electric buzzing and the flash in his right hand.

The mobile.

Illuminated all of a sudden, the device vibrated in Palandt's latex fingers and it took him a while to realise what he was seeing on the display: an image of two people. A man. A woman. Sitting snug side by side. Secretly photographed in a restaurant as the two of them, in an affectionate pose, are forking a potato cake. The potato cake photo signalling a call from Philipp!

35

The full significance of what he was looking at trickled into Palandt's consciousness between the fourth and fifth ring.

'What the devil…?' he said quietly. Emma put out both her hands, but this time it was Palandt who recoiled.

'I can explain,' she said, trying to get hold of the mobile, but he withdrew his hand.

'You?' Palandt exclaimed, pointing to the display.

The switch had been flipped again. From one moment to the next Palandt had lost his temper. Unlike back in Emma's living room, however, his blind rage wasn't directed at the blackmailers. But at her.

'That's you!'

Emma nodded. 'Yes, but it's not what you think!'

'You were here?'

'Yes…'

'You broke into my house?'

'No…'

'So it was your voice I heard in the bedroom!'

'Yes, but...'

'Your shrill scream...'

'Yes.'

'You were trying to scare me to death!'

'No.'

Emma's vocabulary had shrunk to that of a small child.

Was she in danger?

The expression in Palandt's eyes had drastically changed. Nothing about him now was reminiscent of a loveable, elderly uncle suffering from a serious illness. He looked as if he were in another world.

'Why can't you lot just leave me alone?' he bellowed.

You lot?

Emma tried to salvage what was salvageable and adopted a calm, friendly tone, almost like when her patients used to flare up in their consultations.

'Please give me a moment to explain.'

Palandt wasn't listening. 'Where were you?' he shouted. 'Were you outside too?'

'Outside?'

'In the garden. Did you find it?'

'Find what?'

'Don't lie to me!' he screamed, striking Emma the first blow. A slap, right in the face. For a second he seemed to be shocked by what had got into him and Emma hoped this meant he'd calmed down. But the opposite was the case; he became more aggressive, like a fighting dog losing all inhibitions about biting. He yelled at her even more loudly and his clenched fists hovered above her head.

'Of course you did. That's why you opened the package too, isn't it? To get me sent down? But you won't succeed. It won't work!'

Emma wanted to retreat further, but she already had her back against the wall. Palandt grabbed her shoulders.

'I'm not going to prison. Never!'

He shook her so violently that if Emma had been a baby she'd have likely suffered lifelong brain damage. Then, in a further sudden onset of fury, he pushed her away from the wall. She stumbled and grabbed onto the coatrack. Although it was screwed to the wall, it wasn't secured tightly, and so she ripped out the fixings and toppled to the floor with it.

Palandt had now completely lost it. 'You fucking bitch,' he cried. He kicked Emma, bent down and grabbed her hair, but slipped because it was too wet *(or was it too short after all?)*. Emma jabbed her elbow backwards, painfully hitting another bone, maybe his chin or the side of his head. She didn't know because she wasn't looking behind, only forwards. But ahead of her the hall was leading in the wrong direction – deeper into the house.

Into the house of the man who was holding onto her ankles (he must have tripped over the coatrack too) and yelling crazy sentences: 'I had to do it. I had no other choice. I haven't got any money! Why can't anybody understand that? Why can't you all just leave me in peace?'

Emma kicked out, ramming her foot into his face. This time she did turn around and saw the blood streaming from his nose as he stayed on his knees.

But Palandt didn't leave her alone; he made Emma tumble again. As she fell she kicked out one of his incisors, which finally had the desired effect: he let her go and, howling, put his hands up to his bloodied face. Emma crawled on all fours to the door that she knew because she'd already stood outside it some hours before.

As she pulled herself up on the doorknob she heard herself scream, a mixture of fear and hatred. She briefly contemplated going to the kitchen to look for a weapon, no longer to defend herself with, *but to bring it to a conclusion.*

Then she thought she saw a shadow behind Palandt, by the front door. She felt a breath of wind on her tear-stained face and watched Palandt regain his balance and wipe the bloody saliva from his mouth. With the expression of a rabid fox he screamed at her, 'You're not going to destroy my life, you whore!'

Emma jerked the door open, shut it behind her straight away and ran past the sofa beneath the goggling horses' eyes on the wall to the garden door. Emma wasn't going to lose any time finding out whether it was still stuck and now she didn't have to worry about making any noise. So she picked up the ugly umbrella stand by the door, ignoring the twinge in her lower back as she lifted it high, and slung the kitsch Labrador statue through the pane of glass.

The shatter sounded like a scream, but maybe that was her imagination, a faulty signal from her completely distorted senses. Turning her back to the garden and shielding her face with her arms, Emma pressed herself backwards, ripping her puffer jacket on the shards that remained in the doorframe.

She ran across the terrace, into the garden and sank into ankle-deep snow. She wanted to head right around the house, but heard a man's voice coming from that direction. *Not Palandt, but maybe an accomplice?*

So Emma kept running straight, intending to climb over the fence at the end of the garden and turn into the service road that ran between the properties here. A useless path that most neighbours used as a loo for their dogs, but now it might be her chance of escape.

Although it didn't look like that.

Turning around she saw Palandt only a few metres away.

Whereas her path was marked by footprints and feathers, Palandt left a trail of blood behind him.

For a moment she wondered how she was able to see him so well, see his bald head – he must have thrown off his wig.

Then she noticed the light source. Garden lamps that were probably motion sensitive, a relic of his mother who'd kept house and garden in such good nick before handing it over to her son (*the Hairdresser?*).

Emma could hear Palandt behind her, could feel his anger on her neck. She followed the lights in the snowy ground, which led to a grey tool shed. The door was ajar.

Should I?

There was only yes or no, right or wrong. But no time to weigh up the pros and cons. Perhaps it was the fear of slipping on the fence, losing her strength and being pulled down again by Palandt that made her opt for the shed. But maybe rather than make a conscious decision she just followed an innate survival instinct which, in case of any doubt, preferred a lockable door to open ground. That's assuming the shed *was* lockable.

Emma's nose was hit by a pungent cocktail of engine oil, wet cardboard and disinfectant. And there was something else. A mixture of air freshener and rancid liver sausage.

She slammed shut the thin aluminium door of the shed and hunted for a key. It wasn't in the lock nor on the doorframe, although she could hardly see her own hand in the gloom because only a fraction of the light from the outdoor lamps made it in through the small, grimy window.

But even if there had been an 80,000-watt bulb to assist her, Emma wouldn't have been able to search the shed. She didn't have time to catch her breath.

The door that opened inwards was shaking from the

thundering of Palandt's fists. She could have locked it with a thin bolt, but this was only supposed to prevent the door from flying open and shut in gusts of winds. It wouldn't survive a physical attack for long. 'Get out of there!' Palandt yelled. 'Get out of there right now!'

It could only be a matter of seconds before he launched the weight of his entire body against the door and broke it open. Emma would never be able to defend it with her own body.

I've got to push something in front of it.

Her eyes darted around the shed, passing a rubbish-strewn workbench, metal shelving, a military-green box for garden cushions, and alighting on an organic waste bin. A 240-litre container with the city refuse and recycling collection logo. A toolbox sat on the lid.

Emma swept the toolbox to the floor and grabbed the bin, which to her relief was sufficiently full. Even with wheels it was incredibly difficult to pull, but it wasn't very far, *and maybe I'll be lucky and the thing will be the right height so I can wedge it right under the…* 'Haaaaaaandle!' Her thoughts turned straight into a scream when she realised that it was too late. That she hadn't heaved the bin forwards quickly enough and had thus given Palandt a crucial few extra seconds.

He'd thrown himself against the door with all his might, hitting it so hard that the lock broke and he fell into the shed, knocking Emma to the side.

When she caught his elbow in her midriff, she

couldn't breathe and felt faint. To try and prevent her inevitable collapse, she grabbed onto a handle, unaware where it had come from. But as soon as she felt the cold plastic she realised she was clutching the organic waste bin, which tipped over with her.

As Emma fell her head hit the toolbox, but she wasn't granted unconsciousness. Staring upwards she wanted to scream when she saw the sea of air fresheners dangling from the ceiling of the shed. Then Emma really did scream when Palandt was standing beside her holding something that looked like a utility knife.

Now she was bathing in a stench that made her lose her mind, if not yet her consciousness. And in this case, 'bathing' was almost literally correct.

'Nooooo!' she heard Palandt cry. Clearly his mind was already in the no man's land of the soul where Emma was heading too.

Help me, please God, let this be over!

She was lying in a viscous, foetid liquid, which had slopped out of the bin over the floor. A sweetish, rancid, organic and vomit-inducing infusion.

Emma wanted to throw up on the spot, but couldn't. Not even when she saw the lower leg.

With foot but without knee, and very little skin over the calf and shin. It was, however, populated with endless maggots. The slimy worms had nested in the severed limbs that had tipped out of the organic bin along with the decomposed bodily waste and other body parts.

36

With every breath the taste of death made its way into Emma's lungs, clawing itself into the most remote bronchial tubes as if it had talons. Not even the loudest scream or worst coughing could shake it off. Emma knew that even if she survived this encounter (which didn't look likely), deep inside her something would survive forever, a germ of horror, fertile ground for the most appalling nightmares.

'Leave her in peace!' Palandt yelled in a scream-cum-sob. Staring death in the face had afforded Emma some moments of lucidity, and now Palandt's words confirmed her suspicion that the bony foot and decomposing lower leg belonged to a woman. She was also in no doubt that Palandt, brandishing the utility knife above her, must be the Hairdresser.

Emma was lost. She was still sitting on the damp floor beside the toolbox. She was armed now too, having hectically fished from the tool box the first thing she could find that was long, fitted comfortably in her hand and even had sharp jagged edge. But what was she going to do with a jigsaw?

She slammed it against Palandt's leg, but he hardly felt a thing through his thick trousers.

'You'll pay for that,' he cried, punching her square in the face with the fist gripping the knife. As her head jerked back Emma finally lost consciousness, dropped the jigsaw and, paradoxically, was revived again by the pain when her head hit the edge of the tool box for a second time.

Emma could taste blood and felt as if the skin on her head had torn. Palandt's hand was grabbing her hair. She heard a click. Opened her eyes. Saw the utility knife hovering right before her pupils. The edge of the blade was only a tear-width from her eye.

He's going to scalp me, she thought, her mind instinctively turning to Le Zen... *Get out. Before it's too late...* In the same breath she could have screamed because she didn't want this dreadful image of the hotel mirror to be the final memory with which she exited this world.

There were so many nicer, life-affirming moments. Such as Philipp's crumpled skin in the morning, when the pillow had left a wavy impression on his cheeks overnight.

The tiny pair of lamb's fleece boots, size four, that had stood on her dressing table for a while in preparation for having children – light brown, because they didn't know if it would be a boy or a girl. Even the dent in Philipp's company car, which she'd deliberately made with her foot getting out, after a silly argument about *I'm a Celebrity* (which he found funny and she thought was inhuman). Yes, even this ridiculous attestation that she couldn't control her temper sometimes would have been a better final image than the mirror in Le Zen.

Fuck, I don't want to die. Not like this.

Palandt drew his hand back then lunged.

How strange it was, Emma thought, that now should be the moment – for the first time in weeks – when she felt free of anxiety and perfectly calm. It was probably, she concluded, because finally she had proof that she wasn't as paranoid as she'd secretly feared. But maybe she had just given up. Her next thought was her surprise at how utterly painless death was.

'So this is how it is,' she thought as the blade sliced open her forehead and the blood created a waterfall before her eyes. A red veil, behind which Palandt vanished.

Emma closed her eyes, heard her own breath, but this sound strayed from her, mingling with a deep, guttural scream.

Palandt's voice had changed since he'd readied for the second thrust. It was deeper, as if he'd gained weight.

'Emma!' he cried from what seemed like further away, while an unbearable weight fell onto her body.

Her head rolled feebly from the toolbox and for a surreal moment she feared it had been severed, but then, in a near-death experience, she saw Palandt floating away from her.

Her neighbour, who had just (for whatever reason) lain on her, thus expelling the air from her chest, was moving away from her.

Or me from him?

Emma's eyes saw a light, not in the distance as people always claimed, but close and blazing, edged with red. It was shining straight into her eyes.

Then the light moved to the side. Presumably now came that part of the afterlife when you saw the people who'd been most important to you in life, although Emma wondered why this particular man should be the first to appear.

'Salim?' she said to the delivery man.

Who was kneeling beside her.

Who asked if she could hear him.

Who wasn't her final vision.

But her first responder.

And who was shining the torch in her eyes, the torch he'd knocked Palandt out with from behind. Now her neighbour lay beside the waste bin with the female corpse and looked as dead as Emma had thought herself to be only moments before.

'Everything's going to be okay,' she heard Salim say, and with this lie she passed out.

37

Emma felt the snow coming through the seat of her trousers and her underwear getting soaked, but the air out here was so clear and restorative that wild horses wouldn't have got her to leave the plastic garden bench Salim had taken her to.

From here she had a view of everything: the shed, its door secured by Salim's belt; the small window beneath the cheap door lamp, where she expected Palandt's face to appear at any second. But Salim had reassured Emma that her neighbour wouldn't be getting up again in a hurry.

'I knocked that bastard's lights out!'

She couldn't see Salim for the moment. He was wandering around the shed for the second time, his boots crunching loudly in the snow.

'There's no other way out,' he said in satisfaction when he came back around the corner. 'That lunatic is not going to escape.'

Unless he digs himself a tunnel, Emma thought, but

the base of the shed was as hard as concrete and the ground beneath it must be frozen solid. All the same, she didn't feel safe. And this wasn't just because of the acute pain that she now felt from the cut.

To check the bleeding she was pressing to her forehead the blue microfibre cloth which Salim probably used to clean the inside of his windscreen, because it smelled of glass cleaner, but right now an infection was the least of her worries.

'Why?' she asked Salim. In the distance she could hear the rattling of the S-Bahn, which at this time of day would mostly be carrying pleasure-seekers. Young people on their way to Mitte, starting with a few drinks in a bar or going straight to a party.

'I've no idea what got into him. I saw you enter his house with him, Frau Stein, and it looked a bit odd somehow. When you tripped it didn't look as if you were following him willingly.'

'I didn't mean that,' Emma said, shaking her head and wondering how long it would take for the police to arrive. Salim had called them on his mobile.

'Why did you come back? Your shift was over ages ago.'

Your very last shift.

'What? Oh yes.' Salim assumed a guilty expression.

'Because of Samson,' he said contritely, and it struck her that the vet hadn't yet got back to her with the laboratory results.

Or had he?

Perhaps there was a message from Dr Plank on her mobile, which was still in Palandt's hallway, having dropped from her hands a second time during their struggle.

'I'm not sure, but I think I made a terrible mistake,' Salim said, breathing out large clouds of condensation.

'You poisoned Samson!'

To Emma's astonishment he didn't object, but asked with concern, 'So he's in a bad way?'

Salim scratched his beard and pulled a face suggesting he wanted to slap himself. 'Listen, Frau Stein, I'm terribly sorry. I think I accidentally gave the poor thing the chocolate bar from my right-hand pocket and not the dog biscuit I always keep on the left.'

Chocolate.

Of course!

Cocoa powder could be fatal for dogs, even in the minutest quantities.

Now that she knew, Emma recognised the typical symptoms of theobromine poisoning: cramps, vomiting, apathy, diarrhoea.

Samson clearly reacted particularly badly to chocolate.

'I only realised when I was getting changed back home.'

Salim pointed to himself. In place of his postal uniform he was wearing a tight-fitting motorbike outfit – the obligatory Harley jacket, leather trousers and matching steel-capped boots.

'I didn't have your phone number and you aren't in the phone book, so I thought it best to come back in person.'

He pointed to the shed with his tattooed hand.

'I wasn't expecting to find something like that.'

Salim essayed a sad smile. 'I suppose that's what people mean when they say a blessing in disguise, isn't it?' he asked, returning to the shed to check his belt was still securing the door.

At that moment blue lights flickered in the evening sky and danced on the snow in the garden like disco lights.

The police were arriving.

In large numbers but with no sirens.

Three patrol cars and a police van, out of which four officers poured in black combat uniform. They ran up the drive into the garden, towards her, led by an unarmed policeman in civilian clothes, who wasn't dressed warmly enough – a suit, leather shoes and no trench coat over his jacket.

'What happened here?' he asked when he'd got to Emma, and for a moment she couldn't believe that it was him.

'Thank you,' she said, bursting into tears as she got up from the bench and threw her arms around Philipp.

38

In Emma's mind the men in black skiing masks positioned themselves one behind the other in front of the
door to the shed.

Four men, all with their weapons drawn.

The shortest, a compact body-builder type (so far
as one could make out beneath his uniform), probably
stood at the front and had already cut through the belt
with his combat knife. His hand was on the doorknob,
ready to open it for the three others.

Philipp must be standing somewhere away from the
shed, out of her angle of vision through the window.
What luck that he'd come back to Berlin early. He'd
been worried when Jorgo had told him that she'd simply
hung up during her last call. After that she hadn't been
reachable again. When Philipp called her on the mobile
that was in Palandt's hands, he was going to tell her that
he'd be back in ten minutes.

Now he was here for when the officer in charge gave
the order to storm the shed.

As she knew from films, the men behind would enter shouting loudly and their guns cocked. And the torches screwed to the barrels would light up every corner of the shed.

'*Good God,*' Emma heard Philipp exclaim in her head as he saw the tipped-over container with the corpse. Or Palandt lying in a pool of blood because Salim might have smashed his head in. All this, however, was nothing but conjecture.

Emma saw, heard and felt it in her mind only. She sat forty metres away from the action on an ambulance stretcher that had parked outside Palandt's carport.

'That's going to need stitching up,' said a young paramedic or doctor (Emma hadn't been listening when he introduced himself), who resembled a younger Boris Becker: tall, well built and with a mop of strawberry-blonde hair. He'd wiped the blood from her face and treated the wound with a disinfectant spray and a flesh-coloured head bandage. When he was finished she heard an aggressive struggle coming from the garden. No words, only screams.

'What's going on?' Emma asked loudly enough that Salim, who'd been waiting by the ambulance steps could hear her.

'It's happening,' he told her, although surely that could only be a guess.

A uniformed officer ensured that no unauthorised persons could gain entry to the property. But as far as Emma could make out from the open doors of the ambulance no onlookers had dared come outside anyway, perhaps because neighbours were intimidated by the host of flashing police vehicles blocking Teufelssee-Allee. Also, perhaps, because it was snowing more heavily than before and you could barely see a thing.

Emma sat alone with Salim in the ambulance because the Becker paramedic had gone into the driver's cab to write his report, then Philipp turned up.

'Nothing!' he said, his head poking through the door.

'Nothing?' She got up from the stretcher.

'Body parts, yes. But no neighbour.'

'What are you saying?'

That was impossible.

Turning to Salim, Philipp said, 'So you knocked Herr Palandt to the floor and tied him up?'

The delivery man shook his head. 'I didn't tie him up. But he was unconscious.'

'Herr Stein?'

A policewoman appeared behind Philipp and said that the officer in charge urgently needed a word with him.

'Stay where you are,' he said, but of course Emma wasn't going to sit in the ambulance any more.

She followed him for a few steps of the way before the policewoman blocked her path and Emma shouted, 'Please let me through!'

I've got to see it. The empty shed.

Only the fact that Salim had seen him too prevented her from thinking that she'd lost her mind altogether.

'I want to go to my husband. I'm a witness!'

Philipp turned back to her. He was about to call out 'Emma' in that tone with which parents reprimand their naughty children, but then just shrugged and in response to an invisible signal the policewoman let Emma through.

'Maybe you really can help us,' he said, although half his words were swallowed by the strong wind that was making the snow fly around in places.

Philipp stepped into the open shed, where someone had found the light switch.

Besides him there was only one other officer in there, presumably the commander of the operation. His ski mask was over his nose and he waited for the newcomers with an expression that appeared to say, *'Look here, you wimps. I'm standing with my boots in the middle of this corpse liquid, but I can cope with the stink.'*

'You should take a look at this,' he told Philipp.

'There are more body parts here.'

Philipp turned around to Emma. 'You'd better stay outside,' he advised.

As if she hadn't already left enough traces in the shed, *but what the hell? I'll stand in the doorway.*

Outside the stench of putrefaction was easier to bear.

From the door Emma watched her husband step over

the severed lower leg, trying his best to avoid stepping in the rotting puddle beside the overturned organic waste bin, where the rest of the naked female corpse lay.

Squashed like offal.

Despite her disgust, Emma couldn't help studying the body of the woman who'd gone through what she'd been spared.

That could have been me lying there instead of you, she thought, mourning this unknown creature whose name would doubtlessly be on the front page of every newspaper very soon. Together with her own, which the press would no doubt be interested in too.

'Oh, Jesus Christ!' Philipp cursed in the back right-hand corner of the shed.

He'd taken a glance inside the cushion box, its lid positioned in such a way that Emma was unable to glimpse its contents. If her husband's face was turning green, what he was looking at must be even more repulsive than the female corpse on the floor.

'Are there any more crates here?' Philipp said breathily to the officer in charge. 'Storage for more corpses?'

The officer shook his head. 'And no place where the lunatic could hide either. We've searched everything.' Emma's legs were shaking. The sense of déjà vu was unavoidable.

A room with a secret.

'There's nobody here.'

That's impossible.

'He was with the circus,' Emma heard herself say. In a monotone, almost a whisper.

'What was that?'

The two men turned to her.

'His speciality was the suitcase routine.'

Philipp looked at her as if she'd started speaking a foreign language.

'What are you trying to say?'

That he can make himself so small that he can fit in hand luggage.

'Is it dressed?' she asked uneasily, but Emma already knew the answer. Of course. There was no other explanation.

'What do you mean?'

'The corpse, for God's sake. In the cushion box.' She was almost screaming now. 'IS IT DRESSED?'

Because that was the only thing which made sense.

They haven't found any new body parts.

But Daddy Longlegs.

Palandt, who's made himself small and will leap out of the box at any moment…

'No, it's not,' Philipp said very calmly, his words like a needle pricking the bubble of her worst fears.

'There are severed body parts. A torso. A head, a whole leg. Naked. Full of maggots!'

And then he said something that changed everything. 'But there are clothes here, *beside* the crate.'

The commanding officer bent down and lifted a coat with the barrel of his rifle.

A black raincoat with yellow buttons.

So Palandt had got undressed! Why?

At that moment Emma hadn't yet solved the puzzle.

Not even when her gaze fell for at least the tenth time on the waste bin with the sticker, the carrot that served as the 'I' in ORGANIC.

Only when she kneeled by the overturned container and blocked out the stench did the cogs of realisation all click into place, because Emma did the only logical thing and focused solely on the breathing.

Not her own.

But the corpse's.

First its chest moved. Then the entire naked body.

As quickly as only a man could who'd once been known as Daddy Longlegs and who now, despite his illness, shot from his hiding place in the waste bin like a bullet.

'He's alive!' Emma was just able to say before all hell was let loose.

39

Three weeks later

'Seventeen stab wounds.'

Konrad opened the murder squad's investigation report and put it on his lap. To get a better understanding of her testimony he'd fetched the file from his desk after giving Emma a glass of water.

'Three in the eye. Most in the neck and larynx, only two on the forehead and one – the last one – in the left ear.'

Emma shrugged. 'Self-defence.'

'Hmm.'

Konrad looked at the file as if it were a restaurant menu on which he couldn't find anything he fancied.

'Self-defence?'

'Yes.'

'Emma, he was incapacitated after the first cut, when you severed his carotid artery.'

'But still…'

'But still it escalated into a bloodthirsty attack. With the utility knife…'

Looking up from the documents he frowned. 'How did you get hold of that again?'

Till now Emma had been staring impassively out of the window to study the dark, low-hanging bank of cloud above the Wannsee, its grey-black seemingly reflective of her emotional state, although at least it wasn't snowing – for the time being. They had now been talking for three hours, but unlike her Konrad didn't display the slightest signs of tiredness. And he seemed to have a concrete bladder. She really wanted to go to the loo, but couldn't summon the energy even for that.

Over the last few weeks she'd learned bitterly how depressives have to suffer when their illness is misconstrued by those who don't know such intensive sadness. In truth, you were in such a deep psychological hole that you weren't even able to pull the proverbial blanket over your head. This was a reason for the high suicide rate when depressives took medication for the first time to relieve their symptoms. Rather than a new lease of life, all it gave them was the strength to finally end it.

'The knife was still on the floor,' she said in response to Konrad's question. 'Not long before, he'd tried to kill me with it, remember?'

'Yes. But excuse me for pointing out that, as the law

sees it, this attack was definitively over. It had occurred a quarter of an hour before. Your wound had already been treated.'

'And what about when he leaped out of the waste bin smeared in blood. How does "the law see that"?' Emma said, making quotation marks with her fingers.

'As an escape.' Konrad moved the tips of his manicured fingers towards his mouth and tapped his lips with both index fingers.

'Escape?'

'He was naked and unarmed. He didn't pose any danger. That's how the public prosecutor will see it at any rate, especially as there was an armed policeman close by.'

'Who didn't shoot!'

'Because he couldn't. You and Palandt were like a ball on the ground. The risk of hitting you was far too great. Anyway the danger at that moment wasn't from him, but you…'

'Huh!' Emma snorted. 'That's absurd. A sick man dismembers a woman and stuffs her into a bin, gets undressed, stores the body parts in a cushion box so he can disguise himself as a naked corpse. Finally this guy, who'd kicked, punched and practically scalped me, leaps out from his hiding place – and now *I'm* the one in the dock?'

Konrad's answer was laconic and thus doubly painful. 'Seventeen stab wounds,' was all he said. 'You were crazed. Both men together, your husband and the commanding officer, had great difficulty peeling you away from Palandt. You were stabbing with such fury that you even cut them.'

'Because I was beside myself with fear.'

'Excessive self-defence. Not particularly rare, but unfortunately no justification. At best an excuse, which' – now it was Konrad's turn to make quotation marks with his fingers – '"as the law sees it" is unfortunately a weaker argument for the defence than a real emergency.'

The pressure increased behind Emma's eyes, which felt like the harbinger of a flood of tears.

'I'm in real trouble, aren't I?'

Konrad did not oblige her by shaking his head.

'But how could I have known what it all really meant?'

Her eyes were aching more painfully. Emma wiped invisible tears from her cheeks; she hadn't started crying yet.

Not yet.

'You were mistaken. That's human too, Emma. Many of us in that situation would have drawn the wrong conclusions and regarded Palandt as a criminal.'

Konrad closed the file and leaned forwards. 'In truth he didn't mean you any harm. Not to start with at least. And that's why, I'm afraid, it makes my job of defending you so tricky.'

She couldn't withstand his penetrating look. Nor could she gaze into the flames of the fire, which were higher again now and felt like they were burning her face. But perhaps it was just the shame of realisation.

'What happened next?' Konrad asked calmly. The best listener in the world had put on his poker face again.

'You mean how did I find out that I'd been wrong about Palandt?' Sighing, Emma picked up the water glass and moistened her lips. 'If only that had been my worst mistake that evening.' She glanced briefly again at the lake, then closed her eyes.

Emma found it easier to talk about her darkest moments if she shut out the light and the world within it.

40

Three weeks earlier

Emma knew that she was at home, in her own bed. She also knew that she'd sunk into a feverish sleep, physically and mentally exhausted by the consciousness of having killed a man after the skirmishes in Palandt's shed.

So she knew she was dreaming, but that didn't make it any better.

Emma was crouching in the hotel bathroom, looking up from the tiled floor to the message on the mirror.

GET OUT.

OR I'LL HURT YOU.

There was a knock, but it was Emma herself at the door rather than the Russian woman. She looked like a victim of radiation sickness: a bald head, encrusted in places, interspersed with the odd strands and tufts of hair that remained like forgotten weeds, ready to be plucked out.

But worse than what she could see (the dried blood on her forehead and cheek, the blouse buttoned up wrong, the snot in her nostrils) was what she could not see: an expression on her face, life in her eyes.

That life had been switched off in the darkness of the hotel room. All that remained was the buzzing of the electric shaver in her ears and the pressure in her upper arm at the puncture site, now throbbing like a tooth after drilling.

She slammed the door to number 1904. Ran barefoot to the lifts. But when the lift opened she couldn't get in. The cabin was almost entirely taken up by an organic waste bin. A monstrosity with a brown lid and a sticker on the front that said 'EMMA', the second 'M' formed by a bunch of carrots.

Emma heard, *no, she felt*, a noise emanating from the very bottom of the bin, as if it were several hundred metres deep. Something was carving its way from the depths of this well of horror, something which, once released, would never be able to be caught again.

'You fucking bitch,' Anton Palandt howled. 'I had to do it. I had no other choice. I haven't got any money! Why can't anybody understand that? Why can't you all just leave me in peace?'

Emma stepped closer. Looked into the bin, which

was actually a shaft that Palandt was squatting inside. Maggots were crawling from his unmoving eyes. Only his lips were moving. 'I had to do it. I had no other choice. I haven't got any money! Why can't anybody understand that? Why can't you all just leave me in peace?'

'But I haven't got any money!' he yelled from the shaft, and when the naked, blood-smeared corpse, stinking of decay, leaped into Emma's face she woke up.

Her heart was ready to burst out of her chest. Everything about her was pulsing: her right eyelid, the artery on her neck, the cut on her forehead.

She felt for the bandage, happy to find it there. It covered a large section of her head, including her hair – she'd retch if she touched that now.

Emma had been given some medication for this too.

Ibuprofen for the pain, Vomex for the nausea and pantoprazole to stop the cocktail from making her stomach churn.

They had been able to patch the cut. Now the only thing that urgently needed stitching back together was her life, which was ripped into several parts when she killed the Hairdresser. Maybe it had been shredded earlier.

The Hairdresser. The Hairdresser. The Hairdresser.

It didn't matter how many times she repeated this name, he remained a person. A person. A person.

I killed a person.

Emma looked at herself and wouldn't have been

surprised to see her hand chained to the bedframe with a metal clamp.

Philipp had managed to arrange things so that she was allowed to go to bed after giving a short preliminary statement in the living room. Tomorrow morning the interrogation wouldn't finish so quickly.

Nor, in all likelihood, would it turn out to be so friendly when the coroner's report was ready.

She had no idea how many times she'd stabbed Palandt, but she knew that it had been too many to count. And that it hadn't merely been a case of self-defence, but a desire to bring it to an end.

Back in the shed it wasn't only Palandt she would have killed, but anybody trying to stop her from ridding the world of this danger for good.

Revenge.

There was no other response that felt more important when you were done an injustice. And none that left you feeling guiltier once you'd exacted it.

Emma felt for the light switch and knocked a teacup that Philipp had considerately put beside her bed, its contents now cold. It was just after half past ten. She'd slept for more than an hour.

'I haven't got any money,' Emma whispered with a shake of the head as she put a cushion behind her back so she could sit upright in bed.

Why were these the words she'd taken from her dream?

Emma didn't believe in dream analysis as a means of psychotherapeutic treatment. Not every vision that appeared at night had a meaning in the cold light of day. It was just that, even out of a dream, these words made little sense.

Why had Palandt said them?

Even if in some points Philipp's profile analysis didn't match the reality, for example over the question of wealth, there were still universal, almost indisputable, characteristics that defined a sex offender. They were driven less by lust than power, their motor was impulsivity, and money rarely or never played a role with a serial rapist.

And yet Palandt had uttered these words in a state of great distress and agitation. At a point when he could no longer think, only act instinctively like a trapped animal fighting desperately for its life.

And he chooses this moment to articulate his financial problems?

In her own terror, Emma hadn't spent a second thinking about her blocked credit card and the fact that she urgently needed to ask Philipp to top up her account again.

Then there was something else, something really bizarre: Palandt was terminally ill and being harassed by strangers. Even if he'd shown himself to be surprisingly strong on occasion, the whole thing really didn't fit. If the Hairdresser was in such bad physical condition that he couldn't keep blackmailers at bay, how on earth was he able to rape and kill women?

Emma threw back the duvet.

Someone – Philipp, probably – had changed her into silk pyjama bottoms before putting her to bed. She was wearing sports socks, which was useful because she didn't now have to hunt for her slippers before going downstairs to talk to Philipp about what was unnerving her – she was worried that the danger posed by the Hairdresser still hadn't disappeared.

She checked again to see if her bandage was in place and, as she breathed into her hand to see if the smell was as bad as the taste in her mouth, Emma saw the red light.

A small diode on the display of her house phone beside the charging unit.

It showed that the device would soon have to be recharged.

'I don't have any money. I'm not going to prison. Never!' she heard Palandt shouting in her mind, and she couldn't help thinking of the corpse in the bin, another inconsistency.

The Hairdresser's other victims had been left at the crime scene.

This gave her an idea.

Emma picked up the phone on the bedside table, deactivated the caller ID function and hoped that Philipp hadn't reassigned the saved numbers recently.

41

'Lechtenbrinck?'

Hans-Ulrich's voice was unmistakeable. Nasal, almost as if he had a cold, and far too high-pitched for a sixty-year-old professor.

From a single word Emma had recognised the head of the forensic medicine department at the Charité clinic.

She, by contrast, tried to disguise her voice so Professor Lechtenbrinck didn't guess who he was really talking to, even though it was unlikely he would remember her. They'd rarely spoken in the past.

'My name is Detective Superintendent Tanja Schmidt,' Emma introduced herself, using the name of the police officer who'd questioned her earlier in the living room. She gave the name of the department responsible for the Stein/Palandt investigation. 'The body of Anton Palandt, victim of an attack in Westend, was brought in to you this evening.'

'Where did you get this number from?' Lechtenbrinck asked angrily.

'It's in the computer,' Emma lied. In fact it was stored in the speed dial memory of their phone: button 9. Philipp and Lechtenbrinck had cooperated for some time on the puzzle murderer case. Over the course of several months a Berlin serial killer had put a victim's body parts in plastic bags and left them in public places. In the final week, shortly before the killer was apprehended, they'd telephoned each other almost daily and their professional connection became a casual friendship, which was why Lechtenbrinck's private number was still stored in the phone.

'This is outrageous!' the forensic scientist objected. 'This number is only for emergencies and a select few individuals. I demand you delete it at once.'

'I will,' Emma promised. 'But now I've got you on the line...'

'I'm in the middle of a post-mortem.'

Excellent!

'Listen, I really don't want to interrupt you. It's just that we're about to question the suspect, Emma Stein, a second time and it would be of great help to us if we knew the cause of death of the female victim in the organic waste bin.'

'Puh...'

Just from this exhalation Emma knew that she'd cracked him. Forensic scientists couldn't stand the fact that in books and films they were generally portrayed as oddballs who were only ever deployed when it was all too late. They tended to feel that their work was undervalued. After all, they didn't just cut up corpses, but often played a key role especially in the questioning of witnesses and suspects. On one occasion Lechtenbrinck had been able to nail a suspect thanks to a telephone connection between the autopsy room and the interrogation room at the police station. Whenever the murderer tried to depict the death of his victim as a tragic accident, by analysing the wounds Lechtenbrinck was able to advance proof to the contrary, in parallel to the interrogation.

And now the renowned expert didn't seem to want to pass up the opportunity to have a decisive influence on another investigation.

'Well, the cause of death is fairly unspectacular. The report isn't yet cut and dried, but I'd lay money on multiple organ failure as a result of age-related ischaemia.'

'Are you... *having me on?*' Emma almost cried, her panic making her forget to disguise her voice when she next spoke. 'A natural cause of death? The woman was chopped up.'

'Post-mortem. Looks like a classic case of benefits fraud.'

Emma wondered whether Lechtenbrinck had suffered a stroke. Or if she had, because his words made no sense unless he was trying to pull her leg.

'A classic case of fraud whereby the cheat climbs into a bin without legs?'

'Not the cheat. That's Anton Palandt, of course.'

'I don't understand.'

Lechtenbrinck was breathing heavily again, but he seemed to be relishing his role as the experienced scholar able to teach a thing or two to a naïve policewoman.

'Look, Frau Schmidt. I haven't seen the crime scene, but I bet you ten to one that our perpetrator lives in poverty. One day he comes back home and finds his mother dead in bed—'

'His mother?' Emma interrupted Lechtenbrinck, who added with palpable irritation, 'Didn't I mention that? The corpse in the waste bin is almost certainly Palandt's mother. We're still waiting for the final dental analysis, but she's over eighty at any rate.' Then he elaborated on his theory, which Emma listened to as if in a diving bell: muffled, with numbed ears.

'Anyway, after a moment of sorrow, the son says, "Bloody hell, I've got access to Mama's account. Who says I have to ring the police just because she's dead?" He decides to keep his mother alive, as far as the authorities are concerned, so he can cash in on her pension.'

'I haven't got any money!'

'He tells the neighbours about a lengthy stay abroad, spending time at a health resort or something like that, but to tell you the truth in Berlin nobody wonders if an old person stops showing their face. At some point the smell becomes noticeable, which is why the perpetrator organises a burial in a waste bin. He just stuffs the remains into the container, which is a bit of a mess as corpses usually don't fit in without amputations. Then he leaves the waste bin in the cellar or shed, and chucks in cat litter or sprays litres of air freshener. The classic case.'

So my dream put me on the right track, Emma thought.

Palandt wasn't the Hairdresser and she hadn't killed a ripper, but at most a hot-tempered benefits cheat who'd done nothing worse than to prevent his mother from resting in peace just because he needed the money.

Which meant the danger is still very much present!

Emma wasn't sure how she'd managed to avoid bellowing this last thought down the line. She thought she thanked the doctor and said a rapid goodbye, but she couldn't recall another word that was said. Exhausted, she fell back into the cushions and pillows.

I killed a person!

Not the Hairdresser!

Palandt didn't have the slightest thing to do with him.

His wig, the medication, the package... In her paranoia she'd bent the facts, which had cost an innocent man his life.

Emma closed her eyes and couldn't help thinking of the blood that had spurted from Palandt's body. After she'd stabbed him again and again.

Which in turn reminded her of the pool of blood she'd had to wipe up in the living room this morning.

Samson!

She hadn't thought about him once since she'd

woken up. In the uneasy hope that he, at least, was better, she dialled the number to access her voicemail from the landline. Her mobile had been confiscated as evidence by the police.

'You have three new messages,' the robotic voice announced. And indeed the first was from Dr Plank, reassuring Emma that Samson was over the worst. *Thank God.* But they'd have to wait for the definitive results on Monday before she could pick him up, and what was happening now about payment?

The next was from Philipp, sounding concerned and informing her that he'd be back home in a few minutes.

And finally she heard another voice that sounded so agitated that Emma didn't recognise it at first. It didn't help that Jorgo was practically whispering either.

'Emma? I'm sorry about earlier. I mean that I lied to you. Of course I gave you that note.'

The note!

Something else that Emma, in her distress, had temporarily forgotten. The telephone beeped because the battery was low. It needed to be put back on the dock, but then she wouldn't be able to make any more calls, which is why Emma decided to go downstairs where she hoped the second handset would be waiting fully charged.

'Your husband has a spy program on his mobile,' she heard Jorgo say. 'It automatically records every incoming call.'

A spy program? What the bloody hell is that about?

It beeped again three times before she got to the bedroom door.

But there was just enough juice left in the battery for a few more words from Jorgo.

'I didn't want your husband to find out about the note when he listened to our conversation later on. So please call me on my mobile. Please. It's important. We found out something. Philipp doesn't want to tell you, but I think you ought to know. In the hotel, in Le Zen—'

Beep.

The line was dead and the display as dark as the hallway on the ground floor.

Emma felt her way to the light switch as Jorgo's final words echoed slowly in her head.

'We found out something...'

She went into the kitchen first, but the second handset wasn't in the dock.

'Philipp doesn't want to tell you...'

On the way into the living room Jorgo's voice went quiet, but now she thought she could hear the buzzing of the shaver in her head, only that this time it wasn't a long, penetrating drone, but an intermittent stutter.

'In the hotel, in Le Zen...'

Like a drill.

An insect.

Emma went over to the desk where that afternoon she'd ripped open Palandt's package. She couldn't find the second house phone here either, although she did locate the source of the buzzing: Philipp's mobile.

With every ring it rotated to the rhythm of the vibrations. The caller's name flashed ominously.

Emma turned around, but the vague inkling that her husband would suddenly be standing there was unfounded.

She hesitantly picked up the mobile and pressed the green symbol to take the call.

'What did you find out in the hotel, Jorgo?' she asked anxiously.

'Help me!' screamed the voice on the other end.

42

She recognised it straight away, even though Emma had never heard this voice sound so unfamiliar before.

Muffled, choking with gurgling in the background.

'Sylvia?' she said, and her friend started to sob by way of an answer. 'What's wrong?' Emma asked. 'Are you hurt? How can I help you?'

And why are you calling from Jorgo's phone?

'I... I'm dying,' Sylvia slurred. The panic and terror were still in her voice, but the force of her initial scream had dissipated.

'No, you're not. Do you hear me? You're not dying. I'll fetch help and everything will be alright.'

'No. Never... alright... again!'

Emma could virtually hear Sylvia drifting away. The more tightly she pressed the phone against her ear, the quieter it sounded.

In her mind she saw her friend with a utility knife in her neck, sitting in a pool of blood she'd coughed up in a torrent. Sylvia was no longer speaking now, just coughing and gasping, no matter how loudly Emma implored her to say what on earth had happened.

'Where are you?'

Now Emma screamed, because this question could apply to both Sylvia and Philipp, whose help she desperately needed.

Emma hurried through the living room, the mobile still at her ear. She saw Philipp's keys on the chest of drawers, his jacket hanging on the rack, so he couldn't be out. Anyway he'd never leave the house without his mobile, but he had left it in the living room, *which he only does when...*

'Sylvia, are you still there?' Emma said into the phone, and a cold silence washed back.

... he goes down to his laboratory...

Emma looked at the old cellar door. The light from the cellar stairs seeped into the hallway through a large gap between the floor and the bottom of the door.

... where his mobile doesn't get any reception!

'Sylvia, stay on the line. I can't take you down into the cellar, do you understand? The connection will go, but I'll be right back. Don't hang up!'

No reaction.

Emma briefly wondered whether it would be smarter to cut Sylvia off and call the police, but what if her friend wasn't at home? The telephone connection might be the only way of pinpointing her location.

She put the mobile on the chest of drawers, yanked

open the cellar door and yelled as she went down the concrete steps, 'Philipp? Quick. You've got to help me. Philipp?'

The ceiling in the cellar was so low that the seller had agreed to knock some money off the price when he saw that even Emma had to duck as they looked around.

After moving in they cladded the ceiling on the stairs with wood, which meant there was even less room now. Stooped, Emma hurried downstairs, taking the sharp turn to the right and then straight on to the 'laboratory'.

They'd originally earmarked the area as storage for the vacuum cleaner, broom and mop, but then Philipp replaced the old linen curtain with a folding door and made himself a little office behind it. Inside were a tiny desk with a laptop connected to the internet, two metal shelves on the wall, completely cluttered with specialist literature and all manner of stackable hard plastic boxes containing magnifying glasses, tweezers, microscopes and other utensils. These he used for examining photographs and analysing signatures or other evidence essential to his work as a profiler.

Down here in his 'cave', cut off from the rest of the world, Philipp was best able to concentrate. While he worked he usually listened through headphones to music that calmed him, but would have given Emma hearing loss in a few seconds: Rammstein, Oomph and Eisbrecher.

It was no surprise, therefore, that he hadn't responded to her calling. Nor that he got the fright of his life when

Emma opened the folding door and pulled off the headphones.

'What the hell…'

'Philipp… I—'

Emma stared at his hands, which were wearing mouse-grey latex gloves.

Dull bass drumbeats pounded out from the headphones into the tiny room, providing an accompaniment to her fitful breathing.

Emma was gasping for air, which wasn't a result of the few steps and quick dash down here, nor of her concern for Sylvia. The reason was that she couldn't find an innocent explanation for what lay in front of Philipp.

The utility knife.

The gloves.

THE PACKAGE!

She'd wondered where her slippers had got to. The shoebox-sized package with her internet order that you could put in the microwave. Philipp had put away the food delivery in the fridge and her contact lenses were in the bathroom.

But the light package wrapped in normal brown paper? It was down here. Right beneath Philipp's reading lamp, beside his laptop on the mini desk.

The paper cut open.

The flaps opened.

Some of its contents spread beneath the desk magnifier, the rest still inside the box padded with cotton wool.

Not microwavable slippers.

Emma had obviously been mistaken and she'd neglected to check who the package was addressed to.

For the long, thick, lifelike tufts of brunette hair that had been sent in this box were not for her.

But for Philipp.

43

'What's that?' Emma asked.

Her mind was seeking a logical, but most of all an innocent, explanation.

'Were you sent those by the Hairdresser?'

Definitely. The killer has contacted him. He's just doing his work here and examining the trophies.

'What do you mean?' asked Philipp, who'd stood up from his chair.

'You know, the hair,' Emma said. An icy ring closed around her heart when she watched Philipp open a desk drawer and shut the bunch of dark hair inside.

'What hair?' he asked. 'I don't know what you're talking about, darling.'

Then he turned his notebook so that she could see the screen.

'What... how... where...?' she heard herself stammer. Her monosyllabic questions changed in time to the pictures that appeared on the screen as a sort of slideshow.

Photos of women.

Of *beautiful* women.

Escort girls. Secretly photographed outside various doors. *Hotel-room doors*, opened by a man who was always the same, while the prostitutes changed.

'You?' Emma said, still desperately trying to deny the obvious.

'You met these girls?'

The escort girls. The victims?

'So *you* killed them?'

'Emma, are you feeling okay?' Philipp asked with an expression that made her think he was feigning surprise as he pressed the spacebar on his keyboard. And called up a different picture that showed another victim.

Emma screamed when she recognised herself.

With a wheelie suitcase in one hand, right by a dark door she was just opening. Like all the other clips, this was badly lit, but the room number on the walnut veneer was easy to make out: 1904.

'It was you!' Emma screamed into Philipp's face. 'You're the Hairdresser!'

How could have I been so mistaken?

So deceived?

Perturbed by the package for her unknown neighbour, Emma hadn't paid any attention to the second one.

And thus nor to the enemy in her own house.

Having become lost in the labyrinth of her own paranoid thoughts, Emma had destroyed innocent lives.

'You bastard!'

Her husband smiled and spoke with a tone of great concern, which didn't go with his diabolical grin. 'Emma, calm down, please. You're out of your mind,' he said, at the same time pressing his keyboard again, which turned the screen black.

'What are you going to do?' Emma cried, with no idea what *she* should do. She felt paralysed by bewilderment and horror. 'Are you trying to drive me mad?'

'What do you mean? I'm worried you're seeing things again that aren't there, darling.'

Yes. That's it. I don't know why, but he's feeding my paranoia.

Emma looked around, searching instinctively for an object to defend herself with if Philipp attacked her. Then she saw a small camera on the ceiling, which was fixed so that Emma was in the picture the whole time, whereas her husband would not be visible on the film.

'You're filming me?' she said, devastated.

'But darling, you asked me to make the cellar secure,' he replied piously. 'For fear of burglars.'

'I never said anything about cameras,' she yelled at him. And whereas she was still far from clear as to what Philipp's motives could be, she was struck by another, horrendous realisation:

Sylvia.

She didn't call from Jorgo's phone.

But from her own.

On this point, at least, she was sure about the game Philipp had been playing with her the whole time.

It's just like he did with his ex.

He'd saved Sylvia's number under a different name.

What sort of a man would do that?

One who had something to hide.

An affair.

So it wouldn't attract any attention if his lover called several times a day, sent texts or missed calls.

Emma's stomach tightened.

Of course, how clever.

Jorgo was Philipp's partner, so it was only natural that he'd make lots of calls. At least there was an explanation when the naïve wifey at home saw the display and asked.

How clever and deceitful.

For him Sylvia was Jorgo, while Sylvia called him Peter.

And she's got such wonderful long hair. Just like me.

Just like all the Hairdresser's other victims.

'But why did you have to kill them all?' Emma croaked. The revelations seemed to have blocked her airways. 'The whores, your affairs. Even Sylvia? Why did she have to die?'

As if the name of the woman she'd once regarded as her best friend was the cue, the devilish smile vanished from Philipp's face and for the first time he looked seriously worried. 'What's wrong with Sylvie?' he asked, as if really unaware that she'd just tried to call him in the throes of death.

Maybe it was the brief moment of weakness she thought she could detect in his eyes, or the fact that he'd called his latest affair by her nickname that unleashed an aggressive, unrestrained fury in Emma.

But possibly it was just the courage of despair that tore her from her paralysis.

44

'Emma, stop!' Philipp cried, but she had no intention of surrendering with no way out.

She knocked away the arm he was trying to grab her with, turned around and ran up the stairs as fast as she could, but it wasn't fast enough.

Philipp easily seized her foot and held her where she was. He was bigger, stronger and faster than her. And he didn't have a wound to the head that throbbed like a living insect below its bandage, sending out new waves of pain with every movement.

Emma stumbled and the heels of her hands slapped hard against the edge of the concrete steps.

She flipped onto her back and started kicking as she'd done with Palandt just a few hours before. Now, however, she was only wearing socks; without her heavy boots she couldn't even hurt Philipp, let alone shake him off.

'Emma!' her husband cried, now with a grip on both ankles. The edges of the steps dug into her back and yet she kept thrashing about as if possessed.

Until Philipp yelled 'Stop that!', rushed forwards and hit her.

Hard. Harder than this morning when he'd slapped some sense back into her.

Emma's head dashed backwards against the stairs and she saw bright lights. When she opened her eyes again it was as if she were looking at Philipp through a cracked kaleidoscope.

She saw that his lip was bleeding, which meant she'd probably caught him with her foot.

Not good.

The minor injury had only made him furious like a wounded animal, thus giving him more strength than it had sapped.

Emma, on the other hand, had no more resistance to offer. She could hardly bear the pressure of his fingers around her wrists.

She wanted it to stop.

For it to finally come to an end.

The pain. The violence.

The lies!

Her sudden passivity gave Philipp new impetus. He climbed and lay on top of her with all his weight, like a lusty husband desperate to shag his willing wife on the cellar stairs, the only difference being that he didn't want to make love, *but quite the opposite.*

'Help!' Emma cried, although to whom she didn't

know. In her head she was shouting more loudly than in the dimly lit reality of the cellar steps.

She closed her eyes and the simple wooden panelling on the walls vanished, as did the plastic planter below the banisters, the fuse box by the entrance, which she could only see if she tilted her head back, and the door to Philipp's 'laboratory'.

And Philipp vanished of course, although only the sight of him. His words wouldn't go away.

'Everything's going to be fine,' she heard him say. In a gruesomely friendly tone. She heard his breathing, sensed a hand (probably the right one) push beneath her head, felt him stroking her brow (probably with the back of his left) – he ought not to have done that.

The feeling of latex on her face, the typical smell of rubber and talcum powder, was like a dagger to her heart, twisting, twisting and twisting with every movement.

When Emma opened her eyes she saw Philipp smile, presumably the same grin he'd worn in the darkness of the hotel room. His head came closer and she thought about butting her own into his face. But again she was too feeble to do any serious damage; she'd only make him even angrier.

Emma started crying and heard him make shhhing noises, no doubt aimed at pacifying her. But they made Emma think of snakes and the very next moment she rammed her knee between his legs.

Philipp groaned and loosened his grip, which gave

her the opportunity to chop the side of her hand against his jaw.

He screamed, turned to the side, pressed a hand to his mouth and spat out blood. She'd hit him so hard that she must have knocked a tooth out. Or he'd bit his tongue, so heavy was the bleeding.

He'd now let go of her entirely; Emma could no longer feel any pressure on her body or around her wrists and ankles.

Finally she got to her feet, ran upstairs, but once again she was too slow. Once again Philipp caught hold of her, this time her foot, and started to drag her back. To him.

Into the abyss.

Emma felt for the banisters, tried to hold on, but her hand slipped and knocked against a hard edge, which she instinctively clasped.

Even though it felt like a handle, it wasn't fastened to the wall, but why would there be a handle on the cellar stairs, *unless…*

… it belonged to the fire extinguisher.

As she faltered Emma saw her chance. While her body was still busy trying to regain its balance she yanked the fire extinguisher upwards, swivelled on the balls of her feet, swayed and tried to fall forwards, towards Philipp. But gravity had other ideas, and so once more she toppled onto the stairs on her back.

As she fell there was no way she could launch the heavy

fire extinguisher at Philipp, who was over her again.

All she saw was him raising his hand, then everything went white. The cellar, the walls, the stairs, Philipp, herself. Like in a sandstorm, everything was surrounded by a veil of dust from one moment to the next.

Emma heard a hissing, then pressed down harder with her right hand, which evidently had control over the dust and the hissing noise, and for a split second there was a hole in the fog.

In the hole stood Philipp.

Covered with the contents of the fire extinguisher she was spraying right at him. With the foam he was trying to wipe from his eyes Philipp looked like a ghost with a blood-smeared mouth.

'EMMAAA,' she heard him scream as he managed to grab the banister while stumbling. Now he started moving again. Slowly and carefully. Step by step he came closer.

And agonisingly slowly, step by step, Emma crept up the stairs on her belly.

She'd almost got to the top when he seized her foot from behind and tugged her back.

Emma felt for something to hold onto, but only succeeded in pulling over the washing basket, the contents of which poured out onto her.

She was reminded of the corpse liquor in Palandt's shed, could smell the decay clinging to the dirty washing. Jeans, blouse, underwear. Everything that Philipp had taken off her and must have stuffed into the basket.

Nothing that could assist her now, *because how can I defend myself with a dressing gown?*

DRESSING GOWN!

The thought shot through her mind together with the pain she felt as she was dragged down another step and her jaw hit the hard surface.

Philipp was beside himself; he continued to yell something that could have been her name, but also sounded like pain, torture and death.

Emma would not let go, however. Lying on her tummy, she clutched the dressing gown.

Rummaged through the right-hand pocket.

Fuck.

The left pocket.

And finally had it in her hand.

Just as Philipp grabbed her waist to turn her around, her fingers clasped the plastic handle.

Emma yielded to her husband's strength, used it for her own backswing, raising her hand up high.

Holding the bloody blade.

From Palandt's package.

And in one sweeping movement sliced the scalpel across Philipp's throat.

45

Three weeks later

It was strange she wasn't crying.

In the lonely hours in the psychiatric unit the mere thought of Philipp had been enough to bring tears to her eyes, but now that she'd confessed her dreadful deeds to Konrad, recounting for the first time everything in all its detail, it seemed her reservoir of tears had dried up. Although she could feel the dull, headache-inducing pressure behind her eyes, her cheeks remained dry.

'I'm finished,' she said, and both of them knew that she wasn't referring to her testimony.

Two men, both killed by her own hand on the same day.

Just because of a package for the neighbour.

If she hadn't accepted it, she wouldn't have lost her mobile in Palandt's house. And if she hadn't opened the package she wouldn't have had a scalpel.

'Didn't you notice?'

Konrad was looking at her, standing by the bookshelf with the works of Schopenhauer. He was holding a thin cardboard folder and Emma couldn't have said how it got there. She hadn't even been aware that Konrad had stood up and wandered across the room. Two minutes must have passed since she'd uttered her last word, two minutes during which she'd stared fixedly at the tea stain on the round carpet, comparing its contours with the map of New Zealand.

Her hand tingled, her tongue felt numb – typical symptoms of withdrawal. She'd have to take her tablets again soon, but didn't dare ask Konrad for another glass of water, also because the pressure on her bladder was now almost intolerable.

'What didn't I notice?' she asked after some delay. She was tired and she was reacting with the speed of a drunk.

'That it was your own husband who raped you, Emma. Do you really believe you wouldn't have noticed?'

Apart from the fact that he was using her first name, there was no longer any intimacy in his words. In just a single phrase he'd managed once more to change her whereabouts. She wasn't on the sofa any more, but in the dock.

Where I belong, after all.

'I had paralysing drugs in my body that distorted my senses,' Emma said, trying to answer the question she'd asked herself over and over again. Konrad wasn't satisfied.

'Your own husband materialises in your hotel room from out of nowhere like David Copperfield, just to do what he could have got from you far more easily a day later within the own four walls of his house? Voluntarily too!'

'You know full well that for a rapist it's about power rather than sex.'

'Are you telling me that you've caressed and felt him thousands of times, yet on this occasion you didn't even get a whiff of suspicion?'

'I know what you're thinking, Konrad. You said it straight to my face earlier. Once a liar, always a liar, am I right?'

Konrad gave her a sad look, but didn't disagree.

'But you're wrong,' Emma said. 'Yes, I did lie when I foolishly claimed to have been the woman in the Rosenhan video. But in this case things are very different.'

'How?'

'Well, they found hair belonging to all the victims in Philipp's laboratory. All of them!'

'Apart from yours.'

Konrad opened the folder and took from it four large black-and-white photographs.

'What do you know about these photos?' He spread them out on the glass table.

Emma averted her eyes from the women. She didn't

need to see their large eyes, high cheekbones and certainly not their thick hair to recognise them. In the pictures they were laughing, pursing their lips for a kiss or looking brazenly and wickedly into the camera. They had no opportunity to do this in life any more.

'The victims,' Emma said.

'Correct, these are the escort girls that the Hairdresser murdered.' Konrad fixed her with an inscrutable look. 'These women have a lot in common with you, Emma. Dreadful things were done to them. They've got wonderful hair, they even vaguely look like you. But assuming you've told me the truth about the important things, then there's one key difference between you and these sorry creatures, and by that I don't mean that all of them are dead.'

... assuming you've told me the truth about the important things...

Emma felt even more exhausted than when she'd taken the diazepam earlier on.

'What are you talking about?'

'These women had their heads shaved and they were killed, but...' Konrad tapped each photograph in turn and put an exclamation mark behind each of his words: 'But! These! Women! Were! Not! Raped!'

Silence. Not completely, for the office was filled with the constant roaring of the gas fire, but all the same the stillness that followed Konrad's outburst was oppressive.

Emma wanted to say something. She felt that deep

inside her, words were buried, which now had to come together into a meaningful, logical sentence, but she could manage nothing other than: 'You're lying.'

'*I'm* lying?' Konrad said. 'There was no forensic evidence of forced penetration. With none of the victims.'

'But in the news...'

'Forget the news,' Konrad interrupted her. 'The first newspaper that printed the false information, in twenty-centimetre-high letters on a double-page spread lied to increase its circulation. And all the other hastily put-together news tickers, tweets, posts and internet reports, which more people believed and nobody bothered to verify, *these* spread the lie. Later, the serious magazines, weeklies and television features followed. They lied too, but this time at the request of the investigating officers.'

'But... but why?'

'Why was information withheld from the public?' He answered his own question: 'I hardly need to tell you about the problems police have with psychologically deranged nutcases who crow about having committed other people's spectacular crimes.'

Pathological liars.

'Which is why detailed knowledge about killers isn't disseminated in the media. So that confessions can be checked for truth.'

Konrad paused to lend his words more weight. 'Normally this is a way of filtering out people just trying to jump on the bandwagon. It's not as often used for victims, though.'

He got up and strode across his office as if through a courtroom, his hands crossed behind his back.

'Do you have any idea how many women rang the police hotline having cut their own hair off? Women who said they'd been raped but were able to escape?'

'I'm not one of those,' Emma said, making the error of running her hand through her hair as she'd done all her life whenever she was nervous.

'I've spoken to the public prosecutor. Do you know what he thinks? That you were trying to make Philipp stick with you because of your financial worries. He wanted to leave you so you pretended to be pregnant. But because this isn't a lie you can keep up forever, you invented a rape to explain the miscarriage. At the same time you were aiming for sympathy with your psychological trauma. But when you realised that none of this was enough to keep Philipp, you killed him, making you his sole heiress.'

'Konrad... how... how... can you even entertain the... I know what happened. I mean, I'm not mad.'

'No?'

No?

Did he really just ask that?

Konrad took a few steps towards her and now stood so close again that she'd only have to raise her hand to stroke his well-trimmed beard.

'Leave me alone,' she said when she sensed he was going to touch her. 'Go away!' she protested, but more for the sake of it rather than with any force. Nor did she shake his hand off when he put it on hers.

'You were mentally abused,' he whispered softly. 'But not physically!'

'Yes, I was. I was…' She closed her eyes. 'I *was* raped and now I want you to stop your *advocatus diaboli* routine, or…'

'EMMA!'

Konrad shouted so loudly that she trembled.

'Open your eyes and listen to me. This is not a negotiating tactic. I'm not speaking to you as a lawyer, but as a friend.' He took a deep breath. 'Your husband abused you. But only psychologically. He didn't abuse your body. Nor those of the other victims.'

No, no that's impossible.

'Philipp wasn't the Hairdresser?'

'No.'

All she could see in Konrad's eyes was a sad certainty. Emma turned away. She couldn't stand the gaze which seemed to be telling her that in Palandt and her husband she'd killed two innocent men in one day.

46

'So who was it then?'

Emma's entire body was itching. She was desperate to scratch her arms, legs and tummy. Or even better, cast off this skin she no longer wanted to be in.

'Who murdered those women if it wasn't Philipp?' she repeated her question.

'Think about it, Emma,' Konrad said, getting to his feet and picking up the photos of the dead women from the coffee table. He held them in his hands like a fan. 'All these victims – look closely and then you'll see the connection between them.'

Reluctantly her eyes wandered to the photos.

Yes, they look like me. They've got hair like I used to have.

'They're all Philipp's type.'

'Precisely, Emma,' Konrad agreed. 'But unlike you they're prostitutes. High-end escorts. Your husband cheated on you. With every one of them.'

He shook the fan of photos in his hand.

'And this infidelity is the motive. It points the way to the murderer.'

Emma couldn't breathe until a tortured cough freed her passages.

'What did you just say?'

'Think about it, Emma. Who was so close to Philipp that he could discover his amorous escapades? Who was so hurt yet intelligent enough to forge a plan to remove from those women the very thing that had triggered Philipp's desire?'

Their hair.

'You're crazy,' Emma protested. 'You must have totally lost your mind. Do you seriously believe that all these women...'

'... your rivals in love!'

... *were murdered by me?* She wasn't able to say this out loud.

'Put yourself in his position, Emma. Philipp knows that the Hairdresser is after women who he's had sex with. The killer taunts him by sending packages to your home with his trophies, as if trying to say, '*Look what I've done to those women you sleep with.*' If your husband discloses this information and passes the evidence to the investigation team, it gets out that he's been cheating on you. Which is the last thing he wants. So he has to take the matter in hand himself. In his laboratory he examines the pieces of evidence and undertakes research without knowing that the Hairdresser is someone close to him. Even though Philipp knows the women haven't been raped he makes the mistake of looking for a man. And yet any child knows who uses poison, the weapon that that killed the escorts.'

The weaker sex. Women.

Emma crossed her arms behind her head. The scar for which she had Palandt to thank was throbbing and itching, but she resisted the urge to scratch her forehead.

'So why did he show me the photos in the cellar? And behave as if there weren't any hair? Was he trying to drive me mad?'

Konrad nodded. 'I have to say that this is what most bothered me in preparation for our conversation. And it won't be easy to convince the court that Philipp exploited your vulnerable mental state for his own purposes.'

'Which purposes?'

'I think he wanted to obtain a reservation of consent.'

'Have me declared incapacitated?'

'That's another way of putting it.'

'But that makes no sense,' Emma protested. 'Philipp was the one with the money, not me.'

'For that very reason,' Konrad said. 'Your husband had the fortune and because there was no pre-nuptial contract he would have lost half of it if you got divorced. Unless as your guardian he had regained full access to it while you were legally committed to a psychiatric hospital.'

The motive. His cheating had brought it to light.

And yet...

'Okay, you say that Philipp wasn't the one who killed the women. He didn't even rape them, but just slept with them. And someone else, the Hairdresser, shaved their hair and sent the trophies to Philipp to show him that they knew about him cheating on me. And you claim that Philipp then resorted to emotional blackmail to destroy me.'

Konrad nodded. 'That's about right.'

'And you think that the Hairdresser...'

Emma let her words hang in the air and Konrad made a grab for them.

'I think that only an extremely jealous person is capable of such acts. Someone who wants Philipp for herself and can't stand the thought of having to share him.'

'I didn't know anything about Philipp's infidelity,' she told Konrad. 'I didn't know those prostitutes. So I didn't kill them.'

'You?' Konrad asked, perplexed. In a gentle, conscience-stricken voice he said, 'Oh my, Emma, I'm really sorry. You thought I was talking about you the whole time?'

47

Emma's head started spinning.

Konrad doesn't think I'm the killer? He wasn't talking about me? But... but who then?

She mulled over the questions her old friend had just asked her.

Who was close to Philipp? Who was intelligent enough to forge a female's plan of revenge? And who would suffer most from his sleeping with the escort girls if not his wife?

'His mistress!' Emma blurted out, putting her head in her hands at the moment of realisation.

'Correct,' said Konrad, who'd regained his confidence. 'Not a whore, but the woman who was important to him. Who was close to him because he saw her regularly.'

All the hairs on Emma's forearms stood up.

'Sylvia?' she whispered.

Konrad nodded.

Emma laughed hysterically, tapped the side of her head, then put her head in her hands again.

SEBASTIAN FITZEK

'Noooo,' she screamed. 'That's absurd. Impossible. She died while...'

'... while you were in the cellar with Philipp. That's correct. She loved him, Emma. She loved him so much that she wouldn't forgive his flings and dalliances. You found it out yourself: there was no Peter. The man she wanted children with was called Philipp.'

A sound entrenched itself in her ear, preparing to drown out all others, especially Konrad's voice.

'She loved Philipp and she hated the women he consorted with. Unworthy whores who deserved to die.'

'But what about me? She let me live.'

That made no sense.

'She didn't have to murder you, darling. He could separate from you. In all likelihood he'd promised Sylvia to leave you for her. To have children with her. Since that night you hadn't even touched Philipp, had you? I'm sorry to have to say it, but in her eyes you were no longer any competition. Unlike the prostitutes. Sylvia wanted to prevent all sexual contact between Philipp and other women. Which was one of the reasons for sending him her trophies. To show him: *I know who you're fooling around with. Every one of those whores you sleep with will die.*'

Without sinking to the floor, Emma felt as if she were falling.

That's why Philipp reacted so strangely when she mentioned Sylvia's name in the cellar. Emma had asked

312

him why he'd had to kill her, but he'd had no idea that Sylvia was dying.

Konrad gave her cheek a soft caress. 'A moralist would say that your husband had all these women on his conscience. But he didn't murder them. Nor did he lay a finger on Sylvia. When she tried to call Philipp on his mobile and you answered she'd already taken an overdose of sleeping pills.'

'The call was a cry for help?' Emma asked.

She withdrew the hand that Konrad had tried to hold and gazed at the fire. The gas flames were shimmering violet and blue, reminding her of bruises from wounds that would never heal.

'But why did she come to visit me that day? Why did she scream that I'd slipped her the morning-after pills to stop her from getting pregnant?'

Konrad sighed. 'She was mad, Emma. You can't measure the behaviour of a serial murderer by normal standards. But your question contains the answer you're looking for.'

Bang.

It struck her with the momentum of a guillotine.

'Because *he* didn't want her getting pregnant,' Emma whispered in horror.

'And Sylvia must have realised that at some point after having visited you, darling. Now she knew that Philipp didn't want to have children with her. She feared that he'd go back on his promise and never leave you, and her suspicion can only have been reinforced when he abandoned his conference because of you.'

The world before Emma's eyes blurred behind a wall of tears.

'All of that may be true,' she sobbed. 'But your story has one massive flaw. I may well be paranoid and have overreacted to Philipp. But the reason for that goes back to what the Hairdresser did to me in my hotel room. And that wasn't Sylvia.'

'How come?'

Now it was her turn to yell each word with an exclamation mark.

'BECAUSE! I! WAS! RAPED!' She was quaking. 'I felt it. A woman does feel something like that.'

Konrad looked again as if he were rooted to the floor of his office. Very calmly, without making a face, he asked, 'Are you quite sure, Emma?'

'Yes, one hundred per cent sure.' She turned to the window and gave a fake laugh. 'I know I have a fertile imagination. And sometimes I tell stories, yes. But on this point I'm absolutely sure! It was a man. Inside me. That's why I lost my baby. I can still feel...'

She couldn't breathe. Images flickered before her eyes and veils drifted past her field of vision as if she'd spent too long looking at the sun, rather than the Zehlendorf winter landscape behind Konrad's desk.

'What's wrong?' Konrad asked, sounding more intrigued than concerned.

'The light,' Emma said, pointing out at the Wannsee. *Ought it not to be much darker?*

'How long have I been here in your... in your...' Once more she was unable to complete a sentence, and this time it was because of the man on the promenade. And the large mastiff on its lead. Which opened its mouth as if intent on catching snowflakes on its tongue. '... in your practice?' Emma mumbled, seized by a surreal, completely irrational feeling of having got caught up in a time loop.

She wasn't just looking at a similar backdrop, but exactly the same one she'd seen at the start of her session. She stood up. It took some effort, but this time she found the strength to stay on her feet.

'What's going on here?' she asked, wandering over to the window.

Behind her Konrad started talking to someone, even though he was alone in the room.

'That's enough now,' he said sternly. 'I repeat, that's enough.'

She heard footsteps approaching from the corridor outside. At the same time her nose again picked up a smell of fresh paint and other renovation work as she got closer to the window. Just as the doors were opened behind her and she was about to touch the glass with her fingertips, the lake vanished before her very eyes, and with it the walker, the snow, the mastiff, the promenade, everything. Even the window wasn't there any more.

Just a black hole in the wall.

'Frau Dr Stein?' she heard a man's voice say. It wasn't Konrad's and she ignored it.

'But I know who I am,' she insisted, starting to cry as she heard the electrostatic clicking of the high-resolution television her head was leaning against.

'Please don't be afraid, Frau Stein,' the man said, but when she turned to him and saw her psychiatrist in a white coat with two nurses standing beside Konrad, that's exactly what she felt: a fear that took hold of every cell inside her body and seemed to have settled there for good.

Emma felt faint and, when her knees gave way and she was losing consciousness, she tried to hold onto something for support, but failed.

48

'Splendid. That was splendidly done.'

Dr Martin Roth pointed to the screen on the table in front of them, having just turned down the volume. On it they could see the mock-up office where Emma was being attended to by two nurses. After passing out, she'd come around again soon afterwards and now was lying on the sofa with her legs bent. If Konrad hadn't known better he would have actually believed he was watching his office by the Wannsee on the security camera. It was incredible how perfectly the carpenters and builders had reproduced it.

And as for the technicians!

Up till the very last minute he'd been sceptical, but in the end they'd been proved right: in truth the picture on an ultra-HD television was no longer distinguishable from reality.

Time and again during the experiment he'd caught himself gazing pensively out of the window until he remembered that the 'view' from his office was just an ultra-HD film processed with a new playback technology that allowed the perspective to change according to the position of the viewer.

'We can't be certain, of course, but there's a very good chance that Emma Stein's treatment has been a success.'

Dr Roth appeared to be trying to encourage Konrad with a broad smile as well as his words. The exhausted lawyer let the psychiatrist's praise bounce off him. He'd listened to Emma for almost four hours, trying all the while to follow the doctor's instructions. It might not be obvious from looking at him – he couldn't afford to show any weakness in public – but in truth Konrad's head was droning in the wake of this marathon session, and the last thing he fancied now was an analytical conversation with the senior doctor who looked far too young, but whose reputation was legendary in professional circles. Ten years ago Dr Martin Roth had apparently succeeded in treating a schizophrenic patient by using his own hallucinations, thereby laying the foundation for his reputation. He sometimes attempted unusual therapies to help out his patients.

Such as the one today.

To make the hoped-for breakthrough with Emma Stein, Dr Roth had ordered a full-scale replica of Konrad's office to be built in the clinic's small gym, where the physiotherapists did their rehabilitation exercises.

Such an effort was necessary because they hadn't been able to get legal authorisation for an interview outside the clinic, while Emma had refused any contact within the institution.

'I need a beer first,' Konrad said, pulling over a folding chair. Here, right behind the scenery walls, which from Emma's side created the perfect illusion of his office in Zehlendorf, it looked like a building site.

Large posts prevented chipboard panels from toppling over. The wires for the hidden microphones and miniature cameras (almost all of which were on the bookshelves) ran across the lino of the gym floor like threads of yarn.

In fact the whole place looked very much like a film set. On a camping table were juices, pretzels and pre-packaged sandwiches: the catering for the Konrad & Emma Show. Dr Roth had no doubt made himself comfortable while observing his patient from here.

'A cold beer and a cigar,' Konrad extended his request.

'You've earned both,' Roth said, pulling a radio from the belt pocket of his white jeans. 'Now, there's a strict smoking and alcohol ban here in the Park Clinic, but as its head I'm sure I can make an exception today.'

He pressed a button and relayed the order, presumably to his bow-legged assistant who Konrad had spoken to regularly on the phone over the past few days to finalise the details. The woman was tediousness and slowness personified. If she organised the beer and cigar with the same speed she'd arranged for the furniture to be moved here from his practice, he'd be taking his first puff tomorrow morning and first sip next week.

'They'll be here in five minutes.'

Hmm. Who'd have thought?

After Roth had scribbled a few notes on a clipboard, he also fetched himself a folding chair and sat opposite Konrad, his back to the monitor.

'I thought it was all over when Emma knocked over the cup and wanted to clean up the mess,' he said, smiling.

Konrad agreed. 'Yes, she was this close to visiting the non-existent loo.'

For plumbing reasons this detail of the mock-up office hadn't been possible. A replica loo would have been okay, but a functioning WC with flush and running water? The premises hadn't permitted such an installation. If Emma had shaken the fake door that led to a non-existent lavatory, the entire illusion would have been dispelled. In actual fact this had been part of the plan, to open Emma's eyes to the situation, just not so early, but as a dramatic climax and as close to the end of the session as possible.

'So how do you feel now?' Dr Roth asked, with emphasis on the *now*, for to begin with Konrad had been very much opposed to the psychiatrist's treatment methods.

'I still don't feel comfortable that I had to lie to Emma and make her believe in a pretend world. But

THE PACKAGE

I have to admit that your unusual idea did have the desired outcome.'

The fact that Emma had refused any visit on her ward had presented her helpers with an almost insoluble problem. She hadn't made a statement, nothing that a decent defence team could work with. The public prosecutor, on the other hand, was in possession of a video that showed Emma slitting her husband's throat in the cellar of her house after she'd hurled totally crazed, partly babbled accusations at him.

Roth hadn't made any progress with his therapy either until it dawned on him how they could kill two birds with one stone – have Emma give a testimony and engage in conversation therapy at the same time. He figured that Emma was a person who opened up to very few people, and to nobody more than her paternal friend.

But this on its own wasn't enough. To ensure a truthful statement she also needed familiar surroundings.

If the patient won't come to the mountain, the mountain must be moved, he'd said to Konrad ten days ago on a damp, cold Friday afternoon, by which time Emma hadn't been under his supervision for even two weeks. Konrad recalled wanting to take a closer examination of Dr Roth's mental state too, when the latter laid out his plan in detail:

'Let's assume that Frau Stein trusts you. She's going to find it extremely difficult to dish up lies to her closest confidant, especially in an environment where she's

always felt secure. There are still many things we can't explain. Whether Frau Stein was really attacked in a hotel room or whether she gave herself those injuries somewhere else. Or how exactly she came to kill the two men. Was it intentional or carelessness? If you, Professor Luft, were to undertake a lawyer's consultation that we might be able to observe, it would give us the priceless opportunity to analyse Emma Stein's testimony from a psychiatric perspective.'

Konrad had laughed and looked around for one of those cameras he and Emma had been filmed with for the last few hours.

'You want to completely replicate my office? You're having me on!'

'Not at all, and if you care to do some research into me you'll discover that I sometimes go down unconventional paths to—'

'Wait a second, stop!' Konrad had interrupted him, propping himself up on his desk with his elbows and looking down at Roth. *'Are you seriously suggesting that I deceive my client? Breach my lawyer's confidentiality?'*

Roth had vigorously shaken his head.

'We're in this together. Your client is my patient. That means your client confidentiality overlaps with my patient confidentiality. Emma Stein is accused of the manslaughter of Anton Palandt and her husband. At the same time she appears to suffer from severe paranoia, perhaps even pathological lying.'

'*And with my help…*'

'*We can kill two birds with one stone. We discover what really happened, and maybe we'll come up with not just a defence strategy, but also a therapy plan. But this will only work with your help. It's a "condition without which it wouldn't be possible". That's a specialist legal term, isn't it?*'

'*A "condition sine qua non",*' Konrad had confirmed.

'*Your lawyer–client interview would also be a psychotherapeutic analysis. It's a means of both discovering the truth and making her better. And no third party would get wind of any of it. The two of us would be the only ones with access to the recordings. There are no cameramen, just fixed lenses.*'

This was the chat that had finally persuaded Konrad, even though he asked for a weekend to think it over. But in fact he knew he'd give his consent when, just before leaving, he'd asked Dr Roth, '*You want to move my entire office?*'

'*Just the furniture,*' the psychiatrist had said calmly, as if it were a perfectly normal procedure paid for by statutory health insurance. '*We'll build the rest of the office.*'

And so Emma had been sedated in her room with the promise of seeing her old friend again, who might be able to save her from a prison sentence. When she awoke, having apparently been transported, she imagined herself to be in Konrad's practice.

SEBASTIAN FITZEK

But was all the effort really worth it? Konrad wondered.

He heard a muffled knocking, which surprised him because the door to the gym they were sitting closest to was made out of glass. And nobody was behind it.

'What was that?' Konrad asked when the noise sounded again, only this time it sounded more like stamping. He turned to the monitor.

Emma.

She wasn't on the hospital bed nor the sofa, but standing in the middle of the room, stamping her right foot. A rather clumsy nurse was trying to hold her arm, but Emma easily shook her off.

'Sound!' Konrad ordered with his authoritative, courtroom-trained voice, and the senior doctor picked up the remote control on the table. Emma's voice grew louder.

'Hello? Konrad?' she said, several times over, turning in a circle. She'd realised, of course, that she was being filmed and listened to, but till now she'd had no idea where the microphones and cameras were.

'Konrad, can you hear me?'

'Yes,' he replied, even though Roth had explained this morning that the mock-up office was so well soundproofed that you could have thrown a plate on the floor out here without anyone inside hearing anything of the smash.

'Konrad?' Emma asked, thick tears running down her cheeks. Her voice strained in the small speakers. 'Please come back, Konrad. There's something I've got to confess.'

49

Emma had a beautiful view from her room in the clinic. Not quite as glamorous as that from his office, but at least it wasn't taped, Konrad thought.

If Emma were standing beside him at the window she'd be able to see a small family of hares hopping across the snowy lawn of the park and leaping two metres out of the beam of the spherical garden lanterns into the darkness, shortly afterwards to leave visible prints in the powdery whiteness once more.

She'd also be able to see his old Saab in which he sometimes used to drive her to university. But to see all of this Emma would have to get out of bed, and at the moment she was too weak. The convertible was covered in a thick layer of snow and stood in the small car park that was actually reserved for senior doctors. Roth had offered him his space.

'Have you searched everything?' he heard Emma ask from her bed. It was wider and more comfortable than the one on which she'd been pushed into the fake office a few hours earlier.

'Yes,' Konrad said.

At her request he'd combed the entire room for hidden cameras and microphones, searching very thoroughly even though Roth had assured him that up here on the ward nothing and nobody was wired up. He wouldn't dare undertake such an intrusion into his patients' privacy.

'I'm sorry,' Konrad said contritely, and that was the truth. In the text books of the future it would look good when people wrote of Dr Roth that he'd treated a supposed liar with a lie. But this didn't alter the fact that Konrad had hoodwinked his best friend and ward.

'No, *I'm* the one who's sorry,' Emma countered wearily. She sounded oblivious to everything around her; the skin around her eyes was sunken and crumpled, as if she hadn't drunk anything in a long time.

'Maybe it would be better if we spoke tomorrow. You look exhausted, darling.'

'No.'

She patted the duvet beside her. 'Please come and sit close to me.'

He moved away from the window bench and was beside her in a couple of steps. He loved being close to her. Now that he no longer had to affect a professional distance, Emma wasn't his client, but his little darling protégée once more.

She whispered as he pushed the bedside table slightly aside so he could sit on the mattress.

'I wanted to speak to you up here. In my cell.'

'In your clinic room, you mean.'

She smiled as if he'd cracked a joke.

Roth had immediately agreed to let Emma return to her room. The mock-up lawyer's practice had done its job. When Emma discovered the HD television was a fake window she realised that humans can lose the capacity to distinguish between fiction and reality. Konrad couldn't judge the psychiatric benefit of this awareness, but he agreed with the head of the clinic that Emma was better off in her hospital bed than down in the gymnasium.

'I didn't want to tell you down there. Not in front of all those cameras. And microphones.'

Konrad nodded.

He took her hand. It was dry and as light as a piece of paper.

'Nobody should hear us,' she said and it sounded as if she had a hot potato in her mouth. Her tongue was heavy. Roth had given her another tranquiliser, which seemed to work slowly, and then left them, saying that he'd wait in the corridor.

'Relax,' Konrad said, squeezing her hand affectionately.

'What I've got to say is for your ears only,' she said.

Konrad felt a pang in his heart, as he always did

when someone close to him was in a bad way and he didn't know how to help. On the battlefield of articles and clauses he always had the right weapons to hand. But when it came to personal problems he was often clueless. Especially with Emma.

'What's troubling you?' he asked.

'Do you know what? As time goes by I'm less and less sure that I was in that hotel.'

He gave her his gentlest smile. 'Well done, Emma. Well done for saying it. And believe me, nobody's going to blame you. We're going to do all we can now to cure you.'

'There's no cure in psychotherapy,' she objected.

'But there is help.'

'I don't want help.'

'No? What do you want then?'

'To die!'

50

Konrad's emotional reaction was forceful.

His hand tensed painfully around Emma's and from his quivering lip she could see how he was struggling to retain his composure.

'You're joking.'

'No, I'm being serious.'

'But why?'

'Lots of reasons. Because of my paranoia I killed Philipp and Palandt. And prevented Sylvia's life from being saved.'

'None of it intentional,' Konrad countered vigorously. 'None of it your fault.'

Emma shook her head, her eyes were red, but clear. She wasn't crying any more.

'Philipp...' she said. 'Without Philipp there's no point to my life. I loved him. I don't care what a shit he was. I'm nothing without him.'

'You're so much more without that cheat,' Konrad said in a surprisingly loud voice. 'If there's anybody who's to blame for your misery, then it's your adulterous, self-absorbed husband. It's bad enough that he was unfaithful and neglected you while he was alive. But even after his death he's plunging you into deep despair.' Konrad then tempered his grip and tone, which was a visible effort for him. 'You're not to blame, Emma. It was self-defence.'

She sighed. 'Even if you were to convince the judges, I still don't want to go on living. Not like this. You have to understand that, Konrad. I'm a psychiatrist. I know the darkest psychological abysses. I could barely cope with looking into them. And now I'm at the very nadir myself.'

'Emma...'

'Shh... Listen to me, please, Konrad. I don't know what to think any more. I was so convinced that I'd been raped. And now? What sort of life is it if you can't distinguish between madness and reality? Not a life for me. I have to end it. But I can't do this without your help. I'm sure you know somebody who can get me the medication I'm going to write down for you.'

'But you're...'

'Mad. Precisely.'

'No, that's not what I meant.'

Konrad shook his head. She'd never seen him look so sad and helpless before.

'Yes, it's true. I'm off my trolley...'

'Just a vivid imagination, darling. And stress. Lots of stress.'

'Others have that too, but they don't hallucinate about being raped in imaginary hotel rooms.'

'But they don't have your power of imagination, Emma. Look. That evening you had a difficult lecture, colleagues were openly hostile and you had to defend yourself. It's only understandable that you lost control in an extreme psychological situation. I suspect you saw a television report about the Hairdresser and your febrile imagination turned you into one of his victims. It's going to take a long time, but together with Dr Roth I'm sure we'll find out the truth.'

'I don't want that.'

Konrad squeezed her hand again as if it were a pump to force new vitality into Emma.

'Emma, just think. You were helped once before. Back when you were a girl, when your imagination was also turning somersaults.'

Arthur.

Gripped by an unexpected melancholy, Emma couldn't help thinking of the imaginary childhood friend, of whom she'd been so frightened to begin with. Much of her memory was a blur. Only the motorbike helmet and the syringe in Arthur's hand had stayed with her, even years after her therapy which – it now seemed – can't have been that successful after all.

Emma's eyes closed and she no longer fought against the tiredness that brought forth more scraps of memory as harbingers of her dreams.

Her father's words: 'Get out right now. Or I'll hurt you.'

The voice in the cupboard: 'He said that?'

Her mother's screams when she lost the child at four months.

The morning-after pill.

Her own voice yelling at Sylvia: 'I was shaved and raped. There was a man in my room...'

'Yeah, like Arthur in your cupboard...'

Emma tore her eyes open. Fought her way back to the surface through the fog of torpidity.

'What's wrong?' Konrad said, still holding her hand.

'How did she know his name?' Her tongue weighed several kilos; she could barely move it any more.

'What?'

'Arthur. How did Sylvia know his name?'

'Are you talking about the ghost now?'

She looked at Konrad's puzzled face.

'Look, I didn't even tell you his name. You heard it for the first time today when I told you about my row with Sylvia. When she came to my house and accused me of stopping her from having a child, she said something about me lying even as a child. When I made up *Arthur*. But I only met Sylvia after I'd been through therapy. I never told her about Arthur.'

Konrad shrugged. 'She had an affair with Philipp,' he muttered. 'She probably heard it from him.'

Emma was blinking frenziedly. 'Listen. Even Philipp

knew nothing about it. I kept Arthur's name to myself. After the therapy sessions in my younger days I never wanted to say it out loud again; it was a superstition. I thought that if I didn't say it then Arthur would never come back, do you understand?'

I only told my parents and psychiatrist about him. So how did Sylvia know the name?

Emma was shaking. For a split second she knew the answer. And this answer pointed the way to such a terrible, blood-curdling truth that she just wanted to run screaming out of her room.

But then the answer had vanished, together with her capacity to struggle any longer against a loss of consciousness.

And all that accompanied Emma on her deep descent into sleep was a feeling of fear, far worse than the one when she'd accepted the package.

51

Dr Roth was delighted. The experiment he'd mostly funded out of his own pocket was a complete success.

He was almost regretting not being able to continue, but the rehabilitation hall he was blocking was urgently needed and, in any case, no more success could be expected from this set-up.

'We're done then?' Konrad asked beside him, watching two removal men like a hawk as they took away his sofa. After his chat with Emma the defence lawyer had gone for a walk in the park to get some fresh air. Now he looked refreshed.

'The charade is over?'

Konrad had to raise his voice because in front of and behind him cordless screwdrivers buzzed as they took apart the wall panels. The air was heavy with the aroma of wood shavings, a smell Roth had loved since childhood. He'd attended a school with a strong artistic focus. Carpentry was part of the core curriculum, which maybe explained his penchant for creative methods.

'Yes, I think we're done,' Roth replied. 'Unless Frau Stein disclosed something else to you that could be important for my work.'

'Client confidentiality,' Konrad grinned, but then waved his hand dismissively. 'No, to tell you the truth she was all over the place. She expressed suicidal thoughts, so you've really got to keep an eye on her.'

'Don't worry, we're geared up for that possibility.' Roth scratched his receding hairline. 'I'm afraid that reaction was only to be expected.'

'Why?'

'We've seriously rocked Frau Stein's world.'

Roth pointed to the bookshelf with the complete works of Schopenhauer. One of the cameras was still in the spine of *The World as Will and Representation*

'And at the moment she can't see any way of putting it back in order,' Roth said.

'Hey, hey. Please be careful!' Konrad excused himself for a moment and went up to one of the removal men who was trying to yank the round O rug from under the coffee table.

'That's for the dry cleaner's, not the dustbin.'

'Is that an *enso*?' asked Roth, who'd followed him.

Konrad gave him an admiring look. 'Do you know about Zen symbolism?'

'A little,' Roth smiled, pointing to the black edging of the white rug. 'In Zen art an *enso*, or circle, is painted with a single flowing brushstroke. Only those who are mentally composed and balanced can paint a uniform *enso*. For that reason, the way the circle is executed gives us a particularly good idea of the painter's state of mind.'

'I take my hat off to you,' Konrad laughed. The worker had now exited with the coffee table under his arm. The other packers too were taking items outside, leaving Konrad and Roth alone for the moment. 'I didn't know you were a philosopher manqué.'

Roth nodded, seemingly lost in thought. His fingers grasped the threads of the *enso* rug again, then he stood up. For one last time he allowed his gaze to roam the replica office, then he asked Konrad, almost incidentally, 'You were practically inseparable from her, weren't you?'

'I'm sorry?'

'You always had to have her there. Be near her.'

'What on earth are you talking about?' Konrad said, slightly put out.

Instead of giving an answer Roth looked at the fluff in his hand, which he'd just plucked from the rug. The fibres were dark brown and unusually thin for a rug. Almost like hair.

'In Philipp's laboratory they found the trophies from all the victims, apart from Emma,' the psychiatrist said, looking Konrad straight in the eye.

The defence lawyer turned pale and seemed to age from one moment to the next. The firm ground of Konrad's self-assurance had suddenly become a trapdoor.

'What the hell are you getting at?'

Roth replied with a question of his own: 'Are you not surprised by all the time and money that's gone into this, Professor Luft?' The psychiatrist opened up his arms as if seeing the set-up for the first time. 'A completely furnished replica lawyer's office, HD television, hidden cameras and microphones. And all just to free a paranoid patient from her hallucinations?'

'What's going on?' Konrad asked flatly. His gaze wandered helplessly across the set, looking for a way out.

But before he'd found one, Roth let the guillotine of truth come swishing down. 'We were observing you, not Emma!'

52

Emma was swimming on the bottom of an oil-black lake, feeling seasick. And yet the waves upsetting her balance were borne by a strange melody.

A voice, half whispering, half smiling.

A madman's voice.

Konrad's voice.

'I love you, Emma.'

Seized by an immense swell of nausea, Emma wrenched open her eyes and threw up right beside her bed.

She was still woozy, seeing the world as if through frosted glass, but she knew who she was (a raped woman), where she was (in the Park Clinic) and what Konrad had confided to her.

'Don't worry, I'll look after you,' he'd said, holding her hand and believing her to be in a state of total unconsciousness, whereas in fact she was just hovering below the surface of sleep.

'I'll protect you like I've always done.'

She kept drifting off, but each time his voice brought her back.

Now that she'd vomited up her medication before it could make its way throughout her body, Konrad was no longer in the room.

But his voice was still in her head. This eerie, whispering sing-song of memory.

'I'm your guardian angel, Emma. I've been watching over you these last few months, just as I have for years and years. Do you understand? I killed the whores for your sake. To restore your honour.'

Only now did the madness in his words make complete sense to Emma. She was still incredibly tired. But the pull of the psychotropic drugs was no longer trying to drag her so forcefully into the quagmire of her consciousness.

'I wanted you from the first second I laid eyes on you. You were far too young, three years old, when you came to my practice with your father. It was furnished almost exactly as it is now. Even the rug was there. You loved playing on the O, but I bet you can't remember as you were too small.'

That's why I felt so at home there from the start.

Right then Emma had tried opening her eyes again, but couldn't manage it.

'I noticed at once that your father was no good for you. You tried to get close to him, but he was always gruff and cold. I, on the other hand, couldn't show my feelings. I had to hide to be able to see you.'

In my cupboard!

'I watched you, cared for you, guarded you and protected you. I was the father you never had.'

Konrad wasn't just the Hairdresser.

He was Arthur too!

That's how Sylvia knew his name. She didn't get it from Philipp, but from the man pretending to be Arthur, Emma remembered her own, very sluggish thoughts, interrupted again and again by Konrad's whispers.

They'd had contact, *of course.* Konrad must have visited Sylvia when Emma was in a bad way, to discuss how they could help her. From one best friend to another.

'Throughout your life I looked out for you, my darling. Like when your ex-boyfriend Benedict was hassling you, do you remember? I so often held my protective hand over you, but you weren't aware of it. Then, when you were old enough, I showed myself to you. But I was worried you'd realise my true feelings and break off contact with a man who was so much older.'

But aren't you gay?

'I only pretended to be gay. I lied so I could always be close to you, but unfortunately it kept us apart too. Oh, the desire I felt for you. All these years.'

Until the night in the hotel!

'I wanted you to leave Le Zen and go home, darling. Back to your husband who was in bed with a whore. So you'd catch him in flagrante. But you stayed. Even though I frightened you with the writing on the mirror, you wouldn't go. So I cut your hair to stop Philipp from wanting you. To stop him from sleeping with you as he always did when you came home.'

At this point Emma thought she recalled Konrad clearing his throat, just as he'd done that night in the hotel.

'I didn't rape you. It's just that when you were lying in front of me, so peacefully…'

Emma had to retch again. She threw the covers back and fell beside the bed when she tried to stand up.

'No!' she screamed at the voice of truth, which had taken hold inside her head.

'I know, it was a mistake,' she heard Konrad say. 'But I couldn't wait any longer, Emma. After all those years of abstinence it was perfectly natural, you see. And it was beautiful, all very gentle. An act of love.'

Emma felt a powerful tugging in her abdomen. She sank to her knees and threw up again.

When nothing more would come from her stomach the voice in her head had vanished too, as if she'd expelled Konrad from her body with the last of the bile.

Gasping, she pulled herself up on the window sill and looked outside.

She almost expected to see Konrad in the park, waving at her, but there was just a snowy landscape. Hare prints in the snow. A lantern giving off a gentle light.

And the car.

The old Saab stood covered in snow in the clinic car park where only the senior doctors were allowed to park.

Emma looked at the door, wiped some spittle from her mouth with the sleeve of her nightshirt and made a decision.

53

The defence lawyer, once so energetic, staggered through the mock-up of his office like a boxer out for the count. He hadn't said anything to Dr Roth yet. And he wasn't able to look the psychiatrist in the eye.

Konrad stood there, trembling. With his face to the false window, from which the television had already been removed and where only a chipboard recess was left as a reminder of the installation.

Turning around, Konrad tried to support himself on the edge of his desk, but slipped and just struggled to fall into his chair.

'You wove Emma's hair into the *enso* rug,' Roth said. Without reproach. Without the slightest hint of sensationalism in his voice. As a psychiatrist he'd come across far more disconcerting abnormalities in human behaviour.

'That... that's...' Konrad stuttered, finding his voice again 'There's an explanation for that.'

'I'm sure there is,' Roth replied. 'Everything will be

explained. Including the issue of the room number. Was it 1903 or 1905?'

'What?'

'Which of the two connecting rooms was it where you replaced the number on the door with 1904?'

Roth could see beads of sweat on Konrad's brow. He'd turned ashen and his skin had a waxy shimmer.

'Yes, I know. Nobody likes it when people see through their tricks,' Roth said. 'Even though it was an excellent ploy to book both rooms via a foreign hotel portal for a family of four. At Le Zen, as in most Berlin hotels, you only have to present your credit card at check-in, so you just needed someone to pick up the key for you.' Roth knitted his brow. 'This is where we don't know for sure how you did it. We're assuming that this mother and her three children actually exist – a former client of yours, perhaps, who you invited to come to Germany. But who left a little earlier, which meant that on the day Emma was checking in you had free rein for your plans. You had all the time to put up the Ai Weiwei portrait, right over the frameless connecting door so that Emma wouldn't notice there was access to the neighbouring room. You waited in there till she went to bed. Unlike in the past you didn't have to hide in the cupboard.' Roth gave a wan smile. 'By the way, I like the name Arthur. I'm a fan of Arthur Schopenhauer too.'

Konrad winced when the provisional office door opened with a loud crunch. A black-haired police officer with Greek features strode confidently in.

'Professor Konrad Luft, I am arresting you,' the policeman said. Jorgo Kapsalos stood two metres from the desk, his hand on the service revolver at his hip. 'I don't suppose I have to inform you of your right to remain silent.'

Konrad looked up and gazed at the tall, broad-shouldered policeman as if he were an alien.

'Why?' he croaked.

Roth, who'd stayed beside the sofa, fancied he could make out a smile on Jorgo's lips, but perhaps it was just the diffuse light of the desk lamp that gave him this impression.

There was nothing sadistic about Emma's husband's former partner. Although Jorgo had been deeply affected by Philipp Stein's death, because he blamed himself for not having made the connections earlier, Roth didn't think that Jorgo was driven by revenge. It was understandable, however, that he was feeling great satisfaction now at being able to arrest the Hairdresser.

'How did you get onto me?'

Jorgo shook his head and he felt for the handcuffs on his belt. 'We'll have plenty of time to discuss all that at the station when we take your confession.'

Konrad nodded, acknowledging defeat.

'Unbelievable,' he said, letting his eyes marvel at the fake office where he'd thought he was helping Emma, whereas the whole time he himself had been under observation. 'You pulled the wool over my eyes,' the lawyer muttered. He looked towards the exit. None of the removal men had come back into the gym; they were obeying the orders Jorgo had given them.

'It wasn't about making Emma feel secure here, but me, here, in my familiar environment.'

Even in the moment of his greatest defeat, Konrad's intellect was working impeccably. 'You would never have obtained a warrant to search my real office. You orchestrated that perfectly. I give you respect.'

Konrad was supporting himself feebly on the desk, and already then Roth ought to have realised. But even more so when the lawyer breathed out heavily and let both arms fall beneath the desktop.

Konrad was crestfallen, so severely affected by having been unmasked that perhaps he'd never recover. But his transformation had occurred too quickly, especially for someone who'd practised all his life being in control of his body and mind.

We made a mistake, Roth thought, then heard these words echo, but with a slight time delay and in a different voice: they were coming from Konrad's mouth.

'But you made a mistake,' he said.

Within the twinkling of an eye the pistol that the defence lawyer had pulled from a secret compartment beneath the desktop was already in position. Konrad was aiming right between Dr Roth's eyes.

54

'My desk. My secret compartment. My life insurance,' Konrad said. 'Actually intended for furious clients whose cases I lost. And when you look at it that way, this is about right.'

The lawyer gave a sad laugh and gripped the pistol more tightly. 'I will shoot,' he said, and Roth knew he was being deadly serious.

'I'll pull the trigger and then rather than removal men you'll need forensic cleaners specialising in spatters of brain.'

'Okay, okay,' Roth said, coming closer with his hands up. This was his area of expertise. Psychologically damaged individuals in extreme emotional situations.

'What do you want?' he asked.

'Answers,' Konrad said with astonishing calmness, now aiming the weapon at Jorgo's chest. Only a throbbing artery in his neck betrayed how worked up he was. 'How did you come to suspect me?'

With a quick glance at Roth, Jorgo checked that he

could answer truthfully, then said, 'We had no DNA, no evidence, nothing. We were poking around in the dark in the Hairdresser case. From the profile that Philipp had compiled we knew that it must be an "older, conservative-leaning man with a high level of education and a pronounced sense of order".'

Konrad nodded and with his free hand motioned to Jorgo to continue.

'I've known Emma for years. I couldn't see her as a deranged copycat just trying to get her husband's attention. Even less that she'd turn violent for no reason.'

'Hardly likely,' Konrad agreed. 'More like Philipp.'

Jorgo nodded. 'But nor did I think my partner capable of physical violence against women.'

'Psychological violence, on the other hand...' Konrad said and Jorgo hesitated briefly, checking again that he could continue to talk. Either he interpreted Roth's look correctly, or as a policeman he was trained to tell the truth to people who were just about to commit an act of violence.

'Philipp started behaving suspiciously, telling me again and again how he doubted his wife's mental state. And when we searched Le Zen together, it seemed as if he was looking for proof of her paranoia rather than the opposite. And he was adamant that Emma shouldn't find out about the connecting door, even though that would have been a balm for her tortured soul. Nor did he tell her that we found residues of glue on the wall, presumably from the picture you'd covered the door with.'

Jorgo shrugged. 'From there the logical step was to investigate Emma's private life. And see: the profile matches, as if Philipp had been looking right at you when he drew it up.'

Konrad grasped his neck. Once again he aimed his eyes and the barrel of his gun at Roth.

'What about you? You're the mastermind behind all of this, aren't you?'

'Well, I'd prefer to say that I was helped on my way by chance. I also attended the conference where Frau Stein talked about the Rosenhan Experiment. I don't suppose you remember, but we happened to bump into each other in the cloakroom. Later, when the police brought me on board I recalled our meeting. I assume you weren't there out of any medical interest, but to change the key cards in Emma's documents?'

Konrad nodded and said, 'That wasn't my question. I wanted to know if the strategy with this trap here was your idea?'

Roth hesitated. Although Konrad would be bound to notice if he lied to him, the senior doctor could hardly be honest without insulting the lawyer.

After he'd been asked by the police for help as a renowned expert, he'd spent the last few weeks looking into the defence lawyer's psyche. He'd studied all of Konrad's seminar videos and films of his public appearances on the internet. Analysed his almost pedantic outward appearance, his deportment which was minutely managed and geared towards maximum success. Soon he guessed that Konrad's biggest weakness would also represent the investigators' best opportunity: his narcissism.

'To nail you we had to put you in a position where you felt powerful,' he said. 'You had to believe that you were pulling all the strings and were the lead actor in a performance, just like in court. I was convinced that you'd agree to my idea of replicating your office, seeing how you'd gone to all that effort with the hotel room so that the police wouldn't take Frau Stein seriously.'

'So none of this was ever about Emma?' Konrad blinked. His eyes were damp, but it didn't look as if he was feeling sorry for himself. Even in this extreme situation he actually seemed to be far more concerned for Emma's welfare.

'Yes, of course I was interested in Frau Dr Stein too,' Roth explained. 'By building your office in here we could kill the proverbial two birds with one stone. After those terrible events Emma was refusing all communication. The fake setting finally made her open up. And condemned you as a murderer.'

Konrad's expression turned hard. For a moment he looked like a lawyer again, cross-examining the other side's witness. 'How did you know? How did you know that I'd take the rug with me?'

Roth gently shook his head. 'I didn't. To be honest, until the moment you tried to stop Emma from cleaning the stain it didn't even occur to me that this might be a piece of evidence. But then on the close-up I saw your pupils dilate. A second later you'd already leaped up, almost on instinct. You didn't want Emma to touch the rug under any circumstances. Herr Kapsalos and I asked ourselves *why?* We took a closer look and discovered the hair that Emma must have pulled out when she cleaned it.'

Konrad rapped his knuckles on the table in admiration, as students do to applaud a professor.

Jorgo slid his hand down to his holster, which didn't escape Konrad's notice.

'That's not a good idea,' he said laconically, and his knuckles turned white as his grip tightened further on the pistol, which was now pointing at the policeman's heart.

At that moment there was a creaking behind Roth. Like Jorgo, he turned around towards the door of the 'office', which here only led to the changing rooms rather than the corridor in the law firm. It opened.

Very slowly, as if the person pushing from the other side was having to battle a powerful wind blowing in the other direction.

Or as if they had no strength.

'Emma!' Konrad screamed so loudly, like a warning, but it was too late.

She was already in the doorway with her short hair, in white slippers, the clinic nightshirt tied at the back.

'What... *are you doing here?*' he was presumably going to ask, but this was lost in the tumult that ensued once the shot had been fired.

Konrad looked, baffled, at the gun in his hand, then wondered what had happened. He let his arm drop and at that moment was knocked to the ground by Jorgo. The policeman had dived across the table with his pistol drawn.

Roth wasn't watching the unequal struggle in which the lawyer, offering no resistance, allowed himself to be pushed to the floor and have his arms twisted behind his back.

All he saw was Emma.

Teetering towards him.

Blood dropped onto the freshly laid parquet floor. A whole torrent, pouring onto the floor like a sticky, red waterfall. Over the leather armchair to where the coffee table must have been and where now just the enso rug lay, onto which she finally collapsed.

55

Four weeks later

'Number three,' said the hollow-cheeked woman with the man's haircut, who was responsible for welcoming visitors at the security checkpoint. She was tall, plump, with nicotine-stained teeth, and hands that she could have grasped a basketball with. But she was friendly, something verging on a miracle when you had to work in the high-security wing of a psychiatric prison.

'You've got five minutes.' The prison officer pointed to the seat with the specified number above the glass separating the free world from the inmates.

Konrad was already sitting there.

Chalky white, gaunt. They'd shaved off his beard, but this made him look even older. Seeing him, many people would have thought of death and how it already scarred some people in life.

The visitors room was awash with the faint smell

of decay, but this was just in the mind of course, an olfactory error, because Konrad's chest was rising and falling, and his nostrils were quivering almost as badly as the age-spotted hand holding the receiver. But nowhere near as firmly as the pistol back in the clinic. It was no surprise that the inmates here were sometimes called zombies by the care workers.

The living dead. Pacified by medication, locked away forever.

Even here in the visitors' area, where relatives sat opposite the particularly severe cases separated by a glass wall, any normal person would feel an unease similar to that when imagining a tarantula crawling across their tongue.

Emma picked up the receiver and sat down.

'Thank you,' said the man who'd shaven four women, killed three of them and given her the most horrific night of her life. 'Your coming to visit means a lot to me.'

'This is an exception,' Emma said impassively. 'I'm coming just this once then never again.'

Konrad nodded, as if he'd been expecting this. 'Let me guess, Dr Roth sent you. He thinks that closure would help your therapy, doesn't he?'

Emma couldn't help feeling admiration for her once-closest friend. In a short period of time incarceration had eroded his health, his commanding presence and his youthful charm, but not his intelligence.

'He's waiting outside,' she said truthfully. With

Samson, who was following her every step again. And Jorgo, who somehow she'd probably never be rid of.

Emma changed the receiver to the other ear and rubbed her left elbow. The bandage had been taken off recently; the edges of the wound from the operation scars were still visible.

Because the single rooms in the security wing of the Park Clinic were only locked at night she'd been able to leave her room that day. But in her state it had taken more than ten minutes to labour the few metres to get to the gym.

Because of the bullet that had been fired accidentally from Konrad's pistol when Emma appeared so unexpectedly in the fake office, she'd be reminded of him all her life whenever she bent her arm. But even if he hadn't shattered her wrist, it was unlikely she'd ever be able to forget him.

'I'm so sorry. I never wanted to hurt you,' he said in the voice she'd last heard while half asleep. In the Park Clinic. The memory his tone evoked was so powerful that Emma had that same taste of gastric acid and vomit in her mouth as back in her hospital room when she'd thrown up. Dr Roth said the medication had given her an upset stomach, but she knew better. It was Konrad's voice that had stopped her from losing consciousness altogether. And it was his confession that had turned her stomach upside down and eventually made her wide awake again.

'What is it really?' she heard Konrad ask. Emma frowned.

'Pardon?'

'What has really brought you here? You're a wilful girl, Emma, that's something I've always admired about you. Your strength, even as a child. You wouldn't allow him to order you here unless you had something on your mind.'

Emma took a deep breath and felt respect for Konrad once more. He hadn't lost his talent for reading her like an open book.

'After everything that's happened, it's really quite unimportant. But the question… it haunts me.'

Konrad raised his eyebrows. 'What question?'

'Philipp. Why did you let him live?'

She picked nervously at her thumb. Her fingernails were neatly trimmed and painted with transparent polish again. Emma had sprayed on some perfume and shaved her legs. External signs of psychological healing. Inside, however, a heavy cold seemed to be looming. She felt as if her facial muscles were contracting and her ears aching, perhaps because she didn't want to hear Konrad's answer.

'I mean, you killed all those women, but not the guy you hated most. He was the adulterer after all. Wouldn't it have just been simpler to get him out of the way?'

Konrad shook his head sadly. 'Darling, don't you understand? I wanted to protect you from any pain, never inflict it on you. Emma, you must believe me when I say I always loved you. And whatever I did, it was never done out of selfishness. Even when I made sure that you remained an only child.'

Now Konrad's head was in a motorbike helmet and rather than a phone in his hand there was a syringe with a long needle, glistening silver in the moonlight.

'*Come on Emma, go to bed now and settle down,*' she heard Arthur say. '*I'll be right back.*'

Emma blinked and the vision from her memory dissipated.

'What was in the syringe?' she asked Konrad behind the glass.

'Something to induce an abortion,' he admitted candidly. 'I injected it into the water glass your mother had put beside her bed. Please don't hate me for it. I mean, how could I allow her to bring another child into the world which might go on to suffer the same psychological abuse your father inflicted upon you? A man who wants to hurt his daughter just because she's afraid?'

'You're sick,' Emma said, then it struck her: 'It was you! You swapped Sylvia's pills too!'

'To stop Philipp from hurting you again by giving her a child.'

Emma's fingers tensed around the receiver. 'You told her about Arthur to further undermine my credibility. And later you told her it was Philipp to make her kill herself.'

'I just wanted Sylvia to keep away from him. I really couldn't anticipate her suicide.'

'But you've got her on your conscience just the same. You're completely insane, do you know that?'

'Yes,' Konrad said. 'But I was never selfish, do you hear? The only thing important to me was that you were alright. Even if that meant your having to be with Philipp, that worthless pleb.'

For a second it looked as if he were going to spit on the glass separating them.

'The bastard left you alone when you were in distress. I had to slip into your house and watch out for you. I even took the package from your desk and hid it in the garden shed for a few hours so that Philipp would see what a state you were in. That he couldn't leave you on your own all weekend! Not in your condition! But the bastard went anyway. Cold-hearted, no scruples.'

'You hid?'

How often did you secretly watch me all these years?

Emma knew that this was another creepy thought, just like her hair being woven into Konrad's *enso* carpet. A thought which, if she was lucky, might fade over the years, but would never totally lose its horror.

'In the shed. In the cellar. When the two of you were in conversation I was in the kitchen, separated from you by just a thin door.'

'Like behind the connecting door in Le Zen,' Emma snorted.

Konrad's eyes turned watery. 'Oh, sweetie, you must really despise me now.' His lower lip was trembling and he started to dribble, but made no attempt to wipe the spit away.

'I wanted him to stop hurting you. I only sent him the hair so he knew what the consequences were of his cheating on you. But instead the bastard just used it to torture you even more. I'm so sorry.'

'What for?' Emma asked. She'd resolved to be furious with him. On the way here she'd run through the course of the conversation and its conclusion in her head. She'd pictured herself leaping up and slamming the receiver against the glass panel again and again until it shattered and she could slit Konrad's throat with one of the shards.

But now that he was sitting there like a little boy whose favourite toy has been taken away, she felt nothing but a great emptiness tinged with pity.

'You're not sorry for having killed all those women?' she asked, and watched as a tear rolled down his cheek. 'Not even for having hounded me all my life?'

He shook his head, weeping.

'And you're not sorry for having sedated and raped me, before dragging my body out of the hotel? So turning me into a paranoid wreck who stabbed innocent men to death?'

'No,' he sobbed. 'I'm only sorry that I didn't confess my love for you earlier. Maybe the two of us would have had a chance.'

Emma closed her eyes, wiped her eyelids with back of her hand and hung the receiver back up.

Of course, she thought. *He's sick. I should understand that better than anyone.*

She opened her eyes and gave Konrad one final look.

And although she'd never learned how to lipread, nor even ever tried, she was able to read from Konrad's lips what he was saying to her from behind the pane of glass:

'Out of love, Emma. I did it all only out of love.'

Ten Years of Sebastian Fitzek

When I was ten years old I was in class 5b at the Wald primary school and as popular as you can only be if you wear the clothes of your brother who's seven years older, while your haircut (a Mum special) is about a decade out of fashion.

Picture, if you can, a sullen young boy with a big nose, bowl haircut, leather trousers and an aluminium briefcase, who likes to spend all his breaktime in the library. Yes, precisely: I was that classic book nerd who nobody wanted on their dodgeball team apart from as cannon fodder.

And then Ender came.

Ender, a German of Turkish origin, was the biggest thug in the school and had to repeat a year twice. When he first entered the classroom I thought he'd come to pick up his child early from school. But then the coolest of the cool boys was seated right next to me.

Our class teacher probably thought that the swot (me) might have a positive influence on the problem child (Ender). But of course the reverse happened. Ender changed my life, first and foremost by liking me, which might have been because I helped him out with homework. Believe me, no coercion was involved, nor did I have to surrender my trainers to Ender. On the contrary, from his dad's sports shop he brought me my first Adidas customisable sneakers and so liberated me from my ugly clodhoppers.

And because he, Mr Popular, became my friend, this rubbed off on the mob that were my classmates, who till then hadn't even wanted to ignore me.

Ender taught me lots of useful things essential to the daily life of a primary school pupil, such as how to smoke a cigar (although it was a bad idea to try it behind the gym as the sports teacher was jogging past). Later he smuggled his father's 18-rated videos out of their apartment (*Rollerball*, *Class of 1984*, *The Evil Dead*, *Dawn of the Dead* and – of course – *Escape from New York* with Kurt Russell). This might give you an inkling of where my passion for thrillers comes from. To cut a long story short, I have much to thank Ender for and – mate – it's great to still be friends with you after all these years. Of course I'll come to visit you next Sunday in prison (just joking).

This is the second time I'm celebrating a ten-year anniversary. And I can rightly say that the last few years have been some of the most intense but also happiest of my life.

I'm often asked what has changed in my life since I became an author. My standard response is: not much. I still drive a Ferrari and sleep in my twenty-room villa in Grunewald. (Here I ought to add a smiley to make it clear that this is a joke too. Preferably one with tears of joy. I'd love to know the last time I laughed quite so much as this overused tears-of-joy smiley, but I'm digressing.)

In truth my life has changed drastically over the past decade, chiefly because I've had the privilege of getting to know so many great people I'd never have met had I not become a writer. And first and foremost this means you, dear readers.

I admit that when I published my email address in my debut novel, *Therapy*, I was utterly naïve. I reckoned on getting a handful of messages. A dozen emails, perhaps, in which readers would point out typos, voice their criticism, or maybe offer some fleeting praise. But how wrong I was! So far I've received over 40,000 emails and have been chuffed about each one.

Now to the acknowledgements. I should like to point out that the thanks I'm offering here are also an apology. So let me say thank you and sorry to (in no particular order of importance): Hans-Peter

Übleis, Theresa Schenkel, Josef Röckl, Bernhard Fetsch, Steffen Haselbach, Katharina Ilgen, Monika Neudeck, Patricia Kessler, Sibylle Dietzel, Iris Haas, Hanna Pfaffenwimmer, Carolin Graehl, Regina Weisbrod, Helmut Henkensiefken, Manuela Raschke and the rest of the family (including Karl and Sally), Barbara Herrmann, Achim Behrend, Ela and Micha, Petra Rode, Sabrina Rabow, Roman Hocke, Claudia von Hornstein, Gudrun Strutzenberger, Cornelia Petersen-Laux and Markus Michalek, Christian Meyer, Peter Prange, Gerlinde Jänicke, Arno Müller, Thomas Koschwitz, Jochen Trus, Stephan Schmitter, Michael Treutler and Simon Jäger, Clemens and Sabine Fitzek, Franz Xaver Riedel, Thomas Zorbach, Marcus Meier, the Krings brothers, Jörn Stollmann and all the booksellers and librarians out there. On this occasion all of you find yourselves just plonked onto a list, even though this book and my ten-year anniversary would have been impossible without all your efforts, love and friendship. But, as you can't have failed to notice, I've needed the space for something more important: my readers.

And you on the sofa at home, in the car, on the beach or on the tram – if you've made it this far then all that remains for me to say to you finally (as I've been doing for ten years at this point) is 'thank you'. Thanks for all your words, the time and the experiences we've shared. Either in real life or in the virtual world.

I hope you will continue to write to me at fitzek@ sebastianfitzek.de, because I'd still love to hear from you.

And I promise that I'll strive to ensure that the reverse remains true.

Best regards
Sebastian Fitzek

On 8 May 2016, forty-four years old, 1.8 metres tall (so long as I don't slouch) and weighing seventy-eight kilos, that's two kilos heavier than when I started *The Package*. (Bloody chocolate bars between chapters.)

About the author

SEBASTIAN FITZEK is one of Europe's most successful
authors of psychological thrillers. His books have
sold 12 million copies, been translated into more than
thirty-six languages and are the basis for international
cinema and theatre adaptations. Sebastian Fitzek was
the first German author to be awarded the European
Prize for Criminal Literature. He lives with
his family in Berlin.

About the translator

JAMIE BULLOCH is the translator of almost forty works
from German, including novels by Timur Vermes,
Martin Suter and Robert Menasse. His translation of
Birgit Vanderbecke's *The Mussel Feast* won the 2014
Schlegel-Tieck Prize. He is also the author
of *Karl Renner: Austria*.

Enjoyed

Ready for your next Fitzek delivery?